TWO Souls

Henry McDonald is a staff writer for *The Guardian* and *The Observer* and has been a journalist covering conflicts around the world, but specialising in the Northern Ireland Troubles, for more than 30 years. He is the author of eight critically acclaimed non-fiction books, including the histories of terror groups ranging from the INLA to the UVF. McDonald grew up in central Belfast and witnessed first-hand many of the key early events of the Troubles from Internment in 1971 to the carnage of Bloody Friday a year later. He was a punk rocker in the 1970s as well as a follower of Cliftonville Football Club, which he supports to this day.

HENRY
McDONALD

First published in 2019 by
Merrion Press
An imprint of Irish Academic Press
10 George's Street
Newbridge
Co. Kildare
Ireland
www.merrionpress.ie

9781785372575 (Paper)
9781785372582 (Kindle)
9781785372599 (Epub)
9781785372605 (PDF)

British Library Cataloguing in Publication Data
An entry can be found on request

Library of Congress Cataloging in Publication Data
An entry can be found on request

Typeset in Sabon LT Std 11.5/15 pt

Cover design by Jeffers & Sons, Belfast

ADVANCE PRAISE FOR *TWO SOULS*

'Go figure that Henry McDonald's new book is the real thing. The real thing is what McDonald does. Vivid, authentic and scabrously funny. Good news for readers, bad news for other writers.'

ROBERT MCLIAM WILSON

'*Withnail and I* meets *One Flew Over the Cuckoo's Nest* with a manic dose of *Clockwork Orange* thrown in for good measure ... You'll not forget this novel in a hurry. I'm still reeling.'

GERALD DAWE

'Starts fast and gets faster, like a good punk song!'

JAKE BURNS, STIFF LITTLE FINGERS

'I couldn't put this book down – a spellbinding ... journey through Belfast's underground punk scene during the 70s and 80s. With David Bowie's "Low" setting the mood and the ... Irish Cup Final ... a theatre of war ... football, sex, drugs and rock 'n' roll – it's all in here in ... with betrayal, hedonism and ultra violence thrown in. This is essential reading!'

PETER HOOTON, THE FARM

'Any novel whose narrator wears an "I Hate Pink Floyd" T-shirt gets my vote any day.'

JULIE BURCHILL

'Buckle up! Henry McDonald's novel takes the reader on a gritty and violent tour through the underbelly of a city where drugs and politics provide a combustible cocktail. It's the author's native city, and he knows its heartbeat ... this book should come with an X certificate.'

MARTIN DILLON

To Charlotte, for everything.

‘Two souls, alas, are housed within my breast, And each will wrestle for the mastery there.’

Faust – Goethe

‘All this happened more or less. The war bits anyway …’

Slaughterhouse-Five – Kurt Vonnegut

1

'BOYS KEEP SWINGING'

28 April 1979

The triangle turns, missiles fire and asteroids explode. Aliens are obliterated and the quickening sound from Space Invaders promises a high score. Pinballs beep and bleep while the shooting galleries clack and crackle. All the lights and strobed neon pulsating from the machines inside the Yankee Doodle pool hall illuminate the face of my friend, Padre Pio McCann. He has just dipped his middle finger down the fanny-flat crotch of his jeans and played pocket billiards with his balls and dick. He whips his finger out, wiggles it right under my nose and croaks, 'Here, Robbie Ruin, smell your ma. Smell your dirty oul ma!'

His face is about to be crushed to a pulp with the purple spot ball that my cousin, Rex Mundi, has picked up from a pool table facing the jukebox, which is blaring out the Buzzcocks' 'I Don't Mind'. As Pete Shelley howls, Rex grips Padre Pio by the lapels of his army jacket and pushes him onto the scuffed green baize.

'Shut your fucking mouth, you wanker. Don't talk about my aunt like that!' my cousin warns him.

Still giggling, Padre Pio wrestles free from Rex Mundi but keeps up the ribbing, not knowing, as per usual, when it's time to stop. He crosses his arms over his chest, rolls up his eyes and barks, 'Here Ruin, who's this? Who the fuck is this? Just keep smelling yer oul ma!'

I try to ignore what he is saying about my late mother, who died eighteen months ago from what Dad tried to convince me was liver cancer but which appeared on the death certificate, stamped in a single word, as 'cirrhosis'. If truth be told, I'm more interested in how the Buzzcocks have redeemed themselves after all those forlorn tunes and sentimental crap on the *Love Bites* LP. I'm well used to how PP tries to outdo me in trading insults, which usually involves trashing our nearest and dearest, even the dead ones. I'm all too aware that I also went too fucking far the time his grandad died and I suggested we scoop the old boy out of his coffin, chop him up and sell his remains for dog meat to the pet-food factory over on May Street. And besides all of that, there is an even greater menace than him lurking inside the Yankee Doodle today.

As my cousin is about to smash the pool ball into PP's sniggering bake, I slide between the two of them. I am in peacekeeping mode because I have just spotted the bouncer who only wears black and has even dyed his blonde hair and moustache black so he can look like Bruce Lee. Everything about him is black: black heart, black soul and cold, snake-like black eyes. The kung fu-fighting, black-belt sentinel of the Yankee Doodle in Castle Street. In all fairness, he'll probably be needed today, it being the cup final, and the Yankee is the first port of call for the remnants of the Red Army who've come from their homes in the east and south, slipping safely past the hordes of Orangemen gathered around Belfast city centre sniffing out their prey.

'Don't listen to that spastic, cousin! He's at that all the time. He loved my ma really. She was more than good to him – more fool her,' I say.

Rex Mundi drops the pool ball into one of the pockets while staring into Padre Pio's beaming face. 'I dunno why the fuck we're going to the game with that retard. If he keeps this crap up, I'll kick his balls in.'

Padre Pio is now arched up against one of the painted murals on the walls. The brilliant-white smiles of John Travolta and Olivia Newton John seem to be resting on his shaven, elfin head.

'Bruce Lee is watching us,' I tell my cousin, nodding back towards the entrance at the top of the stairs.

'Ruin, you just tell that fuckwit to stop insulting my aunt or he is dead,' Rex replies, nodding furiously at Padre Pio. He is clearly agitated, but his flame-coloured Mohican doesn't move an inch – impressive.

'Aye, be cool, Rex,' PP shouts back and sticks up his thumb.

'Cool is for wankers who still watch *Happy Days* and like to think they're the Fonz. Wankers like you!' Rex Mundi shoots back.

He might be a wanker, but Padre Pio is always with us for one reason and one reason only: he is game. In Belfast you might be the biggest windy-licking, back-stabbing, touting, double-crossing, thieving, hooding, joyriding wee bastard, but if you're game then all will be forgiven. Once you prove you're game, you get respect ... and maybe fear.

Game is what we need on this glorious day – because we are the Red Army. This will be the greatest day ever in the history of Cliftonville Football Club, the side that for far too long has been watched only by gaggles of old boys clutching flasks of tea with tartan blankets wrapped around their bony, withered legs. For we are the new Red Army. We are the Zulus who have appeared on the top of the hill. We are on our way to Windsor Park for the Irish Cup Final, and we all need to show that we are game, and there is none more game as Padre Pio McCann.

A group of older Reds supporters once dared him to go on his own to Windsor Park at our last home match against Linfield. We are barred from playing our greatest rivals at our Solitude home for 'security reasons', which is a total fucking injustice. But to make this dare special, they challenged Padre Pio to sneak into the blue end of the stadium. So there we were, just a couple of weeks ago, freezing our balls off on the Spion Kop, where we will stand for the final later this afternoon. At half-time, a brick shithouse of a hooligan from the New Lodge took out his binos for a squint into the North Stand to clock the top boys in the opposition's ranks. Suddenly, he sees our own boy, right there in the middle of a sea of the Orange scummers. A blue-and-white scarf with thin red lines was tied around his scrawny neck and he was joining in the chorus of 'Dirty Fenian bastards, yiz dirty Fenian bastards'. There he was, Padre Pio, packed right up at the end of the Linfield support, being held back from us by the thick black-and-green lines of the RUC riot squad. Now for me that was, and will always remain, well and truly game.

My cousin's nostrils are still flaring and his fists are tightening as Padre Pio shouts out, 'Alex Higgins – one! Ruin's ma – three times a week!'

In a fair dig, Rex Mundi would easily win, but Padre Pio doesn't know the meaning of that word 'fair'. This is because he makes up for being a stumpy wee cunt by being prepared to do absolutely anything in a fight. Padre Pio was and always will be bladed up. Even as a kid, in the slimy primary schoolyard, he shoved the pointy end of a protractor up into the arse of a spud-head twice his size who had knocked his shite in earlier that day. That resulted in him being expelled from St Columba's and placed into a secure 'education centre' set up for the simpletons and psychos that no normal school would keep on their rolls. Even though he became an absent figure at my school, we remained close, and nobody went near him or me in the street. He had a reputation for carrying razors, flickies, Stanley knives and even screwdrivers wherever he went. I once saw him rip open an Orangeman's face with a penknife at a bus stop near Lord Hamill's burger bar after the Prod had grabbed me by the arm and had the audacity to ask if we were Taigs. Later, when he reached the Lagan, where he chucked the knife into the bilious-coloured water, Padre Pio announced, 'God made Catholics, the Armalite made them equal and this blade made us two fearless fuckers.'

I'm worried now that he's secreted steel up the sleeve of his army coat and that it's going to be plunged into Rex Mundi's shiny new biker jacket. I'm even more worried that if we are trapped in here by Bruce Lee, we will never get to the match on time. But then I remember that on the way through town, Padre Pio had gone into Littlewoods' off-licence to swipe a bottle of QC. Bloodshed could be avoided with the promise of fortified wine.

'Let's go into the bogs and knock back that hooch you stroked before Bruce Lee over there kicks off,' I suggest to him.

Enveloped in the stench of eye-stinging bleach, a truce is eventually reached. They take it in turns to gulp down belts of the wine that looks like the colour of an oul man's polluted prostate piss. Outside, Bowie's 'Boys Keep Swinging' blasts from the jukebox. Somebody out there, amid the rows of spides with their middle shades and steel-tipped brogues, has taste. Whoever keeps putting that song on repeatedly with its high hat drum beat start and dissonant electro ending doesn't know that he is doing it for me. For it propels me back to last summer, to her, to a time I thought I had finally escaped Padre Pio, to the months before I joined the Red Army.

The Bowie track only reminds me now that I am trapped with him here once again, unable to free myself from his tentacles, yet not wanting to be ungrateful for all that he has done for me since we were small boys cowering in a slippery schoolyard, terrified that the bigger brutes in hand-me-down skinner jeans and Wrangler jackets would turn their malevolent attention on to us. Yet they never did because Padre Pio pulled out a blade and threatened to slit the fucking throat of the first fucker that came anywhere near us. No one ever did. Even after he was expelled and even after I passed the Eleven-plus exam, the sarcastic quips and jealous threats from peers never amounted to anything because they knew they could never turn their back on Padre Pio without risking the spear of cold steel up their holes.

My father could never understand why we were ever friends in the first place and used to call us the 'Hitler–Stalin Pact'. Padre Pio first took shit from the other kids because at the start of the Troubles his father had fucked up a sniper attack. Two of his fellow Provos were captured while he blew south on the run, leaving his son, wife and mother on their own back up north. He never returned, and Dad swore that he had ended up in Canada, married in bigamous circumstances to a woman from Quebec. Of course, this was something you would never dare mention to Padre Pio. My family came from the other side of the fence. We were Hackney Wicks, Five-Card Tricks, Sticks: the Official IRA. Padre Pio and I were never supposed to be friends, but there you go.

Now he is extending his hand out to my cousin and giving up the last belt of QC to him as a peace offering. In turn, Rex takes out a plastic money bag from one of his zipped side pockets. It contains a pile of what looks like rabbit poo droppings.

'Don't skin up yet, Rex,' Padre Pio says, sniffing the fetid air. 'Wait till we get to my cousin Trout's house and then we can get stoned. We can smoke his stuff instead and keep yours for Windsor. Let's get outta here. This kip reeks of keek.'

When we go back into the pool hall, Padre Pio takes out a cylindrical pile of ten-pence pieces and feeds the Asteroids machine. He becomes transfixed with his mission to destroy the threat from the flying debris of the stars. Rex Mundi and I go over to the jukebox where a tall lanky punter wearing a three-quarter-length, grey-blue RAF coat has just put on 'Boys Keep Swinging' for the umpteenth time. I recognise him from The Harp, The Pound and Good Vibrations record shop. I am surprised to see he is one of us in his red-and-white barred scarf. We have spoken before in Terri Hooley's shop in Great Victoria Street while flicking through the boxes of singles and albums, searching for left-field bands such as Television, Magazine and Cabaret Voltaire. We didn't speak about Cliftonville, the Red Army and all the associated aggro of the season. Good Vibes wouldn't have been the place for such a discussion.

'What do you think of "Jimmy Jimmy", the new Undertones single?' I ask him.

'Aye, O'Neill did well there, Ruin,' Lanky Balls replies.

Rex Mundi butts in. 'I think it's fucking shite. Punk's not dead, it's fucking decapitated, mate.'

Lanky Balls surveys Rex Mundi's Mohican and biker jacket with the painted image of the Devil as a goat inside a pentagram on the back of it.

'If punk is dead then why do you still look like that?'

'Because I'd no other clothes when I came here, mate. I'm thinking of shaving my head when I get home to Brighton and robbing some of my English grandad's braces. The skinheads are coming back this summer.'

Lanky Balls drops ten pence into the jukebox and the jackbooted crunch of marching men introduces the Sex Pistols' 'Holidays in the Sun'.

'This was when it used to be good, mate,' Rex Mundi says.

'Yeah I know, but punk died when they let that pantomime junkie Sid Vicious take over the Pistols,' Lanky Balls replies.

'Do you know when I realised punk was dead? When they started selling Sid Vicious T-shirts on the pier in Brighton.'

As we nod in agreement, Padre Pio loses patience with the battle to survive the Asteroid fields and storms back off to the toilet with the QC bottle sticking out of his coat pocket. Bruce Lee is bound to have spotted it by now.

We are about to say our goodbyes to Lanky Balls, when the tramp, tramp, tramp of a line of younger Reds supporters coming up the stairs of the Yankee Doodle distracts us. They are singing in unison, 'Oh Airey's here, Airey's there, Airey's every-fucking-where, na, na, nanna, na, na.'

Their progress is halted by Bruce Lee, who still keeps one sly eye on us over by the jukebox. 'Keep it fucking quiet in here, children. No messing, right? And no fucking party tunes either,' he says, before stepping aside.

This is our cue to scoot before Padre Pio gets any more gameboy notions. He has already left the toilet with the QC bottle miraculously filled half way up again. As we edge towards the top of the stairs, Bruce Lee blocks our route.

'Hey cunty!' He points at Padre Pio and already I imagine I can see the sheen of a PP blade. 'What's that in your pocket, chum?'

'It's a bottle of QC. What's it to you?' PP says.

I can feel my blood starting to freeze.

'Out to fuck. No drinking in here, son. I'm taking that bottle off you.'

I expect it to come smashing into Bruce Lee's face but suddenly it's all peace in our time when Padre Pio puts on his softest altarboy voice. 'No bother, boss. I was only going to give it to you anyway. You have a wee drink of it later when the Reds win the cup, just to celebrate.'

We break our bollocks laughing going down the stairs when I look back and see the bouncer taking his first sneaky sip of Padre Pio's undiluted piss.

2

BLACK CAB BLASPHEMIES

28 April 1979

There's a steamer swelling in my pants that won't go soft. It's all the fault of the oul doll sitting opposite on the flip-down seat in the back of a Falls black taxi. I keep hearing Lou Reed in my head every time I look across at her shiny black-leather boots and the pencil skirt exposing a slash of her naked thigh. She's in her late forties or early fifties, has big bouncy tits and is a bit on the beefy side. Her heavy-handed, aquamarine eyeshadow clashes with the deep red lipstick, which leaves a lurid line around the edge of the unfiltered Park Drive she is smoking.

At first she smiles, almost knowingly, as if she has spotted what's going on inside my army trousers. But then her face suddenly shrivels to a scowl when she pans up to my old school blazer and the upside-down mini crucifix pinned on the pocket where the St Malachy's College badge was once attached, to where *Gloria Ab Intus* is no more. She must think she's stumbled upon a satanic coven when my cousin leaps on board and reveals the back of his biker jacket with the head of a horned goat inside the stencilled pentagram, and the words 'Rex Mundi' below in silver sprayed-on script.

Our progress up the road is held back by Padre Pio chatting to the driver, who seems to know his runaway father. Judging by the way our taxi man rolls his own fegs out of a home-made tobacco tin adorned with Gaelic script and a crude tricolour, he must have done some time for the cause – probably just a few months on remand in Crumlin Road jail by the looks of him. He is way too fat to have been smearing shite all over the walls up in the H-Block.

'Is your da still in Dundalk, son?' he asks PP.

'Nah, New Jersey. The last I heard of him anyway, but you're not supposed to know that.'

The oul babe in boots is slithering along the rough leather seating, inching her arse away from us to the relative safety of the other window. She blows smoke out in short nervous jets into the street, which is filling up with Reds fans, several of whom are horsing back carry-outs before the long walk up the Falls and down to Windsor Park.

'If you're ever in touch with your daddy, tell him Big G was asking after him. Tell him he still owes me a tenner.' The driver laughs.

'Oh aye. Will do, mate,' Padre Pio answers, as he backs away from the front of the cab and into the back with us, dismissing the driver with a couple of sneaky hand jerks behind the glass while mouthing, 'wanker'.

Seated next to me, Padre Pio suddenly points to our fellow passenger and says as loud as possible, 'Hey, what's wrong with that oul bat? What's she staring at?'

Rex Mundi steps in chivalrously. 'Leave the oul bird alone, dickhead!'

The woman has her head out of the window now. She is shaking slightly, and the feg between her forefinger and middle finger is vibrating.

'She probably doesn't like our dress sense, gentlemen,' I say, as the taxi finally begins to move towards Divis Street. We're following a long line of beetle-shaped vehicles stuffed with Reds supporters making the same journey as us, all of them chanting, 'Windsor, Windsor here we come! Windsor here we come!'

Rex Mundi is busy rolling a joint that he informs us we'll only light up at half-time on the Kop, just to soothe the nerves. My cousin has only one metal badge dug deep into the lapel of his leather biker jacket. The only badge he would ever wear was the emblem of his adopted hometown's team: the club crest of Brighton and Hove Albion. Two years ago, he warned me that punk badges were only for posers. We were walking along Hove seafront after *Top of the Pops*, and I was still reeling with shock and awe after having watched Johnny Rotten sing 'Pretty Vacant'.

Our crew don't wear badges or scarves. We were banned from doing that shortly after Padre Pio read an article in *The Sunday Mirror* (or rather that I read out to the ignorant semi-illiterate twat one morning) about the English footie hooligans who never donned their club colours. This meant they could go anywhere, even into the opposition's end, totally unidentified. This, he keeps reminding us all, is exactly what he has done. I suppose that is why, deep down, behind the hostility, PP actually likes Rex Mundi. My cousin has seen some real action on the terraces across the water, especially the aggro between Brighton and their hated rivals Crystal Palace down at the Goldstone Ground, where their serious rucking made those old warring mods and rockers out to be a bunch of fairies. Padre Pio's eyes would widen as Rex relayed the derby day damage; how his older brother Mick nearly blinded a Palace fan with diluted ammonia squirted from a water pistol.

Cliftonville FC are to play in the final today in yellow tops and blue shirts, and this is already seriously pissing off Padre Pio. When he clocks a group of fans wearing home-made, paper mache, stove-pipe hats, painted with yellow and blue hoops, he explodes.

'Yiz look like a bunch of fucking Southampton fans in 1976, ya wankers,' he roars out the window as our taxi passes Divis Tower. 'Fucking clowns. Total fucking clowns. I didn't recognise one of them, Ruin. Did you? Not a single one of them. Dressed up like bastard Southampton fans from 1976, and I bet not one of them has had their legs splashed with somebody else's piss inside the Cage at Solitude!'

'Too fucking right, mate,' I fire back as quickly as possible to placate him.

But on he goes, ranting and raving against a newly found bunch of enemies to berate. 'I bet ya not one of them wankers ever went down to Glenavon or Portadown or had darts thrown at them on the Shore Road when we played Crusaders.'

'Too fucking right, mate,' I repeat, while suddenly remembering the afternoon, not too long ago, we went down to Castlereagh Park to watch Cliftonville play Ards.

We had been too late for the official club coaches and opted instead to jump on a commuter bus full of coffin-dodging pensioners decked out in their greys and creams. When we met at our rendezvous point not far from the spot where I saw firemen shovelling bits of bodies into sacks seven years earlier on Bloody Friday, our group decided to hide our colours. Anybody carrying Cliftonville scarves shoved them into their parkas or tied them under their jerseys. The Ulsterbus was heading into the hun heartland of East Belfast, so we had to keep our heads down. Our safety pact lasted all of five minutes. As the bus crawled up Albertbridge Road, PP had one of his occasional kamikaze notions. When we reached the traffic lights at The Albert Bar, Padre Pio pulled a scarf out of one of the younger kid's pockets, put the red-and-white bars up against the window and started hammering. Two oul boys pinting outside ran into the pub, and before the lights hit amber there was a mob gathered outside armed with snooker cues and pool balls. The windows imploded. Within seconds, clear glass turned into hundreds of shattered fragments, some flying through the air like missiles. I hit the deck and lay on my stomach, only looking up eventually to see three middle-aged bare-chested men trying to yank open the rubber flaps of the automatic doors with pool cues. But they were either too tubby or too pissed to force their way on board. The OAPs inside had been holding up their Co-Op shopping bags to their faces as if they were going to shield them from the flying glass. The driver put the gears into third and moved swiftly onto the Newtownards Road with a large crowd in pursuit. If they had reached us, there would have been a lynching. But as I lay there on the floor, all I could think about was Sabine. She had grown up not too far from here, further up at the posher end of the Newtownards Road, and there I was, going to die in a bus at the grimier end of it.

I had almost hoped, in a brief, self-pitying death wish of a moment, that they would find me cut to pieces near the Connswater River, and she would read about it in the papers before weeping, wailing and feeling sorry for everything that she had done to me. It was the laughter that shook me out of my martyrdom fantasy; it was the demonic, sniggering, spittle-filled laughter from the very back of the bus. Padre Pio had his feet dangling out of the broken window and his body reclined horizontally along the seat. His face convulsed with laughter, and a thin trail of blood and saliva trickled down the side of his mouth.

'Look at your face Ruin, just look at your fucking stupid face,' PP cackled.

Instantly, as if he himself had summoned them up from my own pores, pin pricks of pain pulsed and rippled all over my cheeks. When I put my hands to them there were micro fountains of blood bubbling up from the skin. As I tried to clear my face with the back of my hands, Padre Pio started abusing the elderly passengers, reminding them about Airey Neave's recent 'up and under' demise. Then he began conducting an insane orchestra of insult-songs all the way to the peninsula, singing and chanting to the tune of 'Those Were the Days My Friend' that 'we're gonna burn yer town, we're gonna burn yer town, we're gonna burn, we'll burn your Orange hole down.'

Now we are on the road again, this time up the Falls, on Irish Cup Final day. There is only one thing on PP's mind this afternoon and it is not victory over Portadown. It is not about putting one over all the Prods of various hues who will turn up at Windsor just to see Cliftonville defeated. It will not be about our team lifting the cup in the club's one hundredth-anniversary season. Padre Pio simply wants to be the first one onto the Windsor turf. He wants to be seen on TV dodging the peelers and the security men, avoiding the missiles that will rain down on him from the North Stand. He wants the world to see that he's game.

At the Royal Victoria Hospital, the oul bird leans across the cab and rattles the glass with a coin. The driver breaks suddenly. She gets out, pays the cabbie and then looks back in disgust at us.

'I really hope yiz win today, but yiz are still going to hell, ya bunch of weirdos,' she croaks.

PP leans out and hollers, 'Just you go in there and get your bag plumbed in.'

The taxi is barely across Broadway, which is cordoned off at the bottom near the motorway by a line of battleship-grey RUC Land Rovers and a bottle-green wall of cops in riot gear, when the driver stops again. Our new fellow passenger is a wino in a pork-pie hat and old black Crombie coat. The neck of a brown bottle is sticking out of one of its pockets. There is a pencil-thin film of dried brown liquor caked above his upper lip and his eyes are bleary. When the cab passes by a mural close to Beechmount showing the head of a black man being squashed over a lemon juicer and the words above it, 'Don't squeeze a South African dry!' the wino fishes the bottle of Mundies out of the Crombie and tilts it towards the disappearing wall mural.

'Fuck you, Sambo cunt,' he rasps, before guzzling back the wine.

He continues to down the Mundies while moaning about his plight. 'See they've banned it from the Provie and the Sticky clubs because of this Apartheid thing. So I have ta drink my Mundies on the streets now. They won't even let me take it into the hostel.'

When we ignore his protests he changes the subject. 'Here lads, who's playing up at Casement Park today? That's some crowd going up the road. Any of you lads got a spare feg or a couple of shillings even? I got robbed in Castle Street earlier.'

'I'm not giving you anything for being a silly old racist cunt,' Rex Mundi pipes up while attempting to roll another joint in the back of the cab.

'Ach Jesus, lads. Give me a chance. I defended this district once, you know.'

This produces gales of laughter from us, but the wino suddenly has a serious face on.

'It was nineteen hundred and sixty-nine, not that long ago. A few of us were out that day and we did our bit. We stopped the Orangemen burning people in their beds. Then in nineteen hundred and a seventy-one there were a few of us left taking on the British Army down in the Lower Falls too,' he says, taking another swig of the South African hooch.

'Oh aye, grandad,' PP interrupts. 'Just like nineteen hundred and sixteen when we beat the Brits!'

Padre Pio then swivels around, drops his trousers and Y-fronts and spreads his arse cheeks apart right in front of the wino's face, close enough for the oul boy to peer right up his chocolate alley.

The wino looks terrified and rattles the glass to be left off the road.

'Casement's for Gaelic football, ya stupid oul soak,' PP shouts out while he pulls his monks and trousers back up in one rapid movement.

I'm amazed we haven't been booted out of the taxi, but our driver has ignored us all the way towards the Donegall Road. Maybe he is still scared of PP's da, maybe he is scared of PP – and if he isn't yet then he really should be.

When PP signals for the driver to halt just before St James he reminds us that there is still plenty of time before kick-off to get more drugs and drink ahead of our trek down to Windsor. I'm left to pay the fare while PP is having a last word with the cabbie.

'You keep quiet about my da now, comrade. I probably shouldn't have told you where he is hiding out these days in case the Brits ask the Yanks to send him back.'

'No worries, son. No worries. You can trust me. See that oul boy by the way.'

'Aye, what about him? Pain in the arse.'

'I never charge him. Wanna know why?'

'Aye, why?'

'He was picked up eventually in 1971 and never recovered over what the British did to him. He couldn't hold a pint glass straight, even back then, let alone shoot straight with a rifle. He was just the first person the Brits picked up that day and they decided to do a number on him after one of their squaddies got killed near the Falls Park. Next time you see him in the back of a black hack or walking the road, don't give him such a hard time, son.'

'I will stand and salute him instead,' Padre Pio promised as he gave a military-style farewell to our driver.

3

THE KINGDOM OF TROUT

28 April 1979

At first it seems no one in the house has remembered to take down the Christmas crib in the front window. However, on closer inspection, there are no multicoloured lights, sheep, shepherds, Mary, Joseph or baby Jesus in the manger. Instead, there is a naked, cockless, bearded Action Man waving out to the street from the inside of a clipped together Airfix stronghold that's been smeared with splashes of brown paint. He is sitting on a white-framed Sindy doll bed, but the giant 'S' on the headboard has been painted over and replaced with 'H' in the same smudged scrawl as the streaks slashed over the plastic walls.

I look over to Padre Pio and expect him to burst his ballicks laughing at the sight of it, but instead he's gone all scary. He has that same weird expression on his bake, the one normally deployed when his face starts flaming, his teeth crunch and grind, and just before some poor sap gets a dropkick to the balls or a butt in the head.

'That's there for his big brother – my cousin. He's a fucking hero so he is!' PP says, turning to me in what is threatening to be a sudden burst of angry-head. 'Welcome to the Kingdom of Trout.'

We dander into the house without knocking or ringing the bell. There is a whiff of burning dope wafting from the kitchen.

'I'm in here, dickhead, and close the big door behind yiz,' somebody yells out.

Rex Mundi and I follow PP into the kitchen where a black-and-white portrait of a dark-haired woman in a polo neck is hanging up over the back wall; the word 'Mord' is written underneath it.

'Who's that oul boot?' Padre Pio asks, pointing up at the austere face.

A man in his early twenties, with liver lips and petrol-flecked thumbs, is skinning up joints and fiddling with roaches. He stops his work and glares up at PP.

'That, you ignorant fucker, is Comrade Ulrike Meinhof, who was murdered by the neo-fascist West German state. She was a political prisoner just like your cousin in H-Block, Long Kesh.'

Rex Mundi plants himself down on a chair facing our host. He is greedily casting his eyes over the strips of Lebanese Gold lying on tinfoil beside the yellow and red remains of breakfast slashed across a plain white plate. He zips down his biker jacket and reveals his latest T-shirt. It is Britain with a visored helmet on top of where Scotland should be, wielding a baton over a ragged, bear-shaped Ireland. The blood-red splats on white cotton are accompanied with the words, 'Troops Out'.

'Like yer T-shirt, mate,' our host says sticking his hand across the kitchen table. 'I'm Trout. Welcome to the kingdom.'

Rex Mundi nods and asks, 'How did you get a name like that, matey?'

Trout ignores the question and returns the serve with one of his own. 'So, have we a Brit in our midst? Are you one of them toy town Trots that MI5 occasionally sends over to spy on us by any chance?'

'No, mate. He's Belfast born and bred. He was burnt out by the Orangemen in '72 and had ta get the boat ta England,' I say, intervening on my cousin's behalf after an elbow in the ribs from Padre Pio.

Returning to his meticulous rolling, carefully sprinkling little grains of dope through the tobacco along each and every one of the joints, Trout doesn't even look up when he asks, 'So why did the snouts target you and your family then?'

'It was my brother they were after. He was on remand at the time in Crumlin Road jail. It was in the papers. They put a picket on our house one day and then that night they arrived with petrol bombs,' Rex explains.

'So ... what happened next?' Trout asks in half-belief.

'Ruin's dad is my uncle. He saved us. He got certain people to go over to the east and sort it out.'

Trout switches his glare to me. 'His da? McManus? Are you fuckin' takin' the piss? Sure he ran away from the struggle in the same year. What did he do? Did he hit one of the Orangemen over the head with a typewriter?'

Padre Pio sniggers while my cheeks burn with anger and embarrassment. For a second I think my cousin is about to leap across the table and smack Trout one in the bake.

'His dad brought over Big Joe McCann. You might have heard of him. With a couple of his lads and a .45 pistol, which one of them put to the head of one of the loyalists outside our door. The cowardly cunts just scattered after that,' Rex Mundi says.

He and Trout stare each other out for a few moments.

'Sorry comrade, no harm meant. I'm Trout. Didn't catch your name,' Trout says and extends his hand once more towards Rex Mundi.

'Aidan McManus, but everyone calls me Rex Mundi,' my cousin replies.

'Let's just say, Rex Mundi, that I have a mild disagreement over strategy with your uncle and his friends. His oul boy will still be talkin' about class politics and workers unity when we've sent the last of the Orange Boers back on the boat over ta Scotland. Anyway, I really like your T-shirt,' Trout continues, all the while looking slyly at me.

When he hands out a fat spliff, he offers it to me first – probably as a peace offering. We all take turns for a blast, fling our heads back on the chairs and talk shite about the impending final.

'Hey Trout, what has Action Man ever done to you?' Rex Mundi asks, after enjoying a few tokes.

Trout takes a deep draw from the bulging joint before speaking. 'He's there ta represent the struggle for political status in the jails. Not just for my brother but all the republican prisoners. The Provos as well as the 'Erps in H-Block, Long Kesh.'

Padre Pio reconnects with us after several long blasts of blow and adds, 'His brother Mullet is doing a big stretch for trying ta kill a peeler.'

Trout suddenly stubs out the joint into the ashtray and tries to appear serious again. I see his dilated pupils and feel his hooded stare trained on me once more.

'Ask yourselves what's more important today – Cliftonville winning the cup or a chance for us ta highlight what the fuck is going on just a couple of miles up the motorway in the Kesh? Even if one TV camera picks us out singing "Smash H-Block" or shouting "Victory to the republican prisoners" we'll have done something for them. Remember lads: their pain, our struggle. I put that thing in the window to remind the thousands passing by on their way ta Windsor Park that there is still a war on!'

He is getting agitated and I can see the family connection to Padre Pio, who is actually hooked on his every word. It's one of the few times I have ever seen the fruit loop pay attention to anyone for more than five seconds.

'Ask yourselves what's really goin' on here,' Trout continues. 'Ask yourselves this: we are a few weeks away from a British general election and it looks like those stupid English bastards are going ta vote for Maggie Thatcher. And when that happens, the boot is going ta go in ta the likes of us. And the likes of us over there where you live too,' Trout says, pointing to Rex Mundi who is nodding away in total agreement.

'Ask yourselves what she's going ta do here, especially since the republican socialist movement executed her friend and mentor Airey Neave right smack in the Houses of Parliament. It's gonna be worse than Internment when she gets her high heels under the desk. She'll do what the unionist ruling class wants and there'll be mass arrests, repression, more new jails built and prisoners left ta rot and die in their own shit.'

Rex Mundi tries to extract the extinguished joint from the ashtray, but Trout blocks his hand, prompting my cousin to speak up.

'The workers in Britain won't stand for it, Trout. There'll be a revolution in the streets if she takes on and tries to break the unions over there.'

Trout leans across the table. He is so close I can see the blackheads on his bulbous nose. His breath stinks and his nostrils are flaring into our faces.

'We're enterin' into momentous days, comrades. 1979. The year when it all kicks off and we should all play our part.'

I look sideways at Padre Pio who seems distracted from all this talk of repression and revolution. He is studying the back pages of *The Irish News* to find out who will be in Jackie Hutton's team today. When I stare down towards my feet, cautiously avoiding Trout's gaze, I see PP is making wanking signals under the table.

The joint is salvaged again from the ashtray, relit and passed around by Trout.

'We've gotta keep our heads clear before we hit the road, right!' he orders. 'So this is the last one before we go down to Windsor. Cos when we get onto that Kop there's work ta be done,' he continues, while staring at Rex Mundi and myself. 'Here, English boy, which wing of the jail in the Crum was your brother on?' he asks my cousin.

'A-Wing, I think,' Rex replies.

'No, you stupid cunt. Which wing of the 'Ra? The Stick or the Provie one back then?'

'Neither, mate,' Rex Mundi answers. 'He operated with the anarchists and radicals and this one weird dude who was one of her comrades. He was a mate of that old blade on the wall up there,' he adds, pointing towards Meinhof.

On hearing this, Trout breaks into a smile, shoots up from his chair and points over to Rex Mundi. 'Do not move! I've got something for you. It's perfect,' he says, before jabbing one of his fat fingers at PP. 'And don't you go stealing any of my dope while I'm lookin' for it.'

'Lookin' for wha?' PP asks indifferently.

The temperature in the kitchen seems to have dropped by ten degrees the second Trout leaves and I am no longer suffocated by his stare.

'So why the fuck is he called Trout and he has a brother called Mullet?' Rex Mundi suddenly asks.

'Their da is a Kraut,' PP says.

'So? Shouldn't they be called Hitler or Goering then?' Rex Mundi says.

'Where are they today? I mean his ma and da?' I add.

PP shakes his head as if I have just come straight off the windy-lickers' bus. 'It's Saturday, Ruin. Where do ya think they are? They're down the motorway at Long Kesh seeing Mullet on a visit. They're probably on their hands and knees with their rosary beads beggin' him ta give up his dirty protest. It's the best day of the week to be in Trout's house, ta skin up some gear while they're not in. Super Saturday. That's when our Trout always stocks up on his dope. As for our Mullet, well he's a real Action Man!'

I am wondering how the fuck some poor bastard from the Federal Republic of Germany must think about ending up stuck here in this kip, with one son in jail and another floating from one hashish cloud to another and well on his way to joining his brother. I am thinking too that my dad would despise Trout and throw up if he knew we were here smoking his dope while listening to his sermons. I gaze up to Ulrike on the wall. Her face weirdly reminds me of the French teacher at St Mal's, where I have only two months left of my 'sentence' to complete.

After seven long years, I will be free from the stench of floor polish; free from cassocked Christian Brothers with their Embassy No.10 fegs cupped in their hands behind their backs; free from that rat-faced college president with his hysterical screaming pitch; free from the dead-on teachers in their moccasins and corduroy suits; free from the 'Yes' and 'Pink Floyd' fans who control the record players in the Sixth Form centre; free from the sniping sarcasm of the Latin teacher who insists we are a waste of taxpayers' money; free to get out of that school and out of this town. Free to search for her. Free to find her again.

Trout comes back into the kitchen with a present for my cousin. It is a white badge with a red star in the middle and the letters RAF written behind a sub-machine gun. He is definitely warming to Rex Mundi because of the exploits of his older brother Mick, who, while tripping on an acid tab, petrol bombed the Students Union at Queen's University in protest over Internment 1971. Unbeknownst to Trout, Mick nearly topped himself in a West Berlin squat last summer after five days of cold turkey.

'Here my friend, this is for you. It is in honour of your brother and Comrade Meinhof on the wall,' Trout announces.

'Fat chance he will put that on,' I interrupt. 'He won't pin anything on that shiny biker jacket unless it's the badge of Brighton and Hove Albion.'

But Rex Mundi snatches the button badge from Trout's hand and says, 'Balls, Ruin! I will wear this one with pride. For our Micheal and for us too!'

'Us?' I loathe the way he has just said 'Michael' instead of 'Mick'. Next thing you know he will be referring to his older brother in the Irish version 'Mícheál' as if that will impress our suspicious, belligerent host.

'Yeah, us. The Red Army Faction on its way to Windsor. You're coming too, Trout?' the exile-returned continues.

'Too fuckin' right I am. We have chanting that needs to be filmed!'

Suddenly, Padre Pio pipes up, 'Ya haven't got one of them hand grenades ta throw at the Orangemen, Trout? I'm game ta do that.'

This only makes Trout flare up. 'Shut fuckin' up about any talk over hand grenades, dildo brain.'

Dope is supposed to calm the nerves and leave you chilled out, but Trout has that nasty cold suspicious air about him. He is like some stalking predator that also thinks he is being stalked and it is me who he is glaring at again. I am expecting him to start hammering on about fence sitters, traitors, drinkers, cowards and renegades.

'There will be no loose talk about these things in this house,' Trout says with authority before firing a question at me.

'So yer da saved yer cousins' lives. That took balls I suppose, to go over to the east for a rescue mission. Now, no hard feelings here. What do you think the score will be today?' He extends his hand across the table to shake mine.

'2-0 to the Reds!' I reply, only half in belief that this is really going to happen.

'I think it will be tighter, Ruin,' Trout says, uttering my name for the first time.

'More like 2-1 or 3-2, but I can't see us losing. Anyway, win, lose or draw we'll wreck the fuckin' place,' he adds, while beginning another joint that he insists is only for our nerves on the journey down.

Trout looks around the table with a knowing smile that makes me worry about buckets and spades and hand grenades as we hi-ho-hi-ho off to Windsor we go! Maybe he is just mad enough to smuggle a couple of exploding pineapples onto the Kop to be lobbed into a line of riot cops. Or worse still, he could hand them over to Padre Pio and get him to vault over the fence, onto the pitch and hurl them straight into the North Stand. Padre Pio will be up for whatever Trout has planned for him. Meanwhile, he is goose-stepping around the kitchen with his crotch-reeking index finger playing the part of a Hitler moustache, croaking, 'Here's yer da, Trout. Here's yer Nazi oul da.' Understandably, Trout delivers a well-deserved clout to his lunatic cousin's head.

4

'THE SPEED OF LIFE'

July 1978

She didn't dance. She shimmered. She almost stood still, quaking ever so slightly to the same song that DJ Derek put on for her every Tuesday evening after the band had put away their instruments and the punks had stopped pogoing. She quivered as if some force was coursing through her alabaster skin. She always wore the same tight white silk dress with Chinese script curling over it, over her body. She never slipped or slid on her spiked high heels and fishnets. Her dyed, jet-black hair was crimped and shaped in a Cleopatra cut, and her eyeliner swept out in a dramatic cat-eye. She was a moving hieroglyphic.

She was the mystery of The Pound: she sat on her own, with one can of Coke at her table all night, and spurned forever the advances of all the young punks. She never got up for any songs belted out by the three-chord wonders roaring 1-2-3-4 at the top of every tune, or for any other tunes the DJ played before and after the live act. Her interest was singular: she only got up and onto that sticky, treacherous floor when the DJ played the opening instrumental track to Bowie's *Low*. She was addicted to 'The Speed of Life'.

I had only ever seen her once before in 'real life'. It was one grim winter morning a few months earlier on the number 33 bus as it made its way over from East Belfast. I guessed that she came from 'the other side' but knew instantly that she didn't belong to them or to anybody. This is what drew me to her in the first place and why I felt compelled to summon the courage to talk to her that night. I won't deny being helped along the way by the bottle of Merrydown I had knocked back in the Baby Subway before the gig. That night, even the risk of humiliation did not deter me. I waited until Bowie's instrumental opener to *Low* was over to tell her that she had good taste in music, unlike most of them inside here or over in The Harp. I even found the balls to tell her that Bowie was producing his best ever material since he ran away from the sins of America to hide from them all right up against the Wall.

She said nothing at first, just as I had feared, and then I added, 'Should you really be wearing them high heels when you've all that walking to do on Saturday?'

When she finally replied, it was as if she was measuring every word, carefully and cruelly weighing up her riposte. 'Did I ask you to speak to me? Are you retarded or something?'

'No, don't be offended like. I was just thinking you will have sore feet on Saturday if you wear them heels!'

'And what is so special about Saturday?' she asked.

'It's the 12th! The 12th of July. Won't you be out with Orange Lil and all the girls marching to the Field and then coming back pregnant?'

I noticed that she repressed a laugh and was relieved that she hadn't taken offence.

'Either you are being sarcastic or else you are simply a moron. Now which is it?'

'Well, I can confirm that I am not a moron. I'm just asking if you will be OK for the big day.'

'I won't be going anywhere with that lot next Saturday. I don't like crowds, let alone big processions. Are you going?'

'I wouldn't think I would be welcome. I might be the invited guest on top of one of their eleventh-night bonfires, but I wouldn't qualify to be marching the next morning.'

She snatched up her leather handbag with fringes dangling from it and tried to make a quick exit.

'I'm only slagging ya,' I said, standing up with her. 'I've no time for any of that shit, green or orange. I'm not one of them. And by the way, my name's Robbie, but my friends call me Ruin, and I'm dead on.'

She stopped in her tracks and fixed her eyes upon me. They were still loaded with contempt. 'You're a cheeky wee shite. Does your mother know you're out?'

'I bet you're a secret ABBA fan. You can't admit that in here or you will be tried and convicted for being a secret spide. Truth be told, my ma's dead but don't feel bad about it.'

'Snap!' She smiled back at me. 'Snap! Mine's dead too.'

'Excellent. So we really have got something in common as well as Bowie and liking, ahem, ABBA. So, as I said, I'm Robbie. What's your name?'

She gave me a long scrutinising look and said, 'Well at least you're not afraid of the punk thought-police. If you wanna like ABBA, go ahead, but I don't think I've any of their albums up in my place and—'

I butted in to accept what I assumed was an invitation. 'Don't worry. As long you don't play fucking Pink Floyd or Yes, or for that matter Bob Dylan.'

She nodded in approval towards my home-made T-shirt. 'Well, I can see you've got some taste. I'm Sabine. Let's go!'

Outside The Pound, we skirted past my home area then around the closed-off security zone in the city centre. The streets and roads were deserted, except for one army mobile patrol breaking through the traffic lights. The soldiers cooped up in the back of their jeep wolf-whistled at her while flapping their hands towards me, indicating that they thought I was queer, probably because of all the zips and studs. In the distance, I could make out the burning orange lights illuminating the back of the bakery, where only a few weeks earlier I had joined my friends playing midnight football, acting out all the World Cup games we had just watched on TV. We pretended that we were Kempes, Ardiles, Luque and Passarella. Now, just a few short weeks after the World Cup final, here I am, arm in arm with Sabine as we make our way to the black taxi stand at the City Hall. It hit me that all those last blasts of a football-obsessed childhood were fading, corroding faster than I had ever anticipated in this short burst of summer towards something entirely new and out of time altogether.

Even before Sabine, I had concocted a strategy to spend as much time at The Pound as possible. I had told my father I was sleeping over in Padre Pio's house, where I had spent much of June watching the World Cup matches on his colour TV and heading out afterwards to our free floodlit 'pitch' at the back of Inglis's bakery to play five-a-side into the early hours of the morning. PP was always in foul humour when we were going back to his house to bed. He was a shite player and was always picked last. I'd wait for him to fall asleep before creeping back downstairs to the front parlour, where his mother would be waiting for me on the floral sofa – legs open and propped up on the table, just like that first night a few days after we buried my own mother. Her feet in slippers, the half-empty bottle of vodka, a three-quarters smoked cigarette burning in the ashtray and then her slobbering, her urgings, her orders. On my knees eventually and my head in-between her thighs, spearing her moist pubis with the tip of my tongue while she moaned and groaned in a voice rubbed with smoke and Smirnoff: 'It's just a bit of sex, Robert. It's just a wee bit of sex.'

Truth be told, that's why I was confident on that first night with Sabine. I wasn't afraid of this standoffish snob with the crimped hair, the white dress and the fishnets that I longed to rip off with my teeth when we finally got to be alone. Padre Pio's mum had once whispered into my ear when she finally allowed me to bolt inside her that she was giving me 'an education'.

In the taxi up to the Holy Lands, we snogged for the first time and I tasted a sharp clean laboratorial sensation in her mouth.

'I thought you only drank Coke,' I murmured as I tried to slip my hand up her dress.

'At them there prices, no way,' she said. 'They don't have civilian searchers on the door to check what's in your bag. I could get a bomb into The Pound if I wanted to. A half bottle of Smirnoff is easy to smuggle inside,' she continued, while placing her hand on my swelling crotch. 'I wonder why you,' she said.

'Why me what?' I answered.

'I never bother with anyone in The Pound. You're my first. I'm just wondering why you.'

'Cos I'm special?' I ventured helpfully, as I slide my hand further up her dress.

'Maybe,' she whispered and, gliding the tip of her tongue inside my ear, added, 'It's more likely that I'm just feeling particularly horny tonight and I like your T-shirt.'

We must have fucked all night inside 66 Jerusalem Street because when I woke up early the next day my cock was raw and my head was pounding thanks to a half bottle of vodka. Sabine had provided us with a soundtrack for our sex; not Bowie, as I had expected, not even ABBA. Instead we rolled about, she lay astride me, and I took her from behind to the sound of 1950s rock 'n' roll blaring from a C-60 tape she had put on. I recalled too the way she liked to writhe around when she was on top, like the lithe, sinister dancer at the start of *Tales of the Unexpected*. The look on her face told you that she was elsewhere, and wherever that was, she was in charge.

Sabine stirred beside me. 'You've obviously done this before, young man, and there was me hoping you'd be a virgin,' she said with a smirk.

'Sorry about that, love. Damned inconvenient of me all the same,' I replied.

'Where did you learn to screw like that?' she asked.

'I could ask you the same question. You are one fine mount.'

'Oh, I think I was the one doing the mounting, Mr Ruin! But hey, I forgot to ask you something important: what age are you?'

'Fourteen, mam,' I joked and got an elbow in the ribs from her. 'Nah, I'm nineteen. I'm just having a year off before I go to uni,' I lied. 'What about you?'

She had wrapped her legs over mine and started to caress my face with her fingers.

'I am at the art college. It's only the foundation year but I'm thinking of starting first year proper over in London. Maybe St Martin's if I can get in. Where have you applied for?'

'Maybe I'll head to London too. Perhaps the LSE. My dad thinks I should go there and study economics.'

'Didn't Mick Jagger go to the LSE?'

'I'm not applying there because that wanker went to it!' I protested.

Sabine put two fingers across my lips and giggled. 'For fuck's sake, don't be applying to the LSE just to follow me to London then.'

As my eyes got used to the milky morning light, I could make out a whitewashed walled room, pine floorboards and piles upon piles of splashes of paint on rectangular field-grey boards. When Sabine got up to go to the bathroom, I went over to examine a mini-tower of her work propped up beside the record player. *Low* was on the turntable alongside a couple of photos. The most striking image was a side profile of a man, which was blurred by slashes of white, pink and grey streaks shooting off his visage and merging into what seemed to be a kind of gathering storm in the background. I held it up to the window to see it in the morning sunlight.

'I see you're admiring my dad,' Sabine said, as she walked towards me. 'I took those pics shortly after my mum died. Then I based a painting on them too. We were walking along the beach at Holywood talking about her when I got him to stop and pose.'

'They're amazing. I'm jealous,' was all I could say.

'I'd never tell him I based a painting on those pictures.'

'Why?'

'Because he thinks that the pics I took caught him when he was weak. My dad doesn't like to look weak.'

'So what happened to your mum, Sabine?' I asked, suddenly fearing that she might have been killed in the Troubles and Sabine would hold it against the likes of me.

'She got ovarian cancer. She went very quickly, Robert.'

I liked the way she said 'Robert' for the first time. I nearly forgot to answer when she went on to ask about my own mother.

'Well that's a half-snap!' I replied eventually. 'I was told it was liver cancer. Sabine, I ... I was afraid your mum may have been killed in the Troubles. I was afraid you'd—'

'I'd what? Blame you? Well, she didn't and if she had, it would have had nothing to do with you. You are not of them the way I am not one of them, Mr Ruin. We are not like any of them. Our so-called sides. I could tell that about you almost right away.'

'Most people are sick of all this Troubles shite, Sabine.'

'Yeah, but most don't say that loud enough.'

'You'd get on well with me da,' I say, as I place the painting back against the record player.

Before it all got too serious, Sabine held out her hand like a debutante at a ball. I nodded formally and kissed her middle knuckle. Then she went rummaging around the side of the bed for her handbag. She plucked out a blister pack of tiny white pills and swallowed one. It was only then that I remembered I never wore a johnny the night before.

She picked up my T-shirt that I had flung onto the floor when we first leapt into bed. It was one of my home-made ones with a message marked out in black block capitals.

'It was mostly this, you know. Why I took you home,' she said, holding the T-shirt out to me.

'My T-shirt?'

'Yep. I liked the message and that you made it yourself. I hate them punk posers who send their cheques to companies that advertise for 'Boy' bondage trousers and fart-flaps in the back pages of the NME. You really hate Bob Dylan? That's acceptable! Now if you had written 'I hate Bowie' on that shirt I would have ignored you. We'd have been finished before we even got started. And you hate Pink Floyd too – that's an added bonus!'

5

COMMS I

1987

Skyscraper's friends are closing in on us. Although we few in here remain united and strong, we are without a dick to defend ourselves. They imagine their numbers give them the whip hand. Also, it's possible they have brought in gear from the outside, so we can't take any more chances. If we could get a package in here, anything at all – even a Derringer or a Pen Gun – that might make a big difference. Knowing we had something would be a blow to their morale.

For now, only rumour is keeping us alive. We have put it about that our friends beyond these walls have delivered the shopping, although soon the opposition will be trying to provoke us to produce product. We hear from bigger boys – the rosary-bead rattlers – that Skyscraper's people fear being attack on the wings, landings, kitchens and yards, so they stay very close together.

Your name, of course, keeps coming up in their conversations. Even Skyscraper keeps mentioning you. He has his own team convinced that even though you are not in his gang, you are still someone who can be got at – someone who they can put pressure on to make us dissolve and go away. At least, that's what those who follow him around like a pack of docile dogs keep insisting. They're the ones he recruited as kids – who joined his very own merry wee band. They feared him giving them cold steel then; they still fear him now. They might be cowering, callow and stupid, but he's not! You know and I know that Skyscraper isn't as stupid as the rest of them. We believe his so-called faith in you is a front – a cloak to hide his true plot. He's been in to see his boys several times and, like us, has heard that all the charges ranged against them are on the verge of collapse. The only trouble is, by the time we are all released and walking out the jail gates onto the Crumlin Road, there will be blood flowing even before we get to Carlisle Circus.

So, as the Bolshevik's Eagle once asked: What's to be done?

Well, if he wants a purge let's give him one. A first strike seems to be our best option but naturally none of us in here are presently in a position to do that. On the outside, you are the only one we can trust to get the job done. If you can knock him out of the game then the entire rotten structure that he has established will collapse.

If he agrees to a meeting, you stress that you are only a third party and that all you want is the prevention of Irishmen killing Irishmen again – that we are free to operate our own struggles independently of each other and that maybe, just maybe, one day we will all reunite under a minimum programme that we can all agree on in the fight for national liberation ... all the usual sentimental ballicks.

You suggest it should be somewhere he and his clowns will feel safe in. Somewhere far away down in the south – away from the attention of the Brits and the cops up here. But you plan in advance to make the strike en route and be certain to have your own people in place.

Finally, yes, we have all drunk from the bitter cup of factionalism and it is indeed sour. Yet we have no other option given that he and his allies – his wee praetorian guard – will eventually move against us. If what we do is rapid and surgical, we can bring this to an end without a prolonged shooting match. We are

6

THE CROWD

28 April 1979

We are not walking; we are surging all the way down the Donegall Road. We are a throbbing mass of primary colours: all reds, yellows and blues. We are a moving, menacing organism through which courses currents of fear and expectation. We are a jagged forward-marching phalanx of various uniforms from army surplus, denim skinners, snorkels, duffels, plastic, wool, leather, studs and spikes. We slide, stumble and trip over half bottles of Scotch, scrunched up beer tins, broken glass and even splashes of carrot-flecked boke. We spearhead onwards to the swing-gate of battleship-grey and bottle-green, to where the barrier of peelers and Brits will eventually part open, ushering us across the motorway and into the empty brick-studded fields behind Windsor Park. We are in a trance.

I am still on 'our' side of the M1, and Trout is crushed up against my shoulder. We're hemmed in by a line of heavier older men in their twenties, all of whom he seems to know. They swell and bulge out of Wrangler jackets and blue parkas, and sport beards they shouldn't have bothered sprouting until well into middle age. They are 'comrading' this and 'macara-ing' that to each other en route, talking in the Belfast code called 'Braille' about 'jobs', 'gear', 'napperings', 'smokey joes' and 'up and unders'. The last one provokes Trout to cry out, 'Oh Airey's here, Airey's there, Airey's every-fucking-where, na, na, nan, nan-nan, na, na!'

The Brits patrolling close to the rundown redundant football stadium glare at us when they hear this particular chant, and one of them from the back of a jeep sweeps his SLR rifle with a black rubber gunsight across our line as if he is going to take us out; as if we really think he is going to open fire.

'Who's that lying on the dashboard? Who's that splattered on the screen? Who's that all over the wheel?' Trout howls, as two-finger salutes are offered to the Brit patrol. He then pokes me in the shoulder and points up to the side of the decaying old touchline stand with the letters 'Celtic Park' still painted over the giant green background.

'Look at that crowd, son, and ask yourself why! That is what this is about today, Robbie Ruin. They literally kicked and booted Belfast Celtic out of the league all them years ago to put the uppity Taig team in their place, which was off the pitch and out of the league for good. They made sure that that place over there was only good enough for ta run greyhounds around the track beyond the grass. But now we're back and we're on our way to Windsor to fuck them all over,' Trout says.

At that, the beefy-boy brigade on either side of us raise clenched fists in unison into the air and instantly I can see an image of my father back at home, all alone by his radio at the sink, carefully shaving, readying himself for the Saturday ahead with his handful of comrades in the bar. I picture him throwing up at the thought of his son being carried forward by this force pulsating all around me. In my eyes, my da looks more lost than I am now in this moment: isolated, irrelevant, voiceless and being left further behind by the new tide that is propelling me on.

I am bricking it because I have lost sight of Padre Pio amid the thickening numbers that are now bunched up at the security line on the M1. The last thing I want or need is to be stuck with Trout throughout the entire final, listening to his sermons from on high about the sacrifices of his big brother, Mullet, and the struggle in general. Besides, it's Rex Mundi and Padre Pio who have all the drugs we need to get through this day. My bangers are away with it already and we're not even close to kick-off, and those two fuckwits have disappeared into the throng. Trout clocks that I am scouting about for them as the police and army lines eventually open and the traffic is halted on the motorway.

'Don't worry about those two, Ruin,' Trout says slyly, 'PP give me the match tickets to mind in case he got scooped by the peelers on the way down. The two of them dicks can't get into the final without finding me first.'

Suddenly, wheels screech and I leap up above the crowd to see the side window of an ambulance smashed in and PP jumping into the air as if to claim it. A snatch squad of peelers start swinging batons and use Perspex shields to gouge out a route through the crowd to arrest him. We ebb and flow as the riot cops batter their way towards him. But Padre Pio has already bolted, slipping back to the main mass of supporters who are roaring, 'SS RUC, SS RUC'.

Trout and I wriggle our way back to the edge of the crowd and break off towards one of the entries in search of Padre Pio. We finally spot him with his hands around the throat of a kid who looks about fourteen and is wearing a red-and-white stove-pipe hat and a yellow Cliftonville away jersey. The hat comes off first and then the kid collapses to the ground and curls up into a ball to protect himself from the kicks raining down on him.

'Not just the hat, not just the hat. Give me your fuckin' jersey as well. Give me your fucking jersey and you can have my army jacket. Give me the cunting jersey,' Padre Pio screams at the boy on the ground. PP intends to get through that barrier in disguise and not be recognised as the one who hurled the stone at the ambulance passing by.

The kid is now crooked over like a foetus, shaking with fear and pain. At that moment, I really want to lift up the nearest sliver of glass on the ground and slice my friend's throat.

'Give him your hat at least, kid, and he'll let ya go. The peelers are after him and he needs to hide from them.' Trout barks out the order like he was a regimental sergeant major on the parade ground.

Padre Pio is buzzing. He is bouncing on the balls of his feet, ducking and diving, and weaving about like a prize fighter in the ring. 'Aye, you tell him, Trout. If he knows what's good for him he'll give me the Cliftonville shirt too. And you, Ruin, can hold my coat cos this wee fucker isn't getting it,' PP says.

The boy stumbles to his feet. He is reeling from the blows. He rips off his football jersey, throws it into a mucky puddle and stamps on it repeatedly. This makes Padre Pio burst into a fit of giggles. Trout reaches into his army jacket, pulls out a naggin of High Commissioner whiskey and hands it to the boy.

'Keep that, son. You really are game to stand up to that mongoloid there,' Trout says, pointing at the sniggering Padre Pio.

But a thank you doesn't come. Instead, the boy hurls the whiskey bottle against a wall graffitied with 'Victory To The Provos'. 'Shove yer whiskey up your arse, chief,' the kid yells, which now leaves Trout in fits of manic laughter too.

Padre Pio picks up the stove-pipe hat, tips it like a Victorian gentleman towards the boy, pops it on his head and says, 'That wee fucker has game, I'll give him that.'

7

GOD SAVE THE QUEEN

28 April 1979

We are on the Spion Kop, crushed up against the barriers, watching the stone throwing to and fro from the North Stand, where the hardest of the huns are gathered. The missiles are gliding across a no-man's-land of riot cops, barbwire and empty broken-up terraces. The peelers use their see-through shields to bat and swat some of the bricks and bottles out of the way, but from time to time our ammo and theirs breach the lines and someone takes a hit. This is not like the riots on the streets when debris pelts down on the army Saracens, the screeching police tenders, the military snatch squads and the rubber-bullet-firing police phalanxes. Here, in-between the two floodlights, behind the goal at the Kop end, there are short breaks between the salvoes as the Red Army Factions scan the ground for anything to throw. Every time a stone or bottle sails over into the North Stand and the mass ranks of the assorted Prods swell backwards in temporary retreat, a cheer goes up from the Kop. But then you look around and some pissed-up spide from our side is being led away out of the throng, looking stunned, with blood pissing from his forehead and a red-and-white scarf wrapped around his wound for a bandage.

Trout is scouting about all over the place, whispering into the ears of his comrades, planning something very shortly it seems, while Padre Pio stands beside me drawing deeply from another joint. He's glass-eyed and when he sniggers, jets of smoke shoot out of his nostrils. Weirdly, he looks like he's back on the altar serving at a funeral Mass, swinging the incense that curls over some stiff in a coffin.

'This is some fuckin' gear Rex Mundi provided,' PP announces when he comes back to earth. 'This is the fuckin' business. He's a sound man, a sound man. Our Trout doesn't know what he is missing, the stupid cunt.'

I take a blast myself and suddenly there is white noise, bright light and feedback in an echo chamber as the surrounding chants reverberate in beats of four across the Kop: 'Red Army, Red Army, Red Army, Red Army'. The North Stand responds with hymns of praise for the Shankill Butchers. The mass choirs of snouts over there run their forefingers across their throats while they sing, 'One Basher Bates, there's only one Basher Bates, one Basher Bates, there's only one Basher Bates.'

Suddenly, the whole of the Kop surges towards the fence at the goal line and then, instantaneously, the wave retreats, leaving only the hardcore detritus wedged up against the pitch-side barrier. They form into little huddles and start to fireman's lift each other over the wire before the lines of riot cops break off to stop even more fans vaulting over the fence. As the Lebanese gear wears off a bit, I spot Lanky Balls in his RAF coat and DM boots being one of the first to make it over onto the Windsor turf, followed by my own fucking cousin who is already zigzagging past fat, sweating stewards in white coats. He's hoofing it towards the North Stand, stones in hand, ready to fire straight into the ranks of the red, white and blue.

Padre Pio snatches the joint out of my hand and takes another draw while cocking his head up and down to watch the pre-match entertainment on the pitch. 'He may have good blow, but your cousin is one stupid cunt, Ruin. He's hard ta miss with that head a fucking hair on him. A red fucking Mohican! He'll easily get lifted and the peelers will dump him in the middle of the Orangemen on the Lisburn Road. Still, we can keep the rest of his blow if he does get scooped. We can keep the whole batch for ourselves if Trout stays out there in the crowd trying to save Ireland's honour,' he says.

'At least he's got the balls to get over that wire and get into them bastards,' I blurt out in defence of my cousin.

Suddenly everything around the two of us goes quiet, as if time and motion are frozen; as if PP and I have been transported out of this chaotic cauldron of noise, hatred, stoning, hand-to-hand pitch combat, chanting, farting, belching, retching and vomiting; as if we are transported into another one-to-one dimension, to our own private combat zone. Because I know in an instant what is coming when I dared to suggest that Rex Mundi is gamer than Padre Pio.

PP screams into my face, 'I'm not yellow. I'm not a lapper like your da. I'll fuckin' show ya who's game in this ground.'

He charges towards the fence, elbowing children and oul fellas out of his path. Yet before he can climb over the fence, the riot squad are at the barrier and manage to deliver a few winding blows to his kidneys before he collapses onto the dirt track between the first tier of terracing and the barrier.

I try to stop myself from laughing as Padre Pio pukes. In fact, I am praying inwardly that he chokes to death down there on the dirt. Meanwhile, beyond the wire, there are several contests going on between two sets of fans, including Lanky Balls, who is booting the shit out of some spide with fuzzy Starsky hair and a Portadown scarf. Rex Mundi and a handful of other Reds supporters who reached the pitch are now dodging and weaving their way back to the Kop as bottles and stones are showered on them from the South Stand.

The gladiators from either side eventually scatter as the cops chase them down. My cousin trampolines over the fence and into a group of fans who help him hide from the arrest squads. Missiles, toilet rolls, even smoke bombs keep coming over as the peelers grab a couple of stragglers caught on the pitch, including Lanky Balls himself with someone else's blood over his face and fists. While I picture him handcuffed in the back of an RUC Land Rover, Padre Pio is still writhing on the ground. 'Suffer baby, suffer,' I whisper, as Trout reappears beside me. He runs down the steps to pick up PP just as Jackie Hutton appears from the side of the stadium and marches over to our end. Our manager has his hands outstretched like some spirit-possessed American preacher: the voice of reason on the park, appealing for us to let the game get started. His pleadings actually seem to be working miracles: the Red Army suddenly goes quiet and there are no more attempts to invade the pitch. As the fans pay homage to Hutton, Trout is helping Padre Pio back to our spot.

'What the fuck happened to him, Mr Ruin?' Trout asks in an accusatory tone, as if I'm in charge of that fuckwit's welfare.

'Never mind what happened to him, where the fuck is that joint I rolled?' Rex Mundi interrupts, before receiving congratulatory slaps on the back for making it back amongst us after the pitch incursion.

The crowd sing to the tune of 'Guantanamera' – one of my mother's favourite songs: 'One Jackie Hutton, there's only one Jackie Hutton, one Jackie Hutton, there's only one Jackie Hutton ...'

Padre Pio turns his pain into a sudden surge of ire towards me. 'See when this is over today, I'm gonna get you outside, you cunt.'

'Don't talk shite, PP. You're still stoned,' I say, trying to play down his threat.

'Cos I know what you're at with my ma,' he goes on. 'I'm wise to you, lover boy.'

'You are well and truly out of your box, mate,' I say, attempting to calm him.

'Cos she told me, lover boy. She bastard and well blurted it out. She couldn't help herself. She can never help herself, the dirty oul cow,' he hisses, right into my face.

I am sure he is about to make his move when Trout comes to the rescue and delivers a sober-up slap to the back of Padre Pio's head.

'Stop acting the wanker. There's more important work to be done here today than you two squarin' up to each other. We need to get on TV shouting for prisoner rights,' Trout says as he turns to Rex Mundi and me. 'And you two – just ask yourselves what we can do for the struggle today! Ask yourselves how we can show that none of this here in this place is really normal!'

'What are you waffling on about, Trout? Of course it's not normal. That's what's great about it all,' PP interrupts with regained lucidity.

Rex Mundi tears off his biker jacket, jumps up on one of the crush barriers, whips off his Troops-Out T-shirt and starts waving it at the snouts of the South Stand. The assorted Blues and Ports fans retaliate with wank-hand signals, choruses of 'Oh Spot the Loony' and then a piece of flying roof slate skims over the top of the flame-haired punk before slicing into the face of some poor kid standing behind us. In celebration of another injured Taig, the North Stand breaks into what must be now the fifteenth version of 'The Sash my Father Wore'. On cue, the teams file out onto the pitch, the band strikes up a couple of marching tunes and 15,000 spectators wait for what's coming next.

Cliftonville and Portadown players, their managers, their coaches and their team doctors all line up near the touchline facing the South Stand, and the band break into the first bars of a very familiar song. The North and South Stands start to sway in hypnotic unison. Red, white and blue colours are held aloft. Union Jacks and even Orange Order banners with King Billy on his white horse are waving in deference. Their loyal emblems are billowing and swelling in the gentle April wind.

When the upright and vocal Portadown fans and their newly found friends from Belfast find their voice, Trout and his beefy, beardy mates, dotted all over our end of the ground, start roaring at everyone around them, 'Sit down, sit fucking down. Don't stand for it! Don't fucking stand up. Get down!'

Almost everyone in our end suddenly crumples to the concrete, into a defiant protesting seated mass. As 'God Save the Queen' is met by thousands of wanking hands, it occurs to me that this is the big dramatic event Trout has being harping on about. And here was me worried that he'd slipped Padre Pio a few exploding pineapples.

8

'BREAKING GLASS'

July 1978

All through the summer, my father continued to be obsessed with the Dutch midfielder Robbie Rensenbrink. The TV broadcasted images from Buenos Aires of the Argentine masses marking out their team's triumphant progress with ticker-tape and toilet-roll storms and of their manager, Menotti, chain-smoking in the dugout. When their captain, Passarella, eventually lifted the World Cup in the sky-blue-and-white stripes, my dad cursed under his breath and muttered angrily about an 'inch' and a Junta.

For him the 'inch' became the difference between justice and injustice both on and off the field. In the last thirty seconds of normal time, the Dutch midfielder broke through Argentina's defence and almost won the World Cup for the Netherlands, his shot striking the post just an inch away from global football glory. But that inch gave the Argentinians the space to regroup and go on to win 3-1 in extra time, thus allowing the military dictatorship to milk the victory. Even before that if-only moment, I had been subjected to lectures from my father all through the competition about CIA-trained torturers who put electrodes on their captives' genitals, the thousands of 'Disappeared', the reports and rumours of death flights over the South Atlantic and the near total annihilation of his comrades far away across the ocean. After the Argentine team won, he would preface every lecture about the

Junta's exploitation of the World Cup by berating Rensenbrink for missing his chance.

When Rex Mundi arrived back in Belfast after six long years of exile, he brought over a birthday present for me, one which enraged my dad. It was a blue-and-white striped football shirt he had pilfered from an Argentinian student who had fallen asleep bare-chested on Brighton beach, having left the jersey on the pebbled shore. I barely took it off during the tournament, much to the disgust of my dad, who branded me a traitor to the 'Disappeared', the defeated Argentine Left, the Dutch and to Robbie Rensenbrink.

'Take those colours off inside this house! And you, Aidan McManus, should know better than to bring the jersey being used by the Junta Generals. Your brother would be ashamed of you,' my father said, thumping the table during one late Friday-night game and his fifth bottle of Red Heart Guinness.

Rex Mundi reminded me of this a few weeks later as we made our way via the railway tracks running parallel to the River Lagan up to Sabine's house in the Holy Lands. He informed me that his once-firebombing brother cared little anymore for politics anywhere. After his release, Mick had ended up in West Berlin, dossing down in a squat of hippies by the Landwehr Canal, close to the Wall, which sounded even worse than the accommodation he had once shared with other prisoners during that eighteen-month stint in Crumlin Road jail. His brother was now an entrepreneur of narcotics, both a user and a dealer, who sent parcels of dope home to the English south coast with his couriers of hippy trailers, Bowie-disciples and German punks, the latter on their way to pose inanely up and down London's Kings Road.

'At least when our Mick comes home or sends his teams over to England there's always seriously good dope to be had,' Rex Mundi said as he deftly rolled up a joint even while we walk at pace under the shadow of the blue gas tank. The faint reek of Leb

Gold is competing feebly with the pervasive stench of the sulphur from the coal-powered gasworks to our right.

'So tell me about this art-house babe then, cousin,' Rex Mundi continued as we climbed through a broken piece of fencing leading towards the safe territory of River Terrace.

'I first saw her in The Pound. She always dances to the same song every week.'

'What song?'

'"The Speed of Life", the first track on Bowie's *Low*. We listen to the album all the time now.'

'So apart from being a fellow Bowie freak, what's so special about her?' Rex Mundi asked.

'She's just different. So different from anyone I've ever met before. She's a bit like the man himself: when I first saw her on the dance floor she looked as if she might have fallen to earth from another planet too.'

'You are one serious wanker, cuz.'

'Nah, you're just jealous!'

'Well then you're taking a chance introducing me to her. You're a brave man, Ruin. I could end up as second jockey.'

'You can fuck right off and get that idea out of your head now or I'll put you back on that boat to England,' I replied, before changing the subject in case he really did have ideas about her. 'So when did your Mick start losing interest in the revolution? I thought he went to Germany because he wanted to link up with the Baader-Meinhof gang?'

'Yeah he probably did, but he ended up being linked up instead with a load of Turkish geezers who promised to make him really rich. Plus he got into smack, which means he won't end up rich after all.'

'Smack?'

'Smack, yeah. Heroin, Robbie. Not blow or grass or any of that shit. Really serious business. Anyway, never mind about our Mick. What about your bird?'

'Whatever you do, please do not call her a bird,' I pleaded.

'Has Padre Pio met her yet? he asked.

'You must be fucking joking!' I replied. 'He knows fuck all about her, and let's keep it that way.'

'I hear you, cuz. But he'll be feeling neglected by now. I'm surprised he's not making it his business to know what's keeping you from him.'

Rex was right, but I didn't want PP anywhere near my Sabine, my new world. I wanted to leave him behind – him and all his shite. Sabine was a taste of freedom.

When we arrived at 66 Jerusalem Street, Sabine led us into the front room. The table was covered in a red-and-white chequered tablecloth, which boasted a spread of salads, veggie pastas and numerous oddly shaped bottles of Portuguese and French rosé wine. Rex Mundi went straight over, sniffed the food, lifted the bottle of Mateus Rosé and necked a third of it in one greedy gulp.

'Fuck me! All this rabbit food! Is there anything dead on offer?' he asked after slamming the bottle back down on the table.

She looked him up and down. There was instant disdain on her face, which secretly pleased me.

'It must be exhausting being such a cool rebel with your special 'Boy' zips and bondage jacket there,' Sabine said caustically as she delivered a kiss to my forehead.

My cousin planted his DMs on the table perilously close to the pastas and fumbled in his pockets for his red pack of Rizla. 'Still, it's nice in here. Who do you share it with? Have you got any tidy housemates?' he asked.

'By tidy I think he means sexy, Sabine,' I interrupted.

'I know exactly what he means ... and wants. For your information, I live alone or at least I used to be totally alone until this cheeky wee shite came along. Now have you any other equally stupid questions you want to ask?' Sabine said with her hands on her hips. She had that slightly scrunched up stare of defiance on her face that I had come to love. She was the picture of power on her home patch, defiantly underwhelmed by the sight of an original 1976 'English' punk in her living room.

'So, cuz here is invading your splendid isolation,' Rex Mundi replied sulkily.

'Actually your cousin is great company. He's different from the rest of them.'

'Fair play to him. Happy for the both of you,' Rex Mundi grumbled. He began to roll the next joint, like a soldier who has been taught to deftly break apart and reassemble a rifle while blindfolded. He never looked down at the table once as he pieced the reefer together.

'Here's a present from our Mick and his Turkish mates in Berlin,' he said, sparking up and passing the joint to Sabine. 'Hey love, our Mick told me once that no one who lives in the Holy Lands was ever born in the Holy Lands. So where are you from originally?'

His question irritated me. 'People are normally asked that in this town before they get a hole in the head or their throat slashed, Rex. You've been away too long.'

Sabine inhaled the hashish and released the smoke through her nostrils before emitting what sounded like an orgasmic sigh. 'Don't call me love. But just to satisfy your nosiness, I'm from East Belfast.'

'Hey snap! Me too,' Rex Mundi said. 'I'm also from the east. Where abouts exactly?'

'Imperial Drive off the Woodstock Road originally,' she replied, which made my cousin choke as he took his turn to draw on the dope.

'Fuck me pink, love. You were a two-minute walk from my house. You might remember it. It was the big three storey one on the main road that got burned down in 1971. The one just facing the chapel that your neighbours also tried to burn down quite a few times.'

Noticing that Rex Mundi's tone had grown a little darker, I joked nervously. 'Small world, eh! Belfast's a village.'

'Yeah, a village with lynch mobs carrying fiery torches. We were given twenty-four hours to get out of your area or else,' he said, pointing at Sabine.

'It wasn't MY area,' she protested. 'Whatever happened to you and your family had nothing to do with me. Like now, with all this shit around us. I've no interest in any of it. None. The only parade I will ever attend is one that supports my right to control my own body. I won't march behind any flag. So don't lump me in with that lot over what happened to you.'

Rex Mundi deliberately ignored her protests. 'Over what happened to us! I'll tell you what happened to us, shall I? If it wasn't for Ruin's dad and some of his friends we would all be in the ground now. Have you told her about your dad and his old comrades yet, Robbie?'

Sabine sensed that he was turning on me now all of a sudden. 'Leave Robert and his family out of this. It had nothing to do with my family, and besides, we weren't even living in the area back in 1971.'

'Where were you living then, Sabine?' I asked, trying to deflect any questions from her about my dad's old associates.

'In Fallingbostel with the British Army of the Rhine,' she said and immediately appeared to regret telling us this.

There was a silent cessation of hostility between them. A gentle paralysing fug of hashish hung in the air as we listened to *Low* once more, with Rex Mundi constantly going over to the record player and dropping the needle on 'Breaking Glass'. He was trying to convince Sabine that it was a song about Iggy Pop invading the peace and space of Bowie's Berlin hideaway.

After we had downed the third bottle of Mateus Rosé, Sabine gripped on to the side of the armchair and finally staggered to her feet. She grabbed a crumpled up sleeping bag, threw it at Rex and snarled, 'You're on the chair or the floor. Take your pick. I'm fucked and I expect to be fucked by this young man sometime in the morning. I'm off to bed, Robert.'

Rex Mundi ignored us as we snogged good night, preferring to skin up another joint while spearing a few tubes of pasta and popping a couple of olives into his mouth. He only opened his mouth again when I went over to replay 'Breaking Glass' once Sabine was in bed.

'She is some find, mate. I'll give you that. But Rob, a word of warning: don't get too gone on her.'

'What are you talking about? You heard her. She's cracked on me.'

His voice grew strangely softer as he moved over to the other sofa where I was sitting. 'I'm not being funny, but she won't be around forever for you. She'll move on, believe me. And it's got nothing to do with her being a bluenose or me not even getting to be second jockey.'

'Bluenose! What shite you talk! You know she's not a drum-beater so why go on about where she is from? You heard her – she hates all that shit: the Twelfth, the Orangemen, the Queen. It means fuck all to her.'

'Robbie. It's got nothing to do with where she comes from; it's about where she's going. I'm telling you this. I've met her type so many times across the water. All those middle-class art college punk girls, dressed like they're extras from the *Masque of the Read Death* just to piss off their daddies. They all go off to do higher things with richer people, mate, not with the likes of us. And speaking of daddy, don't you think her da was in the Brits?'

'Course he was in the Brits, but so what? By the way, don't go mentioning that ever to her again, please.'

'Why?' Rex Mundi said as he lay back in the sofa beside me and took one final draw from the butt of the joint.

'Because loose talk costs lives, as your uncle often reminds both me and you.'

Tired of his jibing at her, I zipped open the sleeping bag and flung it over to him. A short while later, he conked out. I cleared away the mostly uneaten food, rescued *Low* from the turntable and slipped it back into its sleeve. I walked over to the mantlepiece and picked up the portrait Sabine had painted of her father following her mother's death. I looked back at my cousin, snoring inside the sleeping bag, and wondered why he had only mentioned my mum once since he came back. Rex Mundi had never asked a single question about how she had gotten sick or the way she had finally slipped away. Perhaps his dad had warned him not to pry, given my mother's reputation for causing my father grief over the last few years and subjecting him to ridicule behind his back in the district. To his brother and friends, she was the lush, the bar-room bike, the chaser of hard men, the hunter of all those OCs, adjutants and operators.

Sabine was still awake when I tiptoed into the bedroom and slid in beside her. She slithered over to the side of the wall. I flipped over on my side and ran my forefinger along the contours of her body from the nape of her neck to the small of her back.

'Your cousin really hates me, Robert,' she sniffled.

'He's stoned and still finds it weird being back here, that's all. He gets carried away with being home. For fuck's sake, I had to stop him wearing a Troops-Out T-shirt today when we went round to the Fountain to meet some of my punk mates. My dad went ballistic and said if he wore that we would either be arrested or killed.'

'But he blames me for being burnt out of his house even if that had nothing to do with me. I wasn't even living here then.'

'I know. I know. He's just acting weird and will soon wise up. He was even going to wear that T-shirt down to The Harp. Imagine the reaction of some of the punks to that. He hasn't a clue what it's all about here.'

Sabine turned around abruptly and faced me. 'Well, he's no better than that idiot Joe Strummer wearing his 'Smash H-Block'

T-shirt, is he? And you lot look up to Strummer like he's some sort of guru.'

'I thought Strummer was taking the piss out of all that shite in "Tommy Gun",' I said, feebly trying to defend The Clash frontman.

She started singing in a mocking whisper, '"Oh Tommy Gun, you ain't happy less you got one! Tommy Gun. Ain't gonna shoot the place up just for fun." Total idiot, Robert.'

I continued singing where she'd left off but was met with a short sharp donkey kick into my shin.

'Keep it down and go to sleep. I want you energised for the morning,' she ordered, and then she said, 'Robert? Is that his real name? Aidan? Why the fuck then does he go by Rex Mundi?'

'Next time he wears the biker jacket instead of the 'Boy' gear, you will understand.'

'Understand what, Robert?'

'That he has the Devil on his back, Sabine.'

'More like a chip on the shoulder, if you ask me,' she murmured as she drifted off to sleep.

9

COMMS 2

1987

If the truth be told we were all a bit taken aback by the reticence in your reply. Did I detect a whiff of sentimentality when you reminded us that he brought you into this movement? Are you losing your memory here? Wasn't it me - not him - who saw your potential and gave the go-ahead for you to come into the group? Are you suffering from amnesia, comrade? Don't you recall the way he behaved towards the younger recruits and how he surrounded himself with little yes-men? Have you forgotten what you told me about him and what he is capable of? I might be related to him, but family ties have never blinded me to his failings as an activist.

Have you also forgotten what happened to Duffy over in Amsterdam? Don't you remember how they dumped him like a dog somewhere, probably in a canal? Are you oblivious to the pain his family have gone through searching (and still searching) for their missing son? Don't you think that if he could do that to Duffy he would do it to others too? Was Duffy not a friend of yours as well as mine?

Remember - this network was all down to your hard work. You were sent as an envoy to the Middle East and came back with a master plan. You were chosen because you could articulate our cause politically out there and tell our friends across the sea about our needs. You handpicked Duffy as one of your men to execute that plan, and HE ends up getting executed. Don't you owe his memory something?

Do you imagine that we can really just sit here and rot in these cells with only the cockroaches for company until we walk free one day and straight into an ambush? Can we afford to be complacent about his manic paranoia? Do you really think you and I are immune from his madness?

Yours perplexed ... Comrade T.

10

PLATT HITS THE POST ... BELL NOW RISING

28 April 1979

It's only gone one minute, thirty-seven seconds, and they are already singing from the North Stand, 'You're gonna win fuck all, you're gonna win fuck all, you're gonna win, you're gonna win fuck all!'

Jim Campbell has nodded the ball past our keeper Brian Johnston and that produces an instrumental humming to 'The Yanks are Coming' from all the huns on both sides of the stadium, while bog rolls fly onto the left of the pitch in celebration. There is almost total silence around a numbed and stunned Kop.

Padre Pio has missed Portadown taking the lead as he is still too busy stuffing his wee stubby fingers down his throat trying to make himself throw up again. Trout is bent over beside him. They look like they are huddled in the corner of a boxing ring. I'm smirking as I hear Trout coaching his puke along: 'That's it, PP. Come on, champ. Get it up, son. Get it all out.'

There is no chance now that PP will choke to death on his own boke. Sufficiently restored, he starts to lash rings around him down at the feet of an old peeler guarding the bottom steps leading to the pitch fencing. I look at the oul boy with his big calloused country thumbs shoved up into his flak jacket. There is a look of real disgust on his face; he is clearly saving all this up for his fellow parishioners at Sunday service as yet further evidence of filthy Romanist behaviour.

Padre Pio looks thoroughly pleased with himself as he looks up from the pile of puke he has just left beside the copper's boots, and he croaks out loud for the RUC man to hear, 'Your Mother sucks cocks in hell!' He is oblivious that it is 1-0 to the Ports after less than two minutes, even when the Orangemen start asking us why they can't hear Cliftonville sing. More white streaks of toilet paper curl into the air across the turf as they are dancing to our left and to our right, swaggering and swaying to their umpteenth rendition of 'The Sash' before they finally slow their tempo down and switch to Rod Stewart sailing along with 'U-D-A all-the-way, fuck the Pope and the I-R-A; U-D-A all-the-way, fuck the Pope and the I-R-A.'

As Michael Adair's pass to Tony Bell fails to produce any threat on the Ports goal, I glance over beyond our edge of no-man's-land to where a man in a grey suit is chatting away to a blonde-haired kid of about seven or eight. Both are yapping away happily to each other despite being smack bang in the middle of the frontline. I grip Trout who comes up the step with his 'patient' and I tell him about the man and boy planted on their own between us and the riot peelers holding back the hun-hordes in the North Stand.

'That's their problem, mate,' Trout replies. 'And you know what your problem is, Ruin? You're too fucking soft. I blame all that education you're indulging in. Keep yer eyes on the pitch. The Reds are about to take a free kick.'

Twenty yards out from goal, Ciaran McCurry slides a short ball to John Platt who then hammers a long-range shot into the right-sided post just as a smoke bomb explodes on the sand behind the net. The ball rebounds and it's still 1-0 to the Ports, but at least our crowd have finally woken up. Cliftonville keep pressing forward and the man and boy get up from their arses when the police dogs start yelping at the edge of the Kop. Platt was inches away from scoring ... just like Rensenbrink. The Reds take a corner on the left and when the ball falls to the right, Peter McCusker crosses it back. Tony Bell rises and heads it over the bar.

Trout points over to the empty space where the man and boy were sitting just a few seconds earlier. 'Here Ruin. He was probably one of your da's men, thinking he could hold the middle ground.'

That wanking, liver-lipped bastard! Trout will say anything he can to have a go at my dad and his politics; anything to act the big man in front of his cousin who, of course, gleefully joins in.

'Aye, Trout. Only yer man and that kid had more sense in the end. He got back on our side just before it was too late,' PP quips, and I can hear once more my father's repeated warnings to me about him.

What would my da say if I told him the real reason why I stay over in his house? Padre Pio knows it, or at least hints that he knows. Maybe he has secretly watched us from the crack in the door leading into the front parlour. Perhaps he is really bluffing. Or what if he has seen me down on my knees in-between his ma's legs, licking her minge out under the framed photo of 'Padre Pio the Holy Man' with his hands clasped in prayer and his tightly-clipped bearded chin pointing up to the sunbeams Jesus is shooting down to him from the sky. PP could be waiting for the final to finally do me. He could have the blade planked somewhere down in the grass at the top of the Kop. I must move closer to my cousin, who is probably my only hope of getting away from here today without being bladed.

Padre Pio is whispering slyly into Trout's ear, so I elbow Rex Mundi. We both look up at the floodlight that is full of really game wee Reds men who have climbed up the skeletal steelwork to get the best view of the entire stadium. But as Rex Mundi and I try to sneakily ascend towards the top of the Kop, we are knocked back in the opposite direction by an invisible force and collapse towards the crush barriers closer to the pitch. Thousands are pogoing all around us in joy. When I pick myself up from the ground, I see Big John Platt tearing towards us in celebration. Rex Mundi and I have missed the equaliser, but at least PP has been swallowed up by the throng. I clock him rising up on someone's shoulders to celebrate, to taunt and give two-fingered salutes to the North and South Stands. Trout has to be somewhere down there below him, possibly propping the little emperor up in the air.

Some spide in a brown mangy duffel coat is hugging Rex Mundi and screaming at the both of us, 'Overhead kick from Bell. Platt then nappers it into the net. God Bless big John!' I thank God this pimpled-face loser hadn't gripped Padre Pio instead, otherwise there would have been an 'incident' in the middle of the Red Army's euphoria. In PP's mind, simps like him don't serve any solidarity.

As the Kop bursts into another round of 'We're gonna win the cup', Rex Mundi and I retrace our steps back up towards the top of the terracing. We can see the mountains far off to the west behind us, and the floodlight to our right is quivering and shaking from the wind and the weight of the Reds fans hanging onto it.

In retaliation, the huns on the North Stand – both 'guests' and 'hosts' – are chanting 'Linfield, Champions, Linfield, Champions', to which we respond with 'Shit, Shit, Shit'. Rex Mundi sits down on a clump of grass in the lotus position and begins laying out skins, bits of dope, chopped up blue bits of a Rizla packet and tobacco.

'Fancy a blast at half-time?' he asks.

'For fuck's sake, there's about a million cops in here. Put that gear away until later.'

'So why drag me up here away from all the action down there?' he inquires.

'I just wanted to get away from PP and Trout. They're acting like they are up to something. So it's best to stay clear of them both for a while.'

Rex Mundi gathers up the dope and the gear and puts it all back in various zipped pockets of his biker. He gives me a funny look when he has stored all his stuff away.

'You're as white as a sheet, cousin. Does our Mick's Leb Gold not agree with you or something?'

'Nah, I'm alright. Just up the walls a bit over this match. I can't bear to think about losing it and having to listen to those cunts over there.'

'You sure that's all, mate? I saw that retard saying something to you earlier in the game. Is he threatening you or anything? If he is, I'll kick his shit in.'

'No, no, no sweat. He's just half cut that's all, making no sense. He was crying on about his da and how much he would have loved being here today, especially when we all sat down during "God Save The Queen". But he's not coming back, he's never coming back.'

'I wish our Mick was here too. He would love to see this. It really should be history in the making, as our new friend Trout keeps telling us. For Mick it would have been a chance to get a crack at some of the bastards that burnt us out. Still, he's probably scagged out of his box somewhere up near the Wall with some mad Turkish tunes blaring all around him while he writes his fucking poetry.'

'Poetry?'

'Yeah, fucking poetry. He writes poems every day and even sends some to my da for some God unknown reason. He says he only writes them when he smokes opium, says it opens up his consciousness. He is totally shot away with it if you ask me. Those hippies have a lot to answer for.'

Rex Mundi then sweeps a hand across the entire stadium that is laid out below us and cries out, 'What's so funny about peace, love and understanding? Well there's your answer Elvis Costello, you speccy idiot. They're kicking the shite out of each and they're loving it down there because it's fucking great.'

I really do want to tell my cousin about those dark menacing hints from PP; about his ma; about our supposedly secret nights in the parlour, but I hold back. Padre Pio will probably get too drunk and stoned later to act on any of it. But will I ever be truly free from him now? He has threatened to blade me before but then backed away, claiming he was only raking afterwards. He has had me on the ground, pinned down, barking his manic mantra of 'Submit, submit Robbie, submit McManus' into my face. That was a long while ago, but the memory of it has once more drained the blood from my bake.

A prod in the ribs from Rex Mundi shakes me out of my torpor. 'You look like death warmed up, cousin. Let's get back down there, gather up some ammo from the ground and get back into those other cunts.'

11

'SOUND AND VISION'

July 1978

Amid all the anarchy, chaos and destruction, the word that sliced through us was 'allowed'. Among the spittle-flecked, slashed-up school blazers, studded bikers, torn cheesecloth 'Destroy' T-shirts, the green-and-jaundiced army trousers, spiked Mohawks or just lazily messed up hairdos – they were 'allowed'.

As the punks clashed and then separated in knots of four or five on the dance floor of The Harp to 'Holidays in the Sun', the word 'allowed' ripped right through our company and divided our table into rival factions. The Pistols finished singing, the tempo slowed and the remnants started to jive and sway instead to Bob Marley's 'Exodus', which made Sabine snigger into her illicit vodka-laced Coke tin.

'Hah! The punks are only *allowed* to dance to reggae,' she cried out, provoking Rex Mundi to snort loudly into his pint glass.

'Watch it, you two!' I hissed. We were under the sneering surveillance of the barman, whose contempt for the pub's newfound customers was now enhanced on hearing one of them was speaking in an English accent. 'Tommy Nasty tried to get me thrown out of here last week because he said I was underage.'

'You are underage, cousin,' Rex said. 'Half the fucking punters in here are underage.'

'He's looking for any excuse to chuck one of us out, and by the way he's staring, it might be you this time,' I said.

Sabine was back up on the floor after the DJ paid heed to her request for a track from *Low* by putting his needle down on 'Sound and Vision'. She was joined by the two defiant male Bowie freaks wearing balloonish Turkish Pasha trousers and sporting sculpted, wedged and dyed haircuts. They were the rebels within the rebellion who wanted to be outsiders, even among all of Belfast's other defiant, indefinable misfits.

'Tell me this, cousin. Who the fuck does madam up there think she is? She piss-takes all those kids just because they like to dance to Bob Marley.'

I rushed to defend her. 'She's being ironic. She sees the irony of it all … that they are "allowed" to like reggae but no other music. Look! Not one of them has got up to dance to Bowie.'

'I see you're not getting up with her either! Are you not "allowed" to interrupt her when she's in her Bowie trance?' Rex Mundi sneered back.

At least he had left the Troops-Out T-shirt at home for the evening, swapping it for another one with severed heads wearing gas masks amid reams of bloodied barbed wire. But he wasn't giving up on running down Sabine for her observation, even as he fixed his glare on her figure shimmering and swaying beside her two fellow Bowie fans.

'She's so arrogant that one. Fit and tidy, I'll give you that, but you mark my words, cousin, your little "*Astral Weeks* summer" with her will soon be at an end. First chance and she'll be gone before September.'

'What the fuck are on you on about? *Astral Weeks*?'

'Van Morrison, man. Don't tell me you haven't heard of him?'

'Was he some oul hippy that your Mick made you listen to? Anyway, are you jealous of me and Sabine or something? Why don't you go over there, pick out one of them punkettes you've been leering at all night and leave us alone! Tell them all about your days posing along the Kings Road. There's a couple of free subways down by the Albert Clock you could be taking them down to for a quick ride.' I hit back at him, tired now over his constant carping commentary on Sabine.

However, the look he shot back at me wasn't threatening or menacing, it was loaded with patronising pity instead.

'Cousin. Dear cousin. I'm just saying to watch out for ones like that. They're users.'

'You don't like her because she's an East Belfast Prod, or else maybe you secretly fancy her.'

'I'm just worried about you, that's all.'

'Well don't be, and don't say anything else because here she comes with two pints for us, you ungrateful prick,' I said, as Sabine returned slowly to our table from the bar, carefully click-clacking on her heels, with two pint glasses cupped against her breasts and her tin of Coke tucked under her chin.

Rex Mundi beat a temporary retreat before she arrived with the drinks. 'Alright, cousin. Have it your way. You're cracked on the older woman. Enjoy while it lasts, mate. Maybe I will take up your challenge and poke one of them punkettes over there tonight.'

'Aye, you do that, cuz. Fill yer DM boots.'

Instead of thanking her for the beer when she plonked the pint down beside him, Rex Mundi brushed past Sabine and leapt onto the dance floor to the opening bars of Magazine's 'Shot By Both Sides'.

Sabine appeared stunned by his sudden exit and kept watching him from her seat as he gyrated and slammed into a group of three punkettes in their PVC and leopard-skin trousers.

'What's the matter with Boy Bondage up there? Were you and him having a row about me?' she asked.

'What makes you think we were arguing at all?'

'Because I know he hates me being here with you. He doesn't approve of me.'

'We were talking about my mum, if truth be told,' I said.

I never intended it, but I could see I had landed a blow on her – but that's the trouble with dragging the dead across any floor. Because in this town, the dead are weapons the living can always deploy in defence as well as attack. The dead can be missiles to be constantly launched all over this place, to justify U-turns as well as no surrenders; to certify why yet more others have to be put into a hole; to shame the traitors or the dissenters; to cool the passions of the dangerously belligerent; to ward off the predators and to shoot down incoming fire. Her dead mum, my dead mum. They were enough, I hoped, to stop her asking me more questions about him. My dead ma had become my force field. She had once more served some kind of purpose by, this time, making Sabine feel a little guilty.

Sabine deftly extracted the half bottle of vodka from her fringy bag and poured the remainder into the can of Coke under the table. After taking a sneaky sip, she reached over to my face, caressed it and whispered, 'You can talk to me about her any time you want, Robert. After all, we're in the same sinking boat, aren't we? Half-orphans the two of us!' In one elegant movement, she was sitting on my lap.

I had wanted everyone, including Tommy Nasty himself, to see her on my knee, crushed up into me, smudging her lipstick all over my face, her foundation leaving traces across my cheeks as she softly groaned and writhed. I even wished that all the spides at the local shop corner would walk in and take a good fucking look at me now; the ones who shouted 'fruits' at Rex Mundi and me when our backs were turned in the street; the ones who thought the fucking Village People were cool; the ones whose idea of a good time was a youth-worker-organised fun fest. If they could only take a good fucking look at me now and who I was with!

Yet when I opened my eyes, her gaze was not fixed on me but on the dance floor; on the flame-haired, tall, handsome punk with the English accent pogoing amidst the punkette trio to Howard Devoto's manic wailing and prescient warning. She finished our clinch by cupping my face with her hands and giving me a peck on the lips before returning to her own chair.

'Now there's a tune I really get,' Sabine said, raising her voice to be heard.

'Aye, me too. It's the only place where we should be,' I shouted, as the volume from the speakers appeared to spike higher.

'Caught in the crossfire, Robert. It's a danger zone out in the middle. Hope you have the guts to stay there,' she teased.

'Stay beside me then and we can dodge the bullets,' I called back.

Then Sabine looked back over towards the dance floor where Rex Mundi was pushing and shoving a small punk girl against her taller mate.

'Do you think he's coming back with us tonight?'

'Unless one of them has their own place or he decides to sleep in the subway, he probably will. He can't turn up to my da's place all alone, otherwise there will be a search party sent out for me. I'm sorry but I'm stuck with him,' I replied.

She started searching through her bag before eventually producing a key that she then slapped down on the table.

'Give him this in case he doesn't get lucky. It's a spare. He can come up when he's finished in the subway with them,' she said acidly.

'So, is he "allowed" then?'

There was that scrunched up, recalcitrant expression on her face once again. 'What exactly is that supposed to mean, Robert?'

'For somebody who's convinced my cousin hates you, all you do is keep talking about him, Sabine.'

'Wise up, Robert. Don't get paranoid or worse still, don't start becoming possessive.'

Sabine had delivered this like a cold, hard slap, and I sat seething in my chair, gripping on to the pint glass.

Rex Mundi was now up on the stage, bending the ear of the DJ as the punks were once more 'allowed' to rock to and fro to another reggae classic, this time 'No Woman, No Cry'. He then went to the bar, bought two pints, walked back to the DJ and dropped one beside him. He downed the other in three successive swallows. When Marley's song was over 'Sound and Vision' returned once more and my cousin waved to us, beckoning Sabine up onto the floor to join him. She only accepted his offer though when the two Bowie freaks got up as well, as if to flank her, and, in that instant, I didn't know who I hated the most – him or her.

12

COMMS 3

1987

Your apology is more than accepted, comrade. Sorry to come out all hot and heavy, but it was important to state a few obvious things. The most obvious is that one swift blow to their solar plexus and we will set them reeling. You are our ace in the hole and, deep down, I think you know that. This is what I first saw in you when he brought you to me all those years ago – you keep your counsel, you plan ahead and you operate in near total silence. Skyscraper doesn't know the meaning of silence. He's been heard again and again recently saying, 'I've got these two holes freshly dug ...'

One of these holes is surely for me – his blood relative – while the other, we hear, is reserved for you – his supposed life-long friend. Our neighbours, the bigger boys who rattle the rosary beads, are relaying this boast to us. Remember too – in that wee warped brain of his, he sees betrayal and treachery around every corner.

There may be more than two holes dug in his dark imagination. We hear he has been mentioning your father of late. He whispers to a chosen few of the foolishness of ever trusting you, given how your father ran from the struggle and continues to libel all our actions. Like us, he's well aware of your painful split with your da when you joined the struggle. But this doesn't stop him from wondering whether or not you da could be picked up as a hostage in the ensuing battle. Once he told me you couldn't be trusted given your father's influence on your politics. This is a joke of course, considering that to this day he himself never had any real politics - except those of exercising power and fear over his peers and neighbours.

Finally, just picture Comrade Duffy - terrified, tethered, battered and bleeding - a prisoner in some stinkhole of a garage in an Amsterdam suburb. Feel his pain as he refuses to give access to, or even information about, the gear WE (not them) smuggled out of Czecho and over to Ireland, thanks to our Arab friends. Put yourself in Duffy's shoes as he tries to buy time by offering them bogus information, which Skyscraper pursued to no avail. You and I both know the switch that flicks in his head and ignites anger. We heard he personally took a juiced-up cattle-prod to Duffy's private parts when he found out the leads were fake.

Inside and outside some are saying you have sat on the fence for so long you have splinters up your arse, like your da had. I am not one of them. I do not subscribe to their cynicism or pessimism about you. I trust you implicitly as I have done since your earliest days in our organisation, and I have recognised your loyalty to the principles on which we were founded. It was me who recognised your worth in 1979 - not him. It was me who took your information on that Brit seriously. Skyscraper simply finished the job that you and I set up.

Yours in trust ... Comrade T.

13

TOP OF THE KOP

28 April 1979

The chants, insults and stones are still being traded across the concrete hinterland when the players leave the field at half-time. Our crowd quiver backwards en masse when the missiles launched from the North Stand start to land. Then the other side sways back each time a rock or a bottle makes it over no-man's-land and whizzes above the green lines of riot cops holding the huns back. We yell 'Ole' and 'Yeow' every time one of our salvoes hits a target. Whenever the policemen and the St John's Ambulance Brigade escort their wounded away from the frontline, jeers of joy echo from our end.

I am watching these aerial battles from the fringes of grass at the top of the Kop, on my hunkers beside Rex Mundi, who is sitting in the lotus position skinning up another joint. He has taken off his biker jacket and put it over his head as camouflage to keep nosy peelers at bay while he does his work. There is no sign of Padre Pio or Trout anywhere and for now at least I am calm once more.

'We'll get a couple of blasts before the second half,' my cousin announces. 'I'm not giving any more free gear to that retard.'

'Amen to that, cousin. Cut the two of them bastards out, him and Trout.'

'They are two crashing bores if you ask me,' he adds. 'You'd think Trout was the only one in Belfast who had a brother inside for fuck's sake. And as for that other mongoloid, I really don't know why you keep hanging out with him.'

'PP? He won't leave me alone. He never could. Ever since we were in primary school. He got it into his head from day one that I was his mucker for life,' I say.

'I really thought you had ditched him last summer when you were with her,' Rex Mundi adds.

My stomach plummets and I can't respond. I look at my cousin and I can tell he regrets his last sentence. He knows my break from PP and his madness was as fleeting as my time with her.

He decides to break the silence. 'If you are his mucker for life, then why all the aggression? Why all the threats you tell me about?'

I feel a burning sense of shame that I must have been whining to Rex Mundi about Padre Pio, almost pleading for protection. I stand up to stretch my legs because I have pins and needles, and I scan the crowd below for the two of them. Mercifully, they are not to be seen.

'If I tell ya this, ya must never mention it to anyone, not to my da, and certainly never to PP.'

Rex Mundi shoots up and takes a greedy draw from the newly constructed joint. The initial impact of the blow forces him to roll backwards for a second or two.

I grip his shoulder and move close to his left ear as he recovers and whisper, 'I've been riding his ma!'

My cousin starts to choke with both laughter and an excessive inhalation of the Lebanese blow. I have to slap him on the back of his Troops-Out T-shirt for nearly a half minute before he can breathe again.

'No way man! No shit! That is so fucking great. I never thought you had it in you.'

'What do ya mean? You saw me with Sabine all those weeks last summer. I had it in me then, didn't I?' I reply, stung by his incredulity.

'Yeah, I know I know, but I didn't think you'd be game enough to slide it into some really older bird.'

'Anyway what's game about all that?' I ask him.

'Because you've just joined the crumbly club! Congratulations! Mine starts every Tuesday afternoon back in the Goldstone Flats behind our place. My mate Stemp is over in Horsham seeing his dad, and I go straight into the sack with his mum. You can't whack a lonely divorcee for a fine mount. Welcome to my world, Ruin!'

'Fine mount?' I say into myself, wondering, no, knowing, where he had heard these words before.

We sit back onto the grass, as Rex Mundi looks unsteady again on his feet, and I can't stop thinking where he has heard those words before.

'Go on, lover boy. Tell me all about Mrs Padre Pio.'

What is there to tell, other than those Smirnoff leg-openers, the open-sesame to the parting of thighs? Or that we've never actually gone to bed and fucked, staying instead on the floral sofa? That it only ever takes place in the parlour with the yellowing lace-fringed blinds pulled down to keep out neighbours' eyes as you get a hand-job or give a fingering or both? A gobble hasn't been suggested yet, even though yours truly has been doing all the work with my tongue darting in and out of a sharply clipped snatch, my face and ears tingling with the touch of the cheap material of her floral patterned nightdress that is always tented over my head. Oh and yes of course, the deep, deep kiss at the very end that is laced with Embassy Regal and the taste of vodka that reminds me of the smell of the science lab in school.

'As you say Rex, she's a fine mount. They're your words, aren't they?'

'Well they were your words once, cousin,' Rex Mundi says casually.

Something inside me starts to quake, an uncontrollable sensation that is making my blood race and then freeze so much that I shiver. 'I only ever used those words about one person I've ever known. Someone you probably know too.'

He looks at me genuinely puzzled. 'What is this, the teatime quiz? What are you talking about?'

'You know her too,' I press on.

Rex Mundi then turns to me with a sly, knowing look as the band on the pitch far below play on and the Red Army are engaged in a new wave of wanking signals directed towards the North and South Stands.

'I take it you mean Sabine, cousin,' he says.

'Aye. I told her plenty of times she was a fine mount. How did you pick up on that?'

My cousin turns to face me and has on that same smug expression he bore on the night in The Harp when he warned me about my *Astral Weeks* summer coming to a tearful end.

'Yeah, she told me. She told me one time that you used to say that to her over and over. She thought it was really sweet.'

Sweet! That word has always made me want to chunder on the spot because when a girl tells you that you are sweet you know that it's over, or else it never really began in the first place. Sweet equals just good friends; sweet means being liked but never loved, fancied or desired. Be sweet and, very soon, you are surplus to requirements.

'And when did Sabine tell you about our private conversations then? I thought she hated you, the way she spoke to you last summer.'

Rex Mundi is too busy trying to construct a new joint to give me a proper answer. 'Actually, it wasn't last summer at all. We had a long chat about you when I last saw her, Robbie. She couldn't stop talking about you.'

'When? When did you see her? Where?' I demand. I stand up again, roll about on the balls of my feet, in PP pose, and shove his back, forcing him to spill the contents of the fresh spliff he has been trying to build.

'Watch what you are doing, mate!' he cries out while trying to salvage the green roach, the tobacco and the golden-brown pods of Leb that have spilled onto the grass.

'Fuck them drugs. I wanna know when and where you last saw her!'

'What's it to you anymore?' he says. 'I thought you wanted to talk about Padre Pio's ma. Now that is a really interesting subject.'

'No. I'd rather talk about Sabine. Now tell me where you last saw her!'

He is standing directly in front of me now, and I swear to God there is a smirk on his face. I look down and spot a couple of empty half bottles of booze and I'm priming myself to smash one into the side of his head.

He shrugs his shoulders as if it was nothing. 'Look, it was ages ago in London, maybe just after Christmas. I bumped into her at some poseur nightclub in Camden. It was a place full of weirdos with paint on their faces. Some of them were like Wee Willie Winkies carrying fucking candles. They call themselves Blitz Kids or something. And they are completely full of shit.'

'I thought you hated posers. Isn't that why you are going skinhead this summer?' I remind him to wound.

'We were in London only because Brighton were playing away there and we were pissed after another defeat. We ended up there by accident and, as if by magic, Sabine appears,' he continues.

'A pure coincidence was it then?'

'For fuck's sake cousin, will you lighten up! Just take a couple of draws of this dope to calm down and enjoy the game. We might actually win this match. Besides, best to forget about her.'

'You didn't forget her Rex, did you?'

'But you're the one that keeps going on and on about her all the time, Robbie. Look, she spoke very fondly of you and said you still mean a lot to her.'

'And that I told her she was a fine mount! How was it for you then? Was she a fine mount in the mixed bogs of that trendy club in Camden? Or whatever else you were up to with her?'

'Up to? Would you seriously grow fucking up, Ruin!'

'Judas cunt!'

Rex Mundi grabs the lapel of my torn-up blazer, slides his right foot in-between my legs, kicks my right ankle and ju-jitsus me onto my back in one swift move. Then he's on top of me, pinning me down with both elbows pressing into that neuralgic space between each of my shoulders.

'Cut this shit out, Ruin. Cut it out. I only bumped into her in that club. You fucking hear me? Cut it out. Stop letting her get into your head and in-between us.'

Before my brain even reaches first gear, I gob straight into my cousin's face.

'You dirty little shitkicker!' His fists come raining down on my face and I feel the sharp pain of his kneecaps on my solar plexus. After one final smack to the mouth, blood starts flowing, and someone from above hauls the big lanky bastard off me. It's one of Trout's beardy buck Macaras who has ridden to my rescue.

'Stop that, you two dicks. If there's gonna be any fightin' here today then get inta them black bastards over there,' my hairy-faced saviour shouts, nodding over towards the lines of cops close to the South Stand.

Rex Mundi rolls his Troops-Out T-shirt over his head and wipes away the spittle, while I stagger to my feet, stunned, butter-kneed and bleeding from lips and nose. Close by, the peelers, who were watching on indifferently to our scrap, are now pissing themselves laughing at the sight of me.

Just as Trout's comrade starts to lecture us about the need to stand together 'united in struggle' I feel someone else clipping me sharply on the back of the head. For a terrifying instant, I imagine that Padre Pio is joining in the general assault, but then I hear a familiar voice.

'And that is for being a drunken disgrace!'

I turn around and face my father, who is with one of his comrades. The two of them look ridiculously out of place in their dark suits and stringy ties, like two old original mods who went to sleep in the 1960s and woke up into a style-nightmare. Dad's closest friend, Martin Johnstone, is shaking his head in disgust at me and Rex Mundi.

'Oh, it's you two. We didn't expect ta see the likes of you here today,' the bearded Macara says with a sneer on his face.

My dad stares at Trout's comrade and says, 'We'll deal with them from now on. He's my son and that's my nephew. They're none of your business.'

The man shrugs his shoulders and sneers before pivoting around and melting into the Red Army massed ranks below.

'You see people like that,' my dad says, addressing both myself and Rex Mundi. 'You don't listen to or follow people like that. They've nothing to offer.'

'What are ya doing here?' I ask. 'I thought you said you'd had enough.'

'Well I'm not here cos I want ta be, Robert. I'm here to make sure you don't get arrested or killed ... or follow the orders of conmen like that,' my dad says, pointing to where Trout's Macara has disappeared.

'Why? Because you think I should be following your orders instead?'

Marty Johnstone, over six foot and fifteen stone and someone you'd have never guessed was once on hunger strike in 1971 inside Long Kesh, flares up. 'You speak to your father with some respect, Robert.'

The second I tell Johnty to go fuck himself and mind his own business, my dad delivers a stinging smack to my face. When I turn towards the floodlights, I see the peelers are in stitches once more. I go to walk away but my dad pulls me back; he is not quite finished with me yet.

'Hey you, cunty! Stay at peace for a minute and you too, Aidan McManus. I'm only here because your father rang me up last night and asked me to do the same for you as that dick beside ya. I'm trying to keep you out of jail or even worse.'

Rex Mundi plays Judas Iscariot once more and goes to embrace my dad and then extends his hand out to Johnstone in atonement. Maybe he's doing it in respect for the night my dad sent out the squad that saved him and the rest of his family from being barbecued by their neighbours. Or perhaps it's just to piss me off.

Now it's Johnty gripping the lapels of my blazer as Rex Mundi continues to cling to my dad, whispering, 'I'm sorry, Uncle Peter. I'm really really sorry.'

I can see the broken blue veins that ripple across Johnstone's nose and smell the sour odour of stout and un-tipped fags from his breath as he pulls me closer and whispers, 'Will you wise up, Robert? Will you fuckin' catch yourself on? That man over there is worried sick about you, about the company you keep. Don't you think he has been through enough, losing your mother last year? We only came here today to look after you and your cousin. Cos all he wants is for you to get on, to finish those A levels and get the fuck out of this place for good. So please, today, stay out of real trouble, will ya?'

But I pull away from Johnty, do a quick about-turn and march off in the direction of the pitch fence in search of Padre Pio. When I look back, Rex Mundi is bear hugging Johnstone while my dad is staring after me and shaking his head.

As the band marches off the turf to the applause only of the spectators in the North and South Stands, Padre Pio appears beside me. He spots the blood still seeping from my lower lip and produces a handkerchief out of his army jacket.

'Here Ruin. This is called a hanky. You might not have learned how to use one in your house but you can wipe the blood from your gob with them.'

'Thanks amigo,' I say.

'Who smacked you then? Was it one of them black bastards over there?' he says, pointing towards the RUC officers.

'No. It was Judas up there who did it. That fuckin' two-faced fuck-dog of a cousin of mine.'

A cessation of hostilities has broken out between us because we now share a common enemy, and Padre Pio puts his hand on my shoulder to show solidarity.

All of those dark thoughts about his own mother and me are probably on the back burner of his brain, for now at least. But I am never complacent with PP, ever. There will be more to come on that front later, when he starts to imagine what his ma and me get up to whenever he sidles off to bed. For Padre Pio never really forgets. Things just get postponed. As such, it's best not to mention any two-timing treacherous bitches and Judas bastards who go behind your back for a quick ride, otherwise the switch inside him will flick once more and PP will start to think about what goes on in that parlour with his mammy and me.

'Do you want me to go up there and blade that fucker right now, Ruin?' Padre Pio says in all seriousness, just as both teams come back onto the pitch for the second half amid a welcome paroxysm of cheers, yells and insults from every side of Windsor Park.

14

'BE MY WIFE'

July 1978

The payphone in the hall must have rung about twenty times that morning before Sabine eventually got up and went downstairs in the nude to answer it. On return, she launched us into a frenzied clean-up. Everything had to be spick and span for the arrival of her father and Aunty Iris within the hour, before which, I was informed, I would be banished upstairs to remain quiet. Would she have hidden Rex Mundi away like a dirty secret? I was still angry from watching her dance with my cousin at the end of the previous night, but that paled into insignificance when compared to her behaviour earlier that morning at dawn. My anger had festered to rage. To pay her back and freak her out, I put on track six of *Low*. I wanted her thoughts to be as disturbed as mine. Furiously, I swept the ashtrays with the remains of our joints into a bin bag, along with the empty bottles of Mateus Rosé and the torn sachets of Durex we had left at the side of the sofa when we couldn't wait till we were upstairs. Sabine had come off the pill after reading about another health scare in one of the Sunday papers and we were using johnnies for the rest of that July so I wouldn't knock her up and screw up her plans for escape. She was choking out the living room with jets of orange-smelling air freshener and flashing 'you-naughty-boy' smiles at me as I sang along with Bowie asking someone to be his wife. Sabine hadn't a clue that I was smouldering with anger at her.

After taking a quick shower, Sabine reappeared looking very different to her shimmering Cleopatra persona in The Harp. Her hair was pulled back into a ponytail and her long slender frame fitted into a sombre black dress. She pirouetted in front of me in flat brown sandals.

'Are you trying to tell me something, Robert?' She giggled.

'What do ya mean?'

'I mean "Be My Wife"! Are you dropping hints about your future intentions towards me?' she said, laughing.

I was too stung by embarrassment to answer her back. I had already tried in vain to repress this ridiculous fantasy. Instead, I grabbed *Low* and the head-cans.

'Make sure you keep them plugged in as I don't want my aunt or, worse still, my dad wondering if anybody is up there,' Sabine said, before kissing me on the forehead.

I plugged the head-cans into the record player by the window upstairs and looked outside. There wasn't a sinner to be seen. Jerusalem Street was part of the one district of the city which the political map-makers could never demarcate as either exclusively Orange or Green. How many weeks had I been holed up here in the Holy Lands, in the streets named after cities you remembered from Catechism classes or from the newscasts about the Six Day and Yom Kippur wars in the real Middle East? How many lies had I told, not only to my father about where I had been sleeping the night before, but also to Padre Pio and, worse still, to his mother? Padre Pio wouldn't be caught dead in The Pound or The Harp; he said he didn't want people to think he was a weirdo, or worse still, queer. That suited me. I was concerned, however, that he would follow me up to Jerusalem Street and discover her. If he ever found out I was with a girl from East Belfast ... well ... it wouldn't end well. Padre Pio was defined by difference, relished it and the opportunities it gave to excuse his tendencies. It was coming up to a month already and I wanted to stay with Sabine and never go back to the drab streets of home that now felt like they belonged to my childhood only. I would follow her wherever she chose to go, even if it meant jacking in my A levels and taking the boat across the water.

Yet, looking around, there was nothing of me inside this room, where we fucked, slept, cuddled, debated, read and always, always listened to *Low*. Behind the bed's headboard, there was the poster version of the album sleeve with Bowie's side profile, him so vulnerable and delicate in the anorak and the orange-dyed hair swept to one side that exposed an elfin-like ear, the colours around him merging into the same marmalade sky as the LP's background. Beyond *Low*, there was a series of night-time silhouette photos of the hypodermic-sharp skyline of New York City; this was juxtaposed with an enlarged aerial shot of the Berlin Wall with snow lying deep and commonly shared on either end of the Cold War divide. On the other side of the bed, there was a strange, ghostly photograph of her father standing proud in his British Army uniform with one hand on a younger Sabine's shoulder by the frontier crossing at Checkpoint Charlie. The painted floorboards hosted precariously balanced towers of novels, art books and photography albums, not to mention discarded black lace panties, curled up fishnets and her winkle-picker ankle boots. The one thing that I had bought her – the electric-blue, three-quarter-length, PVC coat – was draped over a chair. We had found it the previous Friday at the Variety Market, at a second-hand stall perilously close to the doors leading out towards my home streets, where Padre Pio must have been sitting, sulking and plotting in response to my long period of treacherous absence from him. I didn't want to go back there, but, looking around, I didn't seem to be here either.

Sabine had been unable to sleep throughout the night, thrashing around in nervous agitation under the single sheet she had thrown around us. In one of her many waking episodes, she had got up and switched on a powerful radio by the bedside table and started fiddling with the dial all the way from Luxembourg to Moscow.

As she soared across continental airwaves, it reminded me of back home when my father tuned into the frequencies from Berlin to Prague to Warsaw and the capital of communism itself. It reminded me of the nights when Mum would come home following a heavy night in the Blackstaff Social and head off to her own bed up in the attic. My father would drown out her snoring and her cries in her sleep by tuning into the news of US imperialist atrocities in Vietnam, the tractor quota targets from Kiev, the advance of the MPLA forces in Angola and the preparations being made to put the first German into space.

Last night, in-between writhing and zipping through radio stations, she elbowed me, urging me to talk to her and help her sleep.

'Robert? Robert? Wake up, darling! Don't tell me you are still asleep,' she said softly.

'Well, I was sleeping until a second ago. What do you want, love?'

'Why do you think he hates me?' she asked.

And there it was: that selfsame hollowness I imagined drove my father towards the comforting escape of Radio Berlin International. She always returned to him.

'He doesn't hate you, Sabine,' I replied with growing alarm in my voice. 'My cousin just likes taking the piss and you just happen to be one of his targets.'

I detected a frisson of concern in her next question: 'Well, what does he say about me then?'

'He says you are just like all those other punk girls he's met in Brighton and London. Rich, arty-farty ones who are only doing it all to piss off daddy,' I replied with some enjoyment.

'I am NOT a punk girl, Robert! I don't even like being called a girl! I am an individual. I won't be pigeonholed,' she said, striking a defiant pose by raising her head up from her pillow.

'Deep down he's just bitter, Sabine,' I replied wearily. 'It's really all about what happened seven years ago. I mean, imagine if you had to run for your life in your pyjamas, being carried into a van by armed men away from a baying mob with petrol bombs in their hands.'

Then she said something that stunned me: 'I refuse to believe that. He's far too intelligent to think my family would have had anything to do with that. Actually, I don't think he hates me at all. I think it's just a big act. Why do you think he left us so suddenly last night?'

'I'm fucked if I know, love. He just turned up this summer during the World Cup without a word of warning. He ends up at our door just as Dad and me are about to settle down to watch the first match. He never shut up throughout the game either. Then he seriously pissed off Dad right at the very end when he took off his biker jacket and showed us his Argentina shirt. My dad was more raging about that than him arriving unannounced from England,' I said.

'Why would your dad be upset with what he was wearing?' Sabine asked.

'Because my dad didn't want Argentina to win. He has nothing against the ordinary working-class Argentinian people; it's their regime he hates. He despises the generals and the admirals who are murdering his comrades over there and then milking the national side's victory. He told Aidan to take off the shirt because that's what it represented to him,' I said and instantly felt proud over telling her a bit about my father and his politics.

'He's really full of surprises,' she said.

'Who? My dad?'

'No, silly. Your cousin. You can never say he's predictable!'

I answered her with barely concealed bitterness. 'Oh aye, he's a bundle of laughs a minute, isn't he?'

She sensed my frustration with talking about him but that didn't stop her from asking for his address in Brighton – just in case she ever found herself there some weekend away from

London. Thankfully I didn't know it, and even if I did, I wouldn't have given it to her.

'Sabine, can I ask you a personal question?' I tried to speak to her once more in the softest of whispers as I steered our chat away from all things about my cousin.

'Yes.'

'I just wanted to know if your mum and dad loved each other right up to the end.'

'Why ask me something like that?'

'Well, what I mean is, does he still miss her?'

'Of course he does, Robert. Doesn't your dad miss your mum?'

I turned around to face her on the pillow. 'Truth be told, no, he probably doesn't, and not for a long time. She was long gone from him before the night we said ... I mean, I said goodbye in the Royal Victoria Hospital. I was the last one to hold her hand – not my dad. I don't think he could bear to be in the same room as her ... even in her death room.'

'Oh my God, that is so sad.'

'No, it's not sad, certainly not sad for him. She was on her own with me, waking up for short bursts and then going back to sleep for hours on end. My dad just sat outside in a red plastic chair, reading a book. He couldn't wait for it all to be over.'

None of what I was telling her was embellished or exaggerated; my father's behaviour really was cold and formal during my mother's final few hours. I suspected it was his last chance for revenge. He had suffered jibes, gossip and whispered asides from both enemies and comrades over his wife's reputation for chasing whomever was the latest flash Harry in the district and beyond. Just before she died, he told me he was never going to be a hypocrite nor would he turn into the mournful widower once she had slipped away.

'Do you wanna know something about my mother, Sabine?'

'Yes, Robert.'

'That last night I really admired her so much. I admired her because she never once cried out for him. She never once asked him for forgiveness or begged him to hold her hand one last time. When she was fit and able and active, I really used to hate her. I honestly hated her! I willed her to die back then! I hated everything she had done from the day my father was released from Long Kesh. I hated the way she fell in love with every macho man swaggering about in an army jacket who came marching down our street. But that night, that fucking night Sabine, just before she passed away, she tore off the oxygen mask and tried to rip out the tubes attached to her neck and arms – I admired her! I never stopped admiring her through those hours. She refused to apologise for the way she was. For her to say sorry would be like an atheist calling for a priest.'

Tears, forced-back tears, were shed shortly after I recounted my mum's last day on earth, but they were not caused by that memory. They were repressed, bitter tears caused only by Sabine's next question:

'And the funeral, Robert? Did your cousin come back to Belfast for the funeral? Did Aidan bother coming over to help you?'

The deployment of the dead had failed me this time. Everything still flowed back to him. I wouldn't give her an answer, even though I could have told her that of course my darling cousin never bothered his bollocks coming home to say farewell. Sabine fell back to sleep, but I couldn't; I watched as dawn broke through the horizontal blinds, sending feeble light shafts flecked with dust particles into the bedroom. And I cried – angry, silent, shameful tears.

Later, when her father and aunt arrived, I put an empty glass to the floorboards of the bedroom and listened to what was going on below. The hubbub of voices reminded me of early childhood when I used to be put to bed at eight o'clock on summer nights but could still hear the tantalising sounds of life just one floor below me.

Amid the clink of cups and plates, I could make out snatches of conversation between them.

'That's a lovely tan you've got, Aunty Iris!' I heard Sabine say.

'Oddly enough, Sabine, it's winter down there, but when the sun comes out I'm still straight over to our William's pool. Did I tell you that William and Darleen had a swimming pool built last year, Campbell?' The aunt was addressing Sabine's father. His name was Campbell. Sabine had never mentioned his name before.

The aunt continued to heap praise on Sabine's dad's younger brother: 'Our William and Darleen said that with the business doing so well in Jo'burg it was really time they built a pool. For the children, of course. They are never out of the water once it's warm enough for a dip. The first sign of the sun and in they go!'

I wondered if Campbell was the type of man who would be happy or annoyed about his brother's rising status.

'Well it must be a difference for them from that wee farm they used to own down in Fermanagh,' he said.

'Oh Campbell, they're very happy down there and the nice thing is that Darleen can work too, now that she has native women doing all the chores around the house. You should take Sabine down there with you to see William. Maybe go down for Christmas when the weather is glorious. I mean, how many years has it been since you saw our William?'

'When do I get a minute to myself, Iris? And sure with what's going on in this society now, how could I justify a holiday?' Sabine's father said.

'Dad hasn't taken a break, Aunty Iris, not since Mum ...'

There was silence as the tea-taking resumed.

I placed the glass back on the bedside table and went over to the record player. I unplugged the headphones, turned up the volume to 8 and dropped the needle back onto the sixth track of *Low*: 'Sometimes you get so lonely. Sometimes you get nowhere. I've lived all over the world. I've lived every place.'

Despite the volume, I heard the commotion downstairs and the thud of Sabine tearing up the stairs. She barged into the room like a woman possessed.

'What the fucking hell are you playing at? I told you to stay quiet!'

'Aye, like one of your uncle's house slaves in South Africa!'

'Have you been listening into our conservation?' Her roar prompted an outburst of muffled chat between her elderly aunt and father downstairs.

Her father called up from the bottom of the stairs, 'Sabby are you alright up there?'

'Campbell, I think there's somebody up there with her,' the aunt piped up.

Sabine stood in front of me with her arms folded, her face scrunched up and her lips tightening until they turned near white.

'Well, given all the noise you were making, you might as well come down and say hello before my dad comes up here to protect his precious daughter. Tell them you weren't feeling well, and put your socks and shoes on. And once you've said hello then you can make your excuses and leave ... you little fucking show-off,' she said before disappearing down the stairs to head her father off.

Fuck her! Fuck her for hiding me away! Fuck her and fuck Rex! I counted to thirty and followed her down into the living room. There, a woman in her sixties, in an ankle-length floral dress, peered up at me over her half-moon glasses. Sabine's father was sitting in the armchair, facing the aunt on the sofa. He had blonde hair, balding towards the middle. He wore royal blue flares, a white safari-style shirt, which exposed a hairless chest, and a pair of light-brown moccasins. The epitome of health and efficiency, he looked as if he was already on holiday with his brother in Johannesburg.

'Is this your young man, Sabine?' the purse-lipped aunt inquired while looking me up and down.

'Robert is just a very good friend of mine, Aunty Iris. He wasn't feeling well when he called around to see me this morning. He felt a bit sick and went up to the bathroom just before you called in on me. I told him he could lie down and rest. He's a bit delicate at the best of times is our Robert,' Sabine jibed.

'Goodness me! How do you keep that hair of yours sticking up like that? Your head looks like a Christmas tree, chum.' Sabine's father snorted, looking across the room towards his aunt for some kind of approval for his quip.

'Now now, Campbell. I've seen this look before, even in Jo'burg, you know. It's all the rage with the youth down in South Africa, this punker image,' the aunt replied. 'Besides, this young man looks like he could do with a good feed more than a haircut.'

'If you're feeling ill I can give you a lift, chum. Where do you live?' Her father's tone seemed unfriendly and over-inquisitive.

'Ah, just the Upper Ormeau. I mean Ballynafeigh. I need a walk up there just to get the air round my head.'

I could see the redness rising around Sabine's neck, throat and eventually cheeks after my reply to her father.

'Ballynafeigh! OK, chum. So long as it isn't that lower end of the road, eh! Bloody Indian territory down there,' he said, jerking a thumb back towards the window.

Aunt Iris delicately placed her cup and saucer on the table, where the night before Sabine and I had been rolling joints before tearing off the Durex wrapper so we could fuck on the sofa. Her aunt put out a bony ringless hand, took mine and squeezed it hard before shaking it.

'Don't you worry, Robert. I'm sure our Sabine will tell us all about you once you've gone out the door. Won't you, dear?'

'Robert's been through a very hard time of late, very similar to us in many ways. His mum passed away earlier this year too.'

Sabine's father butted in, albeit far too cheerily. 'So sorry to hear that, chum.'

Outside on the doorstep, Sabine retreated back into her tight-lipped, scrunched up angry mode.

'Thanks very much, Robert. Now I have to sit in there and be interrogated for the next hour or so all about you.'

'Just tell them I am one of those unclean Fenians from the reservation down below. Tell them I'm one of the natives.'

'Oh, go home and scratch that wee hillock growing on your shoulder, Robert, and then grow up!'

These were her last words to me that day, and I couldn't have given a shit. At least she hadn't mentioned Rex again.

15

COMMS 4

1987

More thoughts from the back channel if you will excuse the pun. I now sense that your stalling is more to do with fear than any residual sense of loyalty towards him. As one of the very few who was never ever afraid of him, let me explain where and how I lost my fear of all bully boys and thugs.

It was the summer of 1971, a few weeks before Internment, and our area, like your own, had gone absolutely ballistic. The new organisation was yet to be born out of the old, but the militants who would carry on a betrayed struggle were the ones taking the war to the enemy, even while others were plotting to run away from it. And, as you can well imagine, my older brother – M – was a busy boy: living, eating, shitting the war, day in and day out. This was long before M was taken into Her Majesty's custody – that happened a year prior to you three landing at my house that Saturday.

One Friday evening, just after 12 July, my brother and his friend 'The Wolf' (you might have heard about him) took me to the chippy at the top of our road for a treat. The Wolf barely made it out of 1971. A few months before the following year's ceasefire, he managed to shoot himself while cleaning a .303 rifle in a safe house – a weapon, which, unknown to him of course, still had a bullet up the spout when he tested the trigger mechanism while the barrel was pointed straight into his guts.

So, off we went to Lily's chippy around teatime, and I couldn't help noticing that even though it was a close summer evening,

The Wolf was wearing a long leather coat that dropped way down beyond his knees. As we joined the queue, in barged a notorious hardman from round our way, whose name struck fear into my and my brother's heart for years - Fra Young. There he was - with muscles bulging out of a tight white T-shirt and him sporting a tan from a recent stint on the boats in South America - thinking he was fucking Marlon Brando in *On the Waterfront*. Just back from sea, he was looking for his first victim of the season - anyone who would object to him bunking the queue. Just as Fra Young ordered a fish supper off Lily, The Wolf called out from the back, 'Here Fra, you have ta wait your turn like the rest of us.' I saw the look of horror on my brother's face. I knew he was afraid because I heard him say a German curse word our da used to say the odd time he was upset. Young used to pick on my brother all the time - on the street and at school. He'd wait for us both at the bus stop before school, and, in front of his acolytes, he'd walk over and make our lives hell. Once he poked my brother in the throat and said, 'Where did ya get that ring?'

In a desperate attempt to humour him, my brother said, 'What ring, Fra mate? Rings are for birds.' Then Young slapped him on the face and said, 'The ring of dirt around your neck, you fucking Kraut!'

Naturally, in the chippy, I feared he was about to humiliate us all over again. But I thought wrong. The Wolf, who had also been a target of Fra Young's schoolyard sadism, stepped out of the line, walked straight to the top of the queue and pulled out a loaded Luger pistol from the inside of his long leather coat and pressed it into his old tormentor's left temple. 'Get on your fucking knees now, you wanking bastard!' The Wolf screamed, and the queue arched back in unison, pressing themselves up against the wall while Lily simply smiled and disappeared into the back of her shop, seeing nothing and saying nothing. The Wolf then summoned us to where Young was lying prostrate on the tiled floor, shaking with fear. 'Now kick him!' The Wolf barked. When my brother flinched, The Wolf lost it and started to scream, 'I said kick him. That is an order from your superior officer! Kick him for fuck's sake.' At first my brother delivered a half-hearted boot into Young's side, which The Wolf followed up with an almighty drop kick into the side of Fra's face. 'Now kick him! Kick him! Kick him! Kick the cunt, kid, kick the cunt! Kick him!' The Wolf snarled. And we started to enjoy ourselves. I joined in too as The Wolf calmly leaned on the chippy counter, called out to Lily and ordered three fish suppers, which he paid for out of a fiver.

Shall I tell you when I really lost the fear? Well, it was not the actual enjoyable sensation of sticking the boot into Young's ribs, balls and face that did it. For me, it was simply something The Wolf whispered into Fra Young's bleeding left ear as we picked up our fish 'n' chips and saluted the rest of the customers: 'You're not in a Charles Atlas cartoon anymore, Fra!' From that moment I lost the fear.

The Wolf would have been a great asset for this movement. Sure, he cultivated that Ringo Starr look with his long straight hair, droopy moustache and flowery shirts, and sure he permanently smelled of petunia oil and incense. Worse still, he was always careless when weapons were around and loved to show off what a crack shot he was at training camp. But - at least he taught my brother and me a valuable lesson: bully boys will crumble if the people's soldiers are around to challenge them.

Think of Skyscraper as your Fra Young. You proved to me you were game a long time ago. Now, lose any remaining fear you may have of him. Because we talk and we talk but no one seizes the time. As the Túpac Amaru freedom fighters have warned us, 'Words divide! Actions unite!'

Yours fraternally ... Comrade T.

16

SAVED BY THE BELL

28 April 1979

In the huns' part of no-man's-land, just before the North Stand, the only things moving are two long streaks of bog roll rippling in the wind. Beyond the gap and the bulky lines of flak-jacketed cops, they have started singing 'The Sash' once more, reminding us all about their victories at Derry, Aughrim, Enniskillen and the Boyne. They are always and forever 'sashing' it over there. A minute or so into the second half, I see Trout preparing to pontificate once more. But big John Platt lobs the ball from the midfield towards Mike Adair, who then wallops it into the Portadown goal. Trout gets drowned out as a new force surges from the back of the Kop down towards the barriers below, where PP and I break free from him and join the Red Army going berserk all around us. 2-1 to the Reds!

When the wave retreats and the game recommences, Trout appears beside us once more and the crowd starts to sing, 'We'll be drinking holy water from the cup.' Is there any escape from him? He puts his arms around us and hands me a pair of binoculars he has either stroked from someone or found amid the broken bits of terracing beneath our feet. Trout starts bending Padre Pio's ear while I peer through the binos at the South Stand. It's easy to distinguish between the culchies and the Belfast spides. The former resemble country-and-western fans in their jet-wing shirt collars, shiny purple and green tweed blazers, exposed chests and gunfighter moustaches – definitely Portadown men over there. Then there are the knots of suede-headed teenagers with near invisible necks poking out of parka and Wrangler jackets, giving two fingers and wanking signs to the Red Army. I also spot a fat, tomato-cheeked bullfrog holding up a stolen Pepsi parasol above his sweaty head. They are all cheering for the red, white and blue, Shankill Linfield fans to a man and boy.

Trout is still busy orating away to Padre Pio, so I slip the binos into my blazer pocket and hope he forgets about them. It's then I notice that the upside-down crucifix that was pinned to my jacket has been snapped off.

'Ask yerself this, cousin,' Trout shouts above the din of delight from the Red Army all around us. 'The last time Cliftonville won the cup was 1909. That's seventy years ago.'

Padre Pio takes the piss: 'Ya don't fuckin' say so, Trout? That's amazing! Seventy years ago.'

But Trout is oblivious to PP's sarcasm. He is too engaged in the historical significance of it all. 'Listen to me, lads. Just imagine this. Ireland was still under the bloody British Empire in 1909 when the Reds won the cup last. World War One was still five years away. Some of their oul grandads and great-grandads over there didn't even know they were all going to get creamed for King and Country against the Kaiser. And the Irish people were still on their knees – although not for long,' Trout announces.

For a second or two I wait for Padre Pio to interrupt and tell Trout to shut the fuck up for being a crashing bore, but once more something flickers within him.

'Too right, Trout. Them stupid bastards at the Somme were getting mowed down for an English king.' He then climbs up one of the crush barriers and yells over to the country-and-western culchies and the Shankill skinner boys, 'Yer granddaddies only got the clap up in Flanders.'

His insults are met with throat-cutting gestures. Trout breaks his ballicks laughing while Padre Pio holds up my crucifix that he has recovered from the ground. He is holding it the right way up and waves it towards the South Stand like some demented exorcist casting out a legion of demons.

It's then I remember that I actually have friends from Portadown: the two punks called Tip and Tap who were named after the mascots of the 1974 World Cup. Every Saturday, they come from Portadown to hang out with the punk crew at the Cornmarket Fountain. They always share their bottles of Buckfast in the Baby Subway. They even gave me *Live at the Witch Trials* by The Fall a few weeks ago, to cheer me up after I told them about an aborted trip to London. Tap had slapped me on the back and handed over the Caroline Music bag. 'Here kid, stick that on the turntable tonight and work up a sweat. Sweat the bitch out of yer system. Let Uncle Mark E. Smith sort it all out.'

Tip and Tap – the two sound men who introduced me to The Fall, Cabaret Voltaire and Television – could very well be over there now, supporting Portadown, not because they were true-blue Prods who sang 'The Sash' or constantly chanted 'Fuck the Pope and the Virgin Mary', but who simply followed their local side because it was the team they grew up with. I just hoped they would not clock me on the Kop as much as I didn't want to spot them with the binos.

Trout is still winding Padre Pio up beside me and suddenly I wonder why our self-appointed leader has not inherited any of his father's Aryan genes. In fact, he reminds me of a white Smokey Robinson with his wire-brush hair, liver lips and pencil moustache.

'See this year is going to be the big one, lads,' he says, wrapping his arms around both Padre Pio and myself once more. 'Next week it all starts. That's when it truly kicks off, boys.'

'What are you talking about?' PP asks in genuine bewilderment as I glance about to see if my own cousin is going to make a reappearance.

'I'm talking about next week when the Brits are going to make the biggest mistake ever. They're going to elect Maggie Thatcher the Milk Snatcher!'

I am trying desperately to avoid seeing the historical significance of all of this, having listened to my dad and his comrades whining on for so long. I am too focused on how Cliftonville are letting Portadown back into this game instead of building on our 2-1 lead. On each side of us the Portadown fans and their friends-for-the-day are taking their minds off their team trailing behind us with yet another chorus of 'The Sash', while on the pitch the ginger snap Ports midfielder Willie Gordon has just snuffed another attack by our Ciaran McCurry.

'Ask yerself this, how much will it take for British workers to rise up once the Tory boot goes in? Ask yerself if you are going to stand on the sidelines when that bitch sticks her high heels into the prisoners in H-Block, Long Kesh,' Trout continues.

Meanwhile, Ian Donegan has his socks back down around his ankles; the Portadown player has a haircut that any punk or New Wave fan would be proud of as he limps about the pitch, bravely tackling our players despite carrying an injury. Secretly, I admire his balls for staying on the park.

'Ask yerself if you are going to play your part because this year is going to see things boiling over,' Trout goes on.

Our keeper Brian Johnston has come too far out and missed the ball, but luckily for us Brendy McGuckian is there to belt the ball away up the field and out of danger.

'Ask yerself if what's happening all over the world won't happen here. The people of Iran have overthrown a Shah. The people of Nicaragua are fighting for their revolution. The Brits are drawing the battle lines now that Thatcher is heading for 10 Downing Street and the prisoners won't—'

Trout is finally silenced by the roar erupting from two-thirds of the stadium as Portadown finally equalise. Gordon takes a shot from twenty yards towards the Kop end goal and strikes the post, but big Jim Alexander follows through by nodding the ball into an empty net and you just know now that it's all going to go their way. 2-2!

Slashes of red and white alongside red, white and blue streaks light up both stands on either side of the pitch as they celebrate the equaliser. On the Kop, heads are in hands and bodies are turned away from the pitch up towards the mountains above; the croppies appear to be lying down again. Everyone around me appears to be plunged into silence. I wonder if Tip and Tap are pogoing up and down in delight on the other side of no-man's-land. The bastards. The bastards – each and every one of them. It has gone very quiet over here, all, that is, except Trout.

'Raise your voices, lads,' he cries out in defiance as the North and South Stands sing in unison, 'Can you hear Cliftonville sing? No, no. Can you hear Cliftonville sing? No, no. Can you hear Cliftonville sing? I can't hear a fucking thing. No, oh no, no, no.'

Trout and a few others raise a feeble response, 'Come on you Reds! Come on you Reds!' He takes full credit for the fight back and urges the mobs around us to keep singing while Padre Pio stands behind him making fresh wanking signs into Trout's back.

'That's more like it, Red Army. That's more like it, lads!' Padre Pio cries out mimicking Trout who is applauding the crowd for their defiance.

Some of the huns in the North Stand are actually making their way to the exits close to the railway end. Maybe they are convinced at this stage the game will end in a draw and we will all be back here next Saturday. Or perhaps some of the harder tickets amongst them are going out to stage a big ambush when we are hemmed in near the brick fields after the final whistle. My stomach lurches when I see Trout signalling towards the top of the Kop. Like a cop directing traffic, he beckons none other than Rex Mundi to join us back towards the steps leading to the goal. Padre Pio swivels around away from the pitch and flashes me a blade he has taken from the inside of his army coat. I shake my head vigorously at him and move over to create a buffer zone between him and my cousin, just before Rex Mundi reaches us. What the fuck am I doing here acting as his human shield? I am in line for a blading to save someone who has just slapped me about in front of my own father.

I am a 'peace-line' between PP and a Judas cunt who has probably been riding Sabine over in London behind my back. I am about to take cold steel for a cousin who must have done the dirt on me. Just as I am about to jump back and create a clear path for Padre Pio to rip into Rex Mundi, the crowd flows forward carrying my cousin along on a tide of red and white. There is a roar all around and I am almost knocked off my feet by the sudden thrust of bodies cascading towards the pitch line. Only Rex Mundi has been able to see the goal go in and he rushes over to grab me by both shoulders.

'One fucking minute to go mate, and we've done it. We've done it,' my cousin screeches into my ear as Trout joins us in a group hug.

'Bell. Bell. Bell. Tony Bell,' Trout screams before flinging both Rex Mundi and myself against the side of one of the blue crush barriers where I almost crack a rib.

'We're still friends, right mate? This is all too fucking important to fall out over nothing – over her,' Rex Mundi says as he opens up his biker jacket once more and beats his chest on the spot of his Troops-Out T-shirt. 'We're still muckers, right! No one will come between us. Absolutely no one. Right?'

Before I get a chance to respond we are thrown back by the force of the crowd again, and I see Trout holding PP in a celebratory headlock.

'Bell knocked it down with his head to Platt then big Platt passed it back on to the eighteen yard line to Bell and wow … what a screamer! He hit a fucking screamer!' Rex Mundi relays how the winner went in.

I am still in too much pain from being crushed against the barrier to take in everything that my cousin is reporting of that last decisive minute of the match and how Bell bent the ball brilliantly into the left side of the net to win the Irish Cup for Cliftonville. I cannot even hear the final whistle being blown a few seconds later as the crowd on the Kop explode with unexpected joy. I look towards the crush barrier and see Padre Pio balancing on top of it, holding aloft a red-and-white bars scarf that he must have snatched off someone while dancing in the throng.

Trout is standing beneath him, an unlit feg between his thick liver lips, clapping on his younger cousin with some serious encouragement. No doubt, he's preparing another fucking speech he must deliver on the further historical significance of 1979.

17

THEY SAID IT COULDN'T BE DONE

28 April 1979

I've never seen so many grown men hug each other before, and to think, just a few weeks ago, we had watched in sullen silence as Linfield paraded the league championship trophy around the touchline, thrusting the Gibson Cup into our faces, trying to remind us who were the real boss men of Irish football. But we don't care anymore, now that we've snatched the cup in their own backyard.

Trout, Padre Pio and Rex Mundi are quickly disappearing into the crowd in front of me, and I take the opportunity to whip out the binos and have a quick scout at the vanquished leaving the North and South Stands. I see a flash of bleached blonde hair bobbing up and down beside a much smaller man with tight-spiked black hair. It's them. They are here. Tip and Tap are on their way out of the stadium. I can guess where they are going because I remember them trying to bring me to a place they boasted about visiting most Saturdays: a 'rub-and-a-tug' knocking shop called The Black Magic Box on Agincourt Avenue not far from where Sabine used to live.

'Get yerself down there big man if ya want to forget about yer ex-girlfriend. The birds in The Box will help ya put her ladyship out of yer mind, especially that wee darkie girl with the healing hands!' Tap once told me down inside the Baby Subway.

It only takes a few minutes to catch up with the others again. Trout and Rex Mundi are standing beside a crouching Padre Pio, who has his trousers around his ankles and is shitting a steaming anaconda of crap on the empty concrete steps.

'Look at me, boys. A present for the Brits,' PP cackles.

'But England aren't playing here for a couple of weeks, you stupid mong. It'll be washed away in the rain. And besides, the Norn Iron fans won't step on your shite,' Rex Mundi says, looking completely baffled.

'Then pray for sunshine until the home internationals, Rex Mundi,' PP says as he pulls up his trousers.

An oul boy in his early sixties, who has been watching this spectacle with disgust, approaches. 'You bloody animals. How dare you sully our club on this great day. You're a bloody disgrace,' he shouts.

Trout saunters over to him, looking all serious and commander-like. 'My advice to you grandad is to go back into the crowd if ya know what's good for you. See, that boy over there likes to blade people, and right now I think he'd really like to blade you.'

'I'll see to it that you lot never get into Solitude again,' the old veteran fan shouts, before beating a hasty retreat.

I don't even realise I still have the binoculars in my hand, until suddenly they are snatched away. A light slap is delivered to the back of my head.

'I was looking for them, thank you very much. Ya do realise, Mr Ruin, that them binos belong to the movement?' Trout says. 'What were you looking at anyway?'

There isn't a chance in hell I'm mentioning Tip and Tap. 'Ach, no one really, Trout. I just wanted to see the shocked expressions on the huns' faces,' I reply.

From his halitosis-polluted mouth, another sermon is about to be delivered. 'Ask yourself this, Mr Ruin. Do ya really think them people over there are going ta see sense anytime soon?'

'What do you mean?'

'Ask yerself why so many of them with absolutely no connection whatsoever with Portadown Football Club would come out today to support a team they've never followed before. Why? Because it wasn't about them – it was all about us!'

'Us, Trout?'

'Aye. Us! They only came to see another episode of the croppies lying down, but this time that didn't happen Mr Ruin, did it?'

'They thought it couldn't be done!'

'They certainly did, Mr Ruin. I'm not being funny, but all that workers unite shite that the likes of your da comes off with, it means nothin' to them over there. Do you think any of them will listen to the likes of him?' Trout says slyly.

'Look Trout, try and leave my da out of this, will ye? I only wanna see the players parade the cup around Windsor. Isn't that enough?'

Trout gives me a look that suggests he thinks he knows more about me than he should. 'You're alright, Mr Ruin. I don't often listen to cousin PP, but when he says you are sound and game I believe him. We should talk again soon.'

'Are you not staying for the cup presentation?'

'Nah, I've got ta go to a meeting down the road. There's a party on later down in the flats. Ask PP to bring you with him. Bring your mad half-English cousin along as well. He seems very game too. Just make sure the two dickheads don't get scooped by the peelers on the way out of here,' Trout says.

'Trout, why did you let PP do that? Why did you let him make a complete wanker of himself by doing a dump?'

He smiles back at the question. 'Listen Ruin, there is nobody that knows him like I do. He's unhinged at times, out of control. You can't imagine how many times I've had to step in and stop the bigger boys from kneecapping him over the last few years. But he can be useful. He can be useful because he is totally game. So he gets a bye-ball.'

'And what about me? Am I meant to be game too?'

'Aye, I think you're game alright, but you're more than that: you're intelligent, educated. The likes of our Padre Pio are only foot soldiers, the infantry. The movement needs officers too, and that's what we've been sadly lacking, my friend.'

'Is PP not an officer?' I ask.

'Your so-called friend, my cousin, is not ta be trusted, certainly not with leadership or power. Even now he thinks he's some form of a fucking general. God help us all if he ever was. He's a loose cannon. Don't be afraid of PP and think about what I just said,' Trout replies before disappearing through the throng of fans waiting for the cup to be raised.

When the team finally arrive to raise the trophy along the touchline of the Kop, I find myself celebrating on my own, free from all of them. I am happily lost amongst people I have never met before, who don't know me, who have absolutely no interest in me beyond sharing in this joy. I feel blissfully alone, wrapped up in the comfort of the cheering, weeping crowd, safely anonymous and unknown.

Diagonally across the pitch, in the middle of the North Stand, I spot a frail-looking lad of about ten or eleven. He is on his own, hunkered down on the concrete. His small frame is drowned inside a blue parka. He appears to be shaking and sobbing uncontrollably. His features appear too soft to be one of the wee hard men from Dee Street or the Lower Shankill. A father is probably searching for this boy who is lost in the grief of defeat. I want to headbutt the smart-arse beside me who has also clocked the boy and yelled, 'Go away home ya wee cry baby! Go back to Portadown, ya wee fruit!'

When I reach the grass-fringed top of the Kop again, I realise that my father and Marty Johnstone have been rooted there since I last saw them. They have been waiting for the final whistle for me to appear once more.

'Any sign of the Brighton Brigade?' Dad says, while Johnty looks on, scowling.

'Haven't a clue where he went and I couldn't care less,' I shout to make myself heard above the metallic whirring of a British Army helicopter flying precariously low over the Red Army as it files out of enemy territory towards the 'border' of the M1.

'You wanna stay and search for him?' Johnty asks my dad while ignoring me.

'We're not staying here any longer, Marty. Looks like trouble is breaking out again,' my dad says and then points at me. 'And you are coming down the Falls with me, lad. Aidan will just have to make his own way home. Let's get out of this place.'

I am flanked all the way back through the brick-studded fields by my dad and his comrade. In turn, lines of transparent Perspex shield us from mini-ambushes of bottles, halfers and stones being thrown at us from the loyalist streets of the Village. Eventually, we reach the motorway and are roughly herded across by the cops. Some people from the houses on 'our' side have come out to cheer us on and welcome us back, to mark our safe passage to home.

When we reach Aldo's fish 'n' chip shop at the junction between the Donegall and Falls Roads, I sense him even before I see him; that depressing familiar figure is leaping up and down, an excited dot of dark vibrating energy tossing chips up into the air.

'Ach fuck, here comes the leader of the Hitler Youth,' my dad announces, and I'm thankful PP is too far away to hear him.

'Ruin, Ruin, Ruin,' PP roars across the street. He streaks through the lines of returning supporters, deftly holding the remains of his fish supper in one hand as if it was a baton he was about to pass in a relay race. 'Ruin, take a few chips, mate, or a whack a fish. Here Mr McManus, do you wanna bite too? What about you Mr Johnstone?' PP says with polite exuberance.

'No thanks,' my dad replies coldly. 'We just wanna get down that road and home safely through the town.'

'Maybe we should get the boys a taxi, Peter? Just to be sure. It's probably dicey for them going through the city centre,' Comrade Johnstone suggests.

Padre Pio's mood quickly switches. 'No, no way. We're going to a Cliftonville victory party, Robbie and me, Mr McManus. We're invited,' he pleads.

For the first time ever it dawns on me that my father has never called PP by his real name or any name for that matter.

'No way, son, and not a chance, Robert,' my dad says.

Padre Pio throws what's left of his supper over the park wall while I keep begging my father.

'If you lend me the money, I promise I will get a taxi home, Dad. We won't be going anywhere near town. We're just going to a party in his cousin's.'

My father presses me up against the park wall, out of earshot of the others, and says,

'You listen to me, Robert, for once in your life. You've got your A-level exams to think of and you've still got time to knuckle down, get decent grades and get the fuck out of this place. Once you get out of here, you won't have to hang about with losers like him.'

'He's my friend,' I protest.

'Like fuck he is. He's a pest and you know that better than me.'

'OK, so he's a pest sometimes. What of it? I am going to study hard but let me go to this party and celebrate Cliftonville's win, please! I promise I won't let ya down on the exam front. And I am going to get out of here once the summer comes, but just let me go and celebrate our win today.'

My father hasn't a clue what my real plans for escape are and how I intend to track her down again, now that Rex Mundi has at least located her in London. I will go over on the pretext of checking out the universities and search the bars and clubs around Camden for her instead. I'll sleep on sofas of oul punk pals who have made it over to London. I'll even try to get a job pouring pints for Irish navvies in the boozers up in the north of the city. I have the contacts, so does my da and Marty Johnstone. There are even a couple of his old comrades living over there who could help me out while I scout about for her.

Dad gets up so close to my face that I can make out the crusted ridge of congealed blood on his jawline. It's always the same spot where he cuts himself most mornings.

'Are you being serious with me here, Robert? Are you going to make a go at these A levels and stop all this acrobating with the Hitler Youth?'

'Honestly, Dad, I will. And you can help me out. You and Marty have contacts all over the place, even London. I could get a part-time job on the building sites or even a bar. I'll go this summer, do a recce job on the universities and come back for the results in August. I just want to celebrate today, that's all.'

He releases me from the black basalt masonry just as Padre Pio starts to clap wildly and laugh demonically at the sight of something coming down the Falls Road. Some Reds fans have kicked in almost all of the windows of a Belfast city bus that they've boarded on its way down towards the city centre. A couple of younger kids are leaning out of the bus, roaring with delight, while an older daredevil is hanging on to it from outside, his black scuffed DMs bouncing off the wheel and his Mohawk swaying back and forward in the wind. Rex Mundi's reappearance, clinging perilously to the space where the bus windows used to be, has left PP in stitches and my father looking on in horror.

'I know where he's heading to, Dad. I'll go after him,' I volunteer, exploiting my chance to break away from my father and Comrade Johnstone.

Padre Pio interrupts us again in his softest altar-boy voice. 'Here, Mr McManus. I bought this for you as a wee souvenir to remember your first Cliftonville match.' He pulls something from his back pocket while all the time keeping his gaze on Rex Mundi's journey hanging off a number 9 bus. He hands it to my dad. It is the cup final programme which shows a picture of John Platt and Jim Alexander on the front with the headline, 'Big Strikers'.

'That's very thoughtful of you, son,' my dad says. 'But you know I used to go to Solitude many years ago when there were only two other men and a dog watching an amateur team.'

'That's amazing, Mr McManus. That means you were one of the original Redmen.' Padre Pio is genuinely taken aback.

'No, son. We only went up to watch football, Marty and me. We used to go over to The Oval as well and cheer on Glentoran. We were there the evening that the Glens drew one all with Benfica and Eusébio playing on their team. That was a truly amazing night and a great year too, before it all went sour. 1967!'

I'm a little stung by the fact that my father never mentioned this game before. 'I don't remember that match! Why did you not take me over?'

'Your mother said no. She thought it wouldn't be safe taking ya over there. I told her ta wise up, but she wouldn't listen. I knew loads of Glenmen, including comrades from the union. There would be no bother from anyone and there wasn't.'

PP butts in with his very own memory of The Oval: 'I went there once too and some really game Orangeman climbed up a big pole like a monkey. He jumped over the rafters and tried ta drop a massive thick plank on our heads. He missed by a couple of feet when it fell onto the terraces, and he didn't even fall when the peelers chased him back onto their side of the ground. Fuck me, he was really game.'

My father glares at Padre Pio as if to say you have nothing in common with me. '1967 was a bit different to 1978, son. The people came from all over this town to support the Glens that night, including your own district. That's the big difference.'

Rex Mundi has fallen off the bus. He gets to his feet near St Paul's chapel and rubs his arse. Then he bolts as the peelers rush out of one of their Land Rovers in pursuit. PP and I watch as my cousin dodges and weaves his way through traffic. Some Redsmen deliberately walk in front of the cops to block their way as they chase down Rex Mundi.

'Does he know where this party is?' I ask Padre Pio as Rex Mundi disappears out of sight.

'Aye, no bother. Trout gave him the address. That's where he's probably heading now,' he replies.

'Here, I didn't see you buy any programme when we went through the turnstiles at Windsor!'

'Are you dumb or what? I swiped it from that oul coffin dodger that was giving us grief about the keek cable I was laying down on the ground. The programme was stickin' out of his arse pocket in the queue inside Aldo's after the match. I couldn't believe my luck when I clocked the oul cunt,' PP says, producing a ten-pound note from his back pocket.

'The programme had this inside it too. I simply didn't have the time to inform the old gentleman that he had lost a tenner,' he adds. 'Now, let's get a carry-out and go over to Dunville Park.'

'Why don't we just go straight to the party with it?' I ask.

He looks at me and shakes his head in mock shock-disappointment. 'Balls to that, Ruin. Are you dumb or what? We'll drink the beer on the benches over there and then we can hoover up whatever my cousin has laid out for free over in the flats. I'm not into handing over my carry-out ta free-loading cunts.'

I stare down at Padre Pio's hands and it hits me that he hasn't washed them since he decorated a little corner of Windsor Park with his own personal waste just an hour or so earlier.

18

'ALWAYS CRASHING IN THE SAME CAR'

July 1978

That morning, when Sabine called with her 'peace offering', Brazil was playing Manchester United on the floor of our parlour. They were the only teams with eleven fully intact players that I had left. The rest were casualties of Padre Pio's frustrations over not being able to properly flick-to-kick: Chelsea forwards were broken; the West German defence and midfield were crushed and poor Franz Beckenbauer was flattened. While Everton away, in yellow shirts and blue shorts, had seven survivors, the all-white Leeds United were down to just four. Almost every box was a monument to PP's rages as well as to my stupidity for resurrecting our Subbuteo league in the first place.

We had started it way back in 1972, after the cup final. We played in our front rooms, often on our bellies, flicking and kicking and updating the scoreboard, while the bullets whizzed past our windows in the gun battles between the two wings of the IRA and the British Army; more often than not, however, it was both IRAs warring with each other.

I had tried to restart the league to stop Padre Pio thinking too many dark thoughts about his ma and me during the 1978 World Cup. Laying out the old green mat, placing the floodlights around all four corners of the pitch, arranging the two plastic dugouts for the managers of each side, and then lining out his favourite side

(Glasgow Celtic, of course!) who would face mine, the mighty Dutch, was my way of keeping him off the streets and out of my head. Unfortunately, in our first contest, the Dutch beat Celtic 6-1 and Padre Pio then took out his frustrations on Cruyff, Rep and Rensenbrink. After that, our league was temporarily suspended and I spent time on my own with the remaining Subbuteo sets in-between bouts of revision in our front parlour. This is why I had been caught unawares, engaged in a solo shoot-out between the Brazilians and Man U, when she called to see me.

Sabine arrived with a brand-new copy of *Low* inside a Caroline Music bag as a present and an apology. She was sporting yet another 'look': a biker jacket with a black vest underneath. She was braless and her nipples were erect. Her tight white jeans were held up by a thin studded belt, and she was wearing brown monkey ankle boots. To my surprise, she had a cigarette wedged between her fingers. Up until then, I thought she only smoked the occasional joint. Sabine took a final drag from her fag, dropped it at the doorstep and stubbed it out with the heel of her boot. She then bent her head slightly and gave me a fake sheepish-but-cute expression of sorrow.

'I thought you might like this for yourself,' she said and handed over *Low* as I stood in the hallway secretly marvelling at the sight of her standing there.

'I never told you exactly where I lived, madam,' I said.

'I know, but I asked some nice boys at the corner shop facing your old school where Robert McManus lives?'

'And what did they say? Hope they didn't ask where you're from?'

'No. They were more interested to know why I was in calling on "that fruit".'

'I hope you defended my honour, Sabine!'

'Oh, I told them that you were my boyfriend and to stop calling my man a fruit.'

'You've passed the test. You can come in,' I responded and took a bow before opening the parlour door for her.

'Wow! Subbuteo. I haven't seen that for years. My cousins used to play it all the time when we were kids. That's really sweet, Robert. I wish I had my camera with me. I'd have loved to take a few shots of you down on your belly flicking to kick.'

I searched for any excuse as to why I would still be playing a kids' football game at my age. 'Ach, I was just bored shitless and brought it down from the attic for a mess about. Anyway, thanks for the album. Shall I put on a track?'

As Bowie sang 'Always Crashing in the Same Car' I neatly folded up the pitch and packed away the floodlights and dugouts. My cheeks were burning with embarrassment over what Sabine had just seen on the floor. I was putting away the Brazilians when Sabine picked up a decapitated Chelsea forward that must have fallen out. Suddenly, I was plunged into a cold panic at the thought of the appearance of another wounded figure.

'Give me a minute,' I pleaded to Sabine before going out and locking our front door. On returning to the parlour I made sure the blinds were pulled down even though it was turning into a blistering July day. Then I went over to the record player, lifted the needle and dropped it back down on 'Always Crashing in the Same Car'.

'I take it you really like that track?' Sabine asked.

'Yeah, it's great. There's something about it that makes you feel like you are lost somewhere, like you're caught up in this endless circle of traffic and you know that eventually you're going to spin out of control and crash again. Like you're always going to fuck it up,' I said.

Sabine replied with something strangely soft and sensuous which came across as 'cir-cul-a-cion'. She pronounced the word in a near perfect French accent and it made me want to fling her against the sofa and tear her clothes off.

'Circulation,' she repeated. 'It's a much better word than boring old traffic. You can see "circulation" in your mind's eye. You can picture a thousand lights at night in a motorway somewhere in the world, at the edge of a vast city, the cars pulsating and winking through the darkness. Being lost is what I like, is what I want, Robert. To lose yourself. You don't have to explain where you're from, only where you're going.' She reached over and delivered a short soft kiss on my lips. 'You are my muse, young man! You've just given me an idea for my next photo-shoot project in art college.'

I never planned my response, but it must have been something to do with remembering why she had brought me a copy of *Low* in the first place. 'What, me? An inspiration? One of the dumb natives from the republican reservation?'

I waited for a comment about chips on my shoulder but instead Sabine slid closer to me and gently caressed my cheek.

'I'm so sorry for being a bitch up in Jerusalem Street the other day, Robert. I get stressed when Dad calls round and even more so when Aunty Iris is in tow. They're always checking up on me.'

'Maybe he doesn't like the idea of me and you.'

'He really knows nothing about you, Robert. Hey, speaking of fathers, where is your dad today?'

'He's at work. Where else would he be? Some of us Fenians really do work for a living you know, despite what your dad and Aunty Iris might think.'

For this I got a deserved elbow into the ribs, but it was followed by another kiss.

'So what does your dad do for a living then?'

'He kills for a living!'

'Don't tell me he is a fully paid up employee of the Provos then?'

I shook with laughter at the absurdity of her question. 'Well, before he kills them he has them stunned. It's a lot more humane than a kneecapping or a car bombing. I hope you're not one of them vegetarian weirdos like Linda McCartney because my father works in the slaughterhouse, the big meat plant down by the docks.'

'There you go again, Robert Ruin! You're a genius muse once more!'

'Jesus, what's next?'

Sabine's tone became all mock-conspiratorial and for the first time I noticed that she spoke with the slightest of lisps. 'I wonder if your dad could get me inside that place. What do you think? Just imagine being able to photograph what goes on inside there. I bet I'd get some great shots that I could turn into a painting.'

'I don't think so. I went down there once with him and nearly threw up after five minutes. You wouldn't fancy it. Stick to traffic ... sorry, I mean circulation.'

'Circulation!' Sabine said, correcting my pronunciation. 'Robert, what if he could take the pics for me?'

'Who?'

'Your dad, you dummy. I could give him a camera and he could take some sneaky shots.'

'Why don't you ask him? You'll have to buy him a few pints first to soften him up.'

She put her hand up my latest creation, my new 'I hate Pink Floyd' T-shirt, and lightly scratched the area above my belly button. 'I can get men to do lots of things for me, Robert. A few pints won't be a problem.'

We sat in silence in the semi-darkness of the parlour with our arms wrapped around each other, listening to side one of *Low*. The shimmering, stinging electro-sounds muffled the sound of the other world outside: the rumble of the bakery lorries, the yelps and yells of the kids pouring out of the summer school around the corner and the clatter of an army helicopter keeping a constant eye on any suspicious movements below. As Sabine started stroking my cheek again, the payphone rang in our hallway. My father had it installed when mum was first admitted to hospital, when the diagnosis was terminal and all kinds of friends and relatives needed to be in touch with us day and night. Reluctantly, I left her to answer it.

There was heavy breathing down the line and the nasal whistle that I instantly recognised but dared not confirm by speaking into the phone. All I said was 'yes' before the caller slammed his phone down and the line went dead. It was a message received and understood without any talking. I now knew that he knew. One of the bastard spides at the corner must have wired him off about a girl in a biker jacket and tight white jeans who had been asking where Robbie McManus lived. Sabine and I had to get out of this house pronto before he landed, hammering on the door, demanding an introduction.

'Who was that, Robert?' Sabine asked.

'Just a wrong number. Hey, why don't we head into the sun? Let's go round to City Hall or even up to Botanic Gardens, love.'

'I thought you wanted to listen to both sides of *Low*, Robert.'

'Sure we can do that later up in your house with your copy.'

'And who says you are invited back up to Jerusalem Street?' she said, her mood darkening slightly.

But Sabine read my panicked reaction and once again touched the side of my face reassuringly with her hand. 'Only joking, Robert. You get one more chance to stay with me tonight, given that you're such an inspiration. We'll go up home and fall asleep together in the Gardens. Have you got any booze in the house?'

I went into the kitchen and liberated the four cans of Harp from the fridge that Dad had left for me when I finished my A-level revision programme for the day. Four cans of Harp for a couple of revised chapters of *The Return of the Native* was the deal, but balls to Thomas Hardy because there was a real life Eustacia Vye in front of me. When I returned to the parlour, I found her poring over the framed photographs on top of the fireplace that we never seemed to use anymore.

'Where's your mum in all these pictures? Most of them seem to be of your father in strange faraway places.'

There was a line of black-and-white pictures from the early 1970s of dad, Martin Johnstone and a few other comrades on tour across the Eastern Bloc: one under the newly built television tower at Alexanderplatz in Berlin; another on a plinth with a giant white wedding-cake building in the background, a gift from Stalin to Warsaw, and a final one of a sombre-looking Johnty and Dad at the tomb of the mummified man of action himself right in the centre of Moscow.

'Your father seems to be an interesting man. A slaughterhouse socialist! I must meet him soon.'

'We can go for a drink with him before The Harp on Saturday, as long as you can put up with him and his mate yapping on about the workers of the world needing to unite.'

'Robert, that would be great. Let's do it, but I want to ask you something and I hope you won't be offended.'

'Shoot.'

'There are no pictures of your mum anywhere in this room. Where do you keep them?'

'Oh just in photo albums, and I think Dad has a special one of her by his bed,' I lied.

'Snap again! My dad has a picture of Mum by his bedside too. He even had it there before mum got sick. He took it everywhere with him, wherever he was sent,' she said.

I was too afraid to antagonise her by asking what and where she meant by 'sent'. Was it when he was 'sent' solo for a few weeks of military training or even a six-month tour while Sabine and her mother were cooped up in a dormitory for a home in Northern Germany? Instead I asked what her mother was like.

'She was a primary school teacher, a supply teacher who mainly taught infants. She was very popular with the wee ones both here and in Germany. She even taught up in the Falls for six months a few years ago, but she had to give that post up,' Sabine informed me.

'Why?'

'She was told she was followed home one evening by an IRA intelligence team, that's why. Someone must have wondered what a woman from the east was doing working in the west. I'm sure it would have been the same the other way around, but don't you think people here in general are such nosey bastards. Everybody is spying on everybody else. It's one of the many reasons I hate this society.'

Her observation made me feel uneasy and I answered her with another question. 'Do you look like her? Are you more like your mum?'

'I'll show you a picture of her and you can judge for yourself. After all, you know what my dad looks like.'

Bowie had stopped by the time our front door started to take a hammering, which meant he couldn't be sure if anyone was inside the house. The blinds were still pulled down and I grabbed Sabine's hand and forced her onto the carpet beside me.

'Robert, if you want to do it on the ground you only have to ask,' Sabine giggled.

In a whisper I urged her to be quiet but she was puzzled by my panic. 'What on earth for? Who are you hiding from? Are you expecting the army to raid?'

'No, just a bogey man. One bad bogey man who is best to avoid. Just pretend no one is in and he will go away.'

Panic and fear surged through me and found a surprising form of expression. By the time I had removed Sabine's jeans and pants and she had torn off her biker jacket and top, the knocking and the ringing had finally stopped. She wrapped her legs tightly around my back as I entered her. She writhed and twisted until she climaxed, her soft moans ensuring that I quickly followed. Still inside her, I caught sight of an indent on her thigh – it was the imprint of a Brazilian snapped off his wedge, lying broken and redundant beside her on the parlour floor. I lifted up the wounded little black man in the yellow, blue and white colours and waved him in her face: 'You've just had Pele crawling up towards your crack!'

'He shoots, he scores,' Sabine replied, laughing.

It was later, as she was enjoying a post-coital cigarette out in the backyard (my father never allowed anyone to smoke ever again in the house after Mum), that Sabine asked about the other absentee from the house that day.

I was stung by her question and replied, 'As I asked you many times before, why, if you say you don't like Boy Bondage, do you keep wondering where he is?'

'Just curious, that's all. Probably because normally he is never away from your side.'

'Well he's up in his other uncle's house, from his mum's side, the rich one. He's probably paying him a visit to see what he can either swipe or con out of the man. I keep telling him to go up to the house in the Malone Road as we're the poor side of his family. Unlike them, we don't have a drinks cabinet in this house.'

'Will he be there on Saturday when we meet your dad?'

I wished I could have told her no, but I knew that Dad would ask him along all the same. 'If there's a free round going and my da is paying, then yes, he will be there.'

'Saturday's a date then. Robert, I'll not see you for the rest of the week. I've got work to do before I head to London at the end of next month.'

I didn't like the way Sabine announced this so casually. 'Next month? What for?'

'For my presentation to St Martin's. I've got an interview but have to show them some of my work and I'd love to present them with stuff from the slaughterhouse. By the way, have those Harp cans gone warm?'

As Sabine rubbed out her fag, I recognised something on the kitchen window sill just by our outside toilet. It was a glass fruit bowl covered with a flat grey plate, which mum had used to set a jelly in one Saturday night. Congealed, tiny wave formations of strawberry jelly were still visible at the bottom of the bowl, crowned with a ring of grey-blue fur. Jesus! It was probably the last thing she had tried her hand at in the kitchen before giving up after the final diagnosis. No one had either remembered or could be bothered remembering that it was still outside in the yard. The phone in the hall started trilling once more and Sabine asked if I should answer it.

'Not a chance, love. Let it ring.'

'It might be an emergency, Robert.'

'Hardly. Just say that word again, please.'

'Which word?'

'That word, not traffic,' I begged her.

She pouted her lips and whispered once more, 'Circulation!' But I was too lost in dark thoughts to appreciate the way she rolled the word around her mouth, the word that recalled pulsating streams of moving lonely light. I knew I would soon pay a price for ignoring Padre Pio. And yet all she could say back to me was, 'That phone call might have been Aidan looking for us!'

19

COMMS 5

1987

Let us offer each other the sign of peace!

And then when they turn around to face the altar again, shoot them in the back.

Let them be the ones labouring under the illusion that the hand of friendship is being stretched back out across the pews. Their acceptance of your offer to talk is a very encouraging sign and, personally, I think it demonstrates a weakness at the very core of their organisation. For despite all their belligerence and disgraceful treatment of Comrade Duffy and his family, it is clear that they really want a deal. Your choice of location for parleying with them is a masterstroke, especially given that we all assume inside this roach-infested hole that they will never reach their destination.

Let us offer each other the sign of peace!

Whenever I hear that shite, I am reminded about a bit of graffiti I once saw scrawled onto a desk inside the library of Queen's University just a few years ago, not long before I was taken into Her Majesty's custody. With the help of a fake student ID card, I was shadowing a full-time cop, who was doing his part-time MA law research in the library. Normally he took time out from his day job in uniform to study on a Thursday or Friday evening. As I waited for him to arrive, I spotted this message from one of our loyalist brethren inked onto the desk where I was pretending to study: 'Let us reach out the hand of friendship across the divide and make peace with our Catholic and nationalist neighbours ... then when they least expect it, let's round up the Fenian scum, put them all into a giant field and annihilate each and every one of the scumbags.'

Whoever wrote that message had clarity of thought, as they wanted to see every man, woman and child of the Romanist faith exterminated. As sick and sectarian as it might have been, this message made me think more lucidly about all the forces that were, and still are, ranged against us. It stripped me of any remaining 'workers-of-the-world-unite' delusions that I might have been clinging to – like the ones your father clung to as he denounced the struggle. For that alone, I am grateful to the bigot who left this missive.

At this critical juncture we – you and I – need this same type of clarity in our vision in dealing with our internal problems. There can be no time for old loyalties, former friendships, or even family ties of blood to obscure what is to be done. Even my family ties!

Fraternally, as always ... Comrade T.

20

UTH

28 April 1979

Padre Pio is puzzled by the sum scrawled on the wall of the abandoned coal yard: 26 + 6 = 1.

For the son of an on-the-run exile, PP is a bit slow on the uptake when it comes to the old rhetoric. He's transfixed on the maths and fails to see the message transmitted in the illogical arithmetic.

We are standing at the entrance towards the 'crying stairs', which the residents of Divis Flats will try to convince you is haunted by the wailing ghosts of two dead British soldiers who were blown up in the stairwell a couple of years ago. Now live soldiers on foot patrol come down from the balconies above. They are accompanied by a heavily built cop with a gunfighter moustache; instantly, he recognises Padre Pio.

'Going up to see cousin Paki, are we?' the peeler asks.

'None of your business where we are going,' PP replies, and I suspect an arrest is imminent.

'You just tell cousin Paki we'll be paying him a visit very soon. It's probably best we do before the 'Erps call looking for him, to put that 9 mill they have into the back of his leg,' the policeman continues.

A black soldier at the back of the patrol smirks at PP and myself.

'What are you smiling at, Kunta Kinte?' PP says.

Fortunately the big brother, who is wearing a radio pack on his back, has a sense of humour. 'I'm just thinking about the last time I was sliding this black mamba into your mum,' he says in a flat Brummie accent, patting his crotch proudly.

'And I'm just thinking about that last show your sister was doing inside The Harp bar last week. Great tits!' I butt in.

The peeler barks at the Brit to move out of the way and then comes towards me. 'I've not seen your unwashed face around here. What's your name?'

'Is this a P-check or what?' I say in a I-know-my-rights tone.

The cop is riled but offers some advice. 'P-check? If I hear any more funny talk like that from you I'll be hauling you into an empty cell in the barracks. Now do yourself a favour and piss off home and don't come back here to the planet of the 'Erps.'

Padre Pio steps close as if to correct the copper. 'Planet of the 'Erps? I wish. You should know better than that, officer. The hoods rule in there. UTH.'

Asserting his authority, the policeman slaps the air to indicate he is tired of talking to us and signals to the soldiers to head towards the Falls Road.

Then it's my turn to look and sound stupid inside the complex as I press the bell for a lift close to a stench-ridden rubbish chute. Padre Pio sniffs the fetid air when I complain about the pong.

'I've said it before and I'll say it again, Ruin, but smell your oul ma!'

I'm still pressing the bell when PP hisses at me, 'For fuck's sake, get a grip, Ruin. These lifts haven't worked since we blew up them two Brits a couple of years ago. We're hoofing it up the stairs.'

I stare up the dark stairwell. 'We'll fucking break our necks. It's pitch black!'

'My advice is to count each step till seven and you should land on the next floor. Just try not to stand on any dog shite.'

Where shafts of light manage to pierce through the slits on the wall overlooking Cullingtree Road, they illuminate graffiti, almost all written in defiance of the Provos, Sticks and 'Erps. There are scratches and scrawls of 'UTH' and even a few 'UTJRS'. Only when we reach the top balcony of the flats do I see one large painted message in homage to the INLA, written by a character who signs his name 'Bonanza'.

When I ask Padre Pio what 'UTJRS' means, he looks perplexed. 'What? Are you some sort of mong? And you're the one that goes to the snobby grammar school, Ruin. Fuck me pink, but you are thick. It means "Up The Joyriders".'

PP then gulders 'Up the Joyriders!', which echoes all over the balconies on the top floor. 'Maybe later we will be in luck and see some serious joyriding,' he says. 'Some of them hoods would give James Hunt a race, they're that tasty behind the wheel. Here, Ruin, do me a favour. When we get into our Paki's flat, don't tell him that peeler mentioned him by name. Our Paki has enough to worry about without the RUC threatening ta raid his flat.'

'You must have cousins up and down the length of this road, PP.'

'Aye, our Trout is on my da's side but Paki here is my ma's sister's son. You know my ma, Ruin, don't ye? The one you spend time with in our parlour after I go up to bed?' he says sinisterly.

His head is once more cocked towards my face, and I am thinking that even if I walted him one and bolted, he would probably have a whole posse of wee flats-thugs to track me down in minutes. So I have to play cool and calm the fruit looper down.

'Look, I've been meaning to talk to you about this. All your mother ever wants is to talk to me. She's been so nice to me since my mum died, PP. Look, I dunno if I should tell you this cos you'll laugh till you shit yourself.'

'Say what, McManus? Say what?'

McManus. That is the alarm button pressed. Once someone uses your surname, its usually a sure sign that despite professing undying loyalty to you they are about to Judas you over.

'Look PP, I once made a fool of myself in front of her,' I plead.

'In what way, McManus? In what way?' he says, continuing with that semi-threatening tone.

Thinking on my feet I choose humiliation as my chosen shield: 'I burst out crying in front of her one night. I bastard and well burst out crying.'

Padre Pio follows suit by bursting out laughing. In fact, he is buckled over with laughter and that familiar sniggering 'sna-ha, sna-ha' he does whenever he is enjoying the embarrassment, the torment, the humiliation of others.

I am about to remind him that we are talking about my mother, who was always good to him, who passed away after a terrible, painful exit, when a door is opened. A face pops out. With his closely cropped hair, clipped moustache and an Indian blue ink dot right smack in the middle of his forehead, this guy would be easily picked out in a line-up.

'Keep the noise down will yiz or you'll have the Village Policemen coming round here and checking on anti-social behaviour, and I am not talking about the RUC,' he says, directing a nasty stare at Padre Pio. He ushers us in and my dear friend, who is still sniggering over how I allegedly broke down in front of his mother about the death of mine, introduces me.

'I know he looks like a right bender with that haircut and them clothes, but our Ruin is alright,' PP says.

'And I'm Paki and I'm dead on. Shut the fuckin' door and come in and join our party,' our host says.

The living room is thick with cigarette smoke, making it hard to see initially how many people are inside. As my eyes grow accustomed to the dim, smoggy light, I can make out Trout sitting in an armchair swilling back a tin of Harp. In another by the kitchen, there is a withered old crone dressed in black and dripping with gold. She's counting out wads of cash on a table with a picture of 'Padre Pio the Holy Man' on it. A younger woman wearing an old man's flat cap is frying food in the kitchen and a grey-haired man is stretched out face down on the sofa, snoring like a hog. Beneath the biggest TV I have ever seen, there is this strange humungous piece of rectangular metal, flashing blue lights and a flat semi-transparent top which exposes one of those new video tapes that is whirring around inside the machine. It is only then that I notice the hardcore blue movie on the screen with the volume turned down to zero. A boy of about eleven or twelve is on the floor, drawing pictures in a school exercise book.

Trout summons Padre Pio over and hands him two cans of lager for us, and I salute back across the room in gratitude. I can't help looking at the black man on the video, armed with something that surely cannot be real, entering up the arse of a short honey-blonde woman whose face we don't see.

'He's got some hammer on him that King Dong!' Paki says in breathless admiration. 'If you'd one like that, sure what else would you do for a living?'

I force a laugh and move towards PP, who has plonked himself down by the living-room door and is horsing back his free gift from cousin Trout.

'Why do they call him Paki?' I whisper to him.

'Because of that Hindu tattoo on his head. Everybody said he looked like one of them Pakis after he'd done it.'

'But why did he do it?' I ask, looking at the indigo dot on our host's forehead.

'Fuck knows why. Probably cos somebody dared him to do it. That's our Paki for ya. He's as game as fuck.'

Paki is sitting balanced on the edge of the sofa where the older man is still snoring.

'Want anything else lads? Cider, wine, dope?' Paki offers.

Padre Pio and I both shake our heads and give thumbs-up signs towards our half-drunk cans of Harp.

'No bother, boys. Make yourselves at home here. Did yiz enjoy the game?'

I'm about to relive the highlights of the final, but PP interrupts, nodding towards the granny counting out the dosh. 'Looks like you had a good day at the office, Paki,' he says.

Paki ignores him and rolls a home-made feg from a tin similar to our taxi driver's earlier. It too was obviously crafted when he was inside at Her Majesty's Pleasure, judging by the Celtic script and the crudely drawn picture of Cuchulain on the front. Although he's probably only in his mid-twenties, Paki looks far older. His thumbs have already turned that petrol colour that heavy smokers develop on their digits, and there are deep canyons around his eye sockets and heavy bags underneath them. He is also wearing a three-piece pin-stripe suit, black shirt, no tie but with a blood-red kerchief poking out of his breast pocket. He looks like he has been auditioning for a part in an adult version of *Bugsy Malone*.

He points down at the snoring drunk, whose belly is protruding from a woolly jumper.

'That's my dad by the way. A fat, lazy, useless cunt. It's as well somebody is here to keep this family going. Isn't that right, cunty?' Paki bellows into the drunken sleeper's ear. His dad doesn't even twitch.

'So were you at Windsor then, Paki?' I ask.

'Windsor Park? Nah! I wouldn't have the time, amigo. I'm too busy working for a living. Cash in hand, of course, to all customers. No taxes or VAT here. Anything the punters want they can just come up to us here in Treasure Ireland, Divis Mansions.'

The granny raises her head and cackles over Paki's advertisement. She is wearing a chain with a golden tabernacle hanging from it; its miniature door exposes yet another image of the saintly Padre Pio inside.

'Seriously, son,' Paki continues. 'If there is anything you're looking for, just come up and order it. We're doing a big line in these new videos and video players at the minute. Blue movies and splatter films are very popular. Our Padre Pio will vouch for our quality assurance.'

Apart from the soak on the sofa, the only other person in the room who doesn't snigger at this is Trout, who is sitting deep in thought, cracking his knuckles. The sound makes me wince. I look down at the kid on the carpet. He has drawn a stick man with a moustache, a blue dot on his oversized forehead and red lines shooting out of his legs.

'Who's that meant to be, son?' I say.

'It's Paki, my dad,' the boy says, looking up at me.

'And what is he doing?'

'Nathin'. He's just bleeding.'

'Bleeding?'

'Aye, are you stupid mister? He's bleedin' like that time when the Provies shat him in each leg,' the boy goes on.

His father comes over and strokes the child's hair while glimpsing up at the video through the fog of feg smoke.

'If I ever meet a leprechaun, my first wish he grants will be ta have a hammer like King Dong's there,' Paki announces, which prompts the woman inside the kitchen to come out and protest.

'Aye, but you still wouldn't know what to do with it,' she says. The woman is a younger version of Padre Pio's mother; thinner, with longer blonde hair, but busty like PP's ma. Her braless tits are packed into a tight, white, grease-stained jumper. For a split second I imagine she might be the woman being rammed in the blue movie, which is still on only inches away from the boy. Thankfully, he doesn't even seem to be aware of what is on the screen directly above his head.

She pulls out a packet of Rothmans and a lighter from her back pocket. 'Any of you boys want a smoke?' she asks, before also ruffling the boy's hair. 'That's our Stephen. He's about the only thing Paki ever got right with me. I'm Colleen by the way. Nice ta meet yiz.'

'I certainly didn't hear you complaining when I put it in and knocked you up the spout,' Paki retorts, and the whole room except Trout and myself start cackling again.

'He's as good as gold, our Stephen. Never goes out anymore onto the balconies or gets inta trouble with the wee hoods. Not since the Village Policemen dragged Paki out of the flat here and shot him in the knees right outside the door, fuckin' bastards. Here, are you boys sure yiz don't wanna a feg or something else I can get ya?' Paki's wife asks, while winking suggestively at me.

'That must have been terrible,' I pipe up.

'What's terrible, love?' Colleen asks.

'To see a thing like that. To see someone shoot your own father,' I say.

Trout clearly can't bear any of this any longer. He stands up, cracks his knuckles and says, 'Mr Ruin's father condemns that kind of practice these days, Colleen. But you and I know fine rightly that Paki got off lightly with that one because I intervened. Otherwise it would have been an OBE.'

'One Behind The Ear,' I hear Paki say in a half whisper.

'Get real, Paki. I had to claim ya as one of us to save ya from an OBE.'

'I know, Trout. I know and I appreciate it, mate.'

'Just don't forget that the movement has ta get a cut of all of this in return. Anyway, can I have a quiet word with ya?' Trout says.

When the two men leave the room, I turn to PP on the floor and whisper as Paki's wife slaps down a plate of fried sausages, bacon, eggs and soda bread swimming in grease on the granny's counting table, between the elastic-banded wedges of one-, five- and ten-pound notes.

'I thought you said this was going to be a victory party. It's more like nosebag time at the old people's home,' I complain to Padre Pio.

'Shut up, McManus. I'm only here ta collect something from Trout and then we're gone, right!' His tone has reverted to one of threat and menace again.

I'm relieved when Colleen interrupts with a plate full of fried food. I decline, but PP hoovers up the burnt offerings with gusto. Up close, Colleen is caked in make-up but you can still make out the encrusted contours of acne below her sharp cheekbones.

'Are you on a diet, love?' she says, staring directly into my eyes. 'Maybe you're in love. Is that it?'

'No, not anymore,' I croak.

'A boy like you shouldn't have too much bother in that department. I see good looks run in the family,' she adds and nods at the floor.

I realise she is referring to something going on downstairs in the lower floor of the apartment, where, it dawns on me, the bedrooms must be.

She switches off the porn film and winks at me. 'There's plenty of real live action going on down there.'

'What do you mean?' I can feel my face flush.

'Is he your brother or your cousin?'

Fucking hell! She's talking about Rex Mundi. I had forgotten about him. He must have ended up in the flats with Trout after he was bounced off the bus with the RUC in hot pursuit. Needing the toilet after all that lager in the flat and in Dunville Park with PP earlier, I ask to be excused and tiptoe downstairs.

When I reach the stand-alone toilet, I switch on the light and shut the door from the outside. Then I creep towards one of the bedrooms on the right, where I can hear the muffled mutterings of Trout laying down the party line to Paki.

'Ask yourself why we have to do this, Paki. If we don't deal with ya again then the Village Policemen will go ape-shit. Do you know every time we have a meeting with the Provos to sort out problems, your name keeps cropping up?'

'For fuck's sake, Trout. Please not again. Not here at least, in these flats.' Paki is begging now.

'Ask yerself what choice do we have. This order has ta be carried out and it's outta my hands anyway.'

'Well, at least do it somewhere else then. Not here. Not anywhere the wee lad knows. I can slip away for a few days after it's done,' Paki pleads.

There is another door, which is ajar. I push it open and see an even larger television on with the same porn flick playing. There are two video recorders attached to each other by a cable; one is feeding the film into another blank video tape. On either side of a single bed are neatly stacked piles of black video cassettes. To the right is a table with a white linen cloth and a silver plinth supporting a glass heart. The holy image of Padre Pio's face is embossed on it. So this is the old granny's room then. Every available space in the room is filled with green shoeboxes, labelled with titles such as 'Jaws', 'Star Wars', 'Rocky' and 'Debbie Does Dallas'.

I exit the room and turn my attention to the last bedroom door. I try to open it quietly but suddenly feel a bony hand on my back pushing me forward into the last room. It's PP right behind me. We fall into a kid's bedroom, startling a young woman naked on the bed. Her legs are spread apart on wee Stephen's Manchester United duvet. A familiar-looking Mohawk is darting in and out of her pubis while she lies there moaning and writhing around the sheets. When PP shouts out 'anyone for second jockey' Rex Mundi takes his mouth away from the girl's clit and angrily barks, 'Get the fuck, you two tossers! Can't you see I'm busy?'

Padre Pio and I bolt upstairs almost knocking over Paki, who looks crestfallen, on the staircase. Trout is waiting for us in the hallway and summons PP by pointing at him.

'I need a wee word with you, cousin,' Trout says, nodding towards the bathroom. The two of them go in and a radio starts to blare out Blondie's 'Heart of Glass'.

'Movement business,' Trout says, poking his head out from the bathroom. 'Go back to the living room and get yourself a drink, Mr Ruin.'

I go and sit in Trout's armchair overlooking the road below. The army foot patrol that stopped us earlier has now been joined by several military jeeps and an RUC Land Rover forming a wagon circle in the crepuscular gloom of early evening. Paki's boy gets up from the carpet and hands me a torn-out page from his exercise book. It's meant to be a footballer, but the figure is so block-wedged that you might mistake him for a robot. Only the yellow and blue colours and the trophy, which is almost as big as the player, give it away.

'It's the Cliftonville captain liftin' the cup today. My da let me listen to it on the radio. He says it's on TV tomorrow and I can watch it. My da says he might even take me up ta Solitude next season,' Stephen informs me.

His father reappears with a large bottle of Johnnie Walker whisky, which he plonks down beside the sofa.

'Here kid, take a swig,' he says.

'No thanks, Paki. I gotta keep a clear head here for wandering through the town to home. There might be Orangemen still about on the prowl for Fenians like us.'

Paki knocks back a couple belts of the Scotch, puts the bottle down and smacks his lips. 'He says it's only goin' to be a wee flesh wound. The Provies said the same thing the last time I got shat.'

'Ruin! Come here!' I hear Trout shouting.

Trout is putting a brown duffel bag on PP's shoulder. 'Go back way down the Grosvenor Road and behind the City Hall. And then take that message to where you said you'd plank it. You cool about that?' Trout instructs PP.

'Aye, no bother, Trout. Tell Paki we'll see him later and not ta be late,' PP adds. He nods at me and opens the front door to leave.

I count to six and seven on the way into the darkness of another stairwell closer to Albert Street and stop near the bottom to face Padre Pio. 'What's happening later?' I ask.

'Paki has an appointment down our way. He asked for it ta be done down there, so he doesn't lose any more face in the flats and that his kid doesn't see anything. He's being shat at eleven o'clock tonight.'

Padre Pio notes the shock on my face and adds scornfully, 'Fer fuck's sake, Ruin. Don't worry about that hoodin' bastard. He's only gettin' a wee flesh wound.'

21

COMMS 6

1987

Let us offer each other the sign of peace! Again! Starting with you and me, comrade.

I owe you an apology. I insulted your father. I forgot that despite your political differences, you still speak to him. Jesus! Do you remember that tiny flat we commandeered for you when he kicked you out for joining the struggle? It wasn't too far from our traitor's old Aladdin's cave.

It seems we all live to disappoint our fathers. Mine still blames me for my brother's ongoing incarceration. He stopped speaking to me once I followed in M's footsteps into this rat hole. No fun visiting two sons every Saturday, I suppose. I think deep down he feels guilty that he chose this place rather than his old Heimat to bring us up in. He knows things would have been different if M and I had grown up in the land of the Audi and autobahn. But hey, us revolutionaries shouldn't get too hung up on blood ties.

Let us offer each other the sign of peace!

Speaking of sentimental shite – at least we all knew where we stood with the Latin-speaking, hellfire-and-damnation clergy. Nowadays, they try to seduce us with their Bob Dylan ballads of brotherly love from the altar rails. But beyond, outside – among the faithful – there is seething hatred and burning resentment due to all the schisms that have split us three or four ways. Even the oul dolls in their headscarves, threading beads through their fingers and whispering their prayers, won't even speak to each other anymore when they leave the chapel because of where their husbands or sons or grandsons stand politically these days. So, why should we be any different? We owe nothing to random things like family or neighbourhood. Our actions should be devoid of these fake loyalties. Let us offer each other the sign of peace? Aye, right!

One of our more enlightened comrades on this wing is currently holed up in his cell studying for his Open University degree. He says he did it thanks to your encouragement when you finished yours. History, wasn't it? Unlike you, he didn't get turfed out of St Mal's and thrown into the Tech though. You were always encouraging the rest of us to get educated. A real Leninist had come into our midst. Your studious fan told me it's no longer acceptable to say 'fraternally' because it excludes our female cadres and is therefore sexist, so ...

Solidarity from Comrade T.

22

THE SILVER LADY

28 April 1979

We make our way down 'bomb alley', where the Provos ship their 'smokey joes' and firebombs from the Wild West into Belfast city centre. Then we amble along Durham Street, around the side wall of Inst. boys school and then past the Tech. After passing the Black Man statue and going towards Wellington Place, we are supposed to follow Trout's orders and go up to the ABC cinema and then over into Great Victoria Street, making a sharp turn at The Crown bar onto the streets leading towards home territory, far away from Brit patrols and any Orangemen still on the hunt for uppity Taigs returning from Windsor Park. But we don't. PP is defying Trout's orders and is clearly ready for a row, any row.

'Before ya even say it – balls to Trout and his so-called commands. We'll make our own way home – our way!' He scowls straight into my face.

'But he said—'

PP prods his right index finger into my chest to interrupt my protest. 'We're going into Lord Hamill's for Hawaiian burgers and nobody's goin' ta stop us. Anyway, one day it'll be me givin' the orders, not that wanker Trout,' he declares, while making a beeline for the fast food joint that last summer I vowed I would never venture into ever again.

When he pulls open the glass door to usher me inside, I freeze at the entrance, and he looks at me with total bewilderment. 'Are you scared of somebody in there, Ruin? Cos there's no need, absolutely no need. I've got all I want in here,' he says, patting the side of the duffle bag slung over his shoulder.

Suddenly, I feel afraid. 'I don't really fancy a Hawaiian burger, mate. I want fish 'n' chips instead. Can't we get fish 'n' chips in our own area?'

He grabs my elbow and pushes me inside. 'I wanna Hawaiian burger and you're gettin' one too, cunty,' he hisses, as the queue of Saturday kids and a couple of menacing spides turn round and stare in our direction.

We take our place, but in about ten seconds PP gets irritated. His right leg starts to vibrate. He's holding his crotch with his left hand. I spot two spides near the front of the queue whispering to each other. One turns around and says loudly, 'Aye, probably Fenians,' and my heart sinks.

PP elbows me in the ribs then nods towards the toilets at the back. I can only hope that he knows another way out of here because the two spides are twice our size and a good bit older. When we get into the bogs, which stinks of piss and stale smoke, PP takes the duffle bag off his shoulder, shoves his right hand into it and uses his left to whip out his cock to start pissing into the urinal. I am too shaky and nervy to even attempt a piss and stand staring at the door just as the two spides come through it. For some reason, I focus on their belts. One has a studded belt with an eagle's head and the American flag on the buckle. The other's is a series of sharp studs that glisten and twinkle underneath the toilet strip lights. The spide with the eagle belt has a thick mane of black hair parted with a middle shade and a scar slashed over his dimpled chin. He asks, 'Are you Taigs?'

I am expecting Padre Pio to answer in the affirmative and follow with a flurry of punches, but instead he looks up at them theatrically and shakes his head, as if he is disappointed, no, even wounded, by the question.

'You are endangering a very important operation, chum,' PP says coldly as he shoots the older spide a venomous glare.

'I asked you a simple question – are you Taigs?' the scarred spide continues.

Instead of replying, Padre Pio drops the duffle bag to the tiled floor but has held on to something he has plucked from inside it. He points it directly into the head of the other spide, who has taken his studded belt off and wrapped it around his hand.

'And you are endangering a very important operation,' PP repeats before adding, 'Now you scoot off and let us get on with what we have to do, or else I am gonna blow your fuckin' mate's head off.'

Like myself, the lad with the belt around his fist is quaking. Sweat breaks out on his forehead and he looks over desperately to his friend. Padre Pio gestures to me to go behind both of them and guard the door. Somehow, I can move.

'We are on an operation for the Young Citizens Volunteers, which I can't talk about any further. So I suggest you and your bum chum get the fuck out of here before I lose my temper,' PP says without a trace of nerves or any fear in his voice.

There is genuine panic in the voice of the lad though, who, just a few seconds earlier, was ready to smash his studded fist into Padre Pio's face. 'They're the YCV, Smokie,' he says to scarred dimple features. 'That's the junior UVF. For fuck's sake, he has a gun.'

'Where are yiz from then? Which battalion do you belong to?' Smokie asks, like a real doubting Thomas. I'm wondering if it's more brains or balls he has.

'East Belfast, chum. Ravenhill Road. I was sworn in at a wee house you might know in Bendigo Street when I was only twelve. Doc Halliday was there himself that day. He actually said I would do the organisation proud just like my grandfather did, fighting in the 36th on the Somme,' PP responds with not a single muscle or nerve moving on his face.

'You know Doc Halliday?' Smokie asks.

'Sure I do. Now take back that insult,' PP says.

'What insult?'

'When you asked if we were Taigs! I don't like being called a Taig,' PP goes on.

Padre Pio then continues to rattle off a number of names he says belong to the UVF East Belfast Battalion, all of them top boys who have taken the war to the republicans. All I can think about, now that the danger has passed, is what happened here last summer. I recall all those times I passed by here in the weeks and months after that day, cursing and swearing under my breath at the sight of this place. I can still hear what was playing on the radio that afternoon. 'Dancing in the city … alleys that we run through … now we've just begun to have fun tonight.' Would I ever be able to blot that fucking song out of my memory?

By the time I shake myself out of this mini-reverie, Padre Pio is already pressing the spides' flesh, slapping them matey-like on the back. Smokie is even offering to buy our burgers as an apology for thinking we were Fenians. When we finally leave the pisser and return to the queue, Padre Pio comes up with an excuse to break away from the spides once we get our Hawaiians and milkshakes.

I thought he had forgotten, but he hadn't. He never forgets anything personal you tell him. High on the gun in the bag, he was simply being cruel, insisting on coming in here.

'Listen boys, our Robert wants ta get out of here pronto like. I always respect you Shankill boys, but my mate isn't too comfortable hangin' about inside this joint.'

Smokie and the other lad, who introduced himself as 'Snow', probably because of his white-blonde hair, both look stunned.

'He has bad memories of this place, lads. Bird trouble,' PP explains.

'You worried she might walk back in here, Robert?' Snow asks.

Quick as a flash Padre Pio produces another gem from the liar locker. 'Worse still. She works here a couple of days every week. Oul Robert here doesn't wanna take any chances of bumping into her. Isn't that right, mate?' PP says all too slyly.

The two Shankill spides nod in understanding and solidarity and say their goodbyes, expressing their best wishes to the 'volunteers from the east'.

It is not until we are far away enough from Lord Hamill's, sitting on a bench inside the City Hall Gardens, that PP starts to howl with laughter. I join him in his mirth because it's easier that way.

'You should have kept that performance up for another few minutes, mate,' I manage to say amid the laughter. 'Them two dumb stupid cunts fell for it. They even offered to walk us home over the Queen's Bridge in case there were any Fenians about. They wanted to be our guards,' I continue, while he sniggers to himself. 'How the fuck did you know all of them names from the UVF over in the east, PP?'

'Trout gives me them. He tells me to be always on the ball in case their names crop up in any conversation. You know like, "Doc Halliday was in the Bodega Bar the other night with this bird" or "Sam Pigface was seen in the Variety Market with his wife last Friday morning". I'm told ta memorise all that. It's called intelligence, Ruin, something you'd be good at ... so says Trout anyway.'

'Well them names definitely came in useful today, PP! What a performance.'

'Aye, sweet,' he says.

'Did you ever think of a career on the stage, PP? I mean that performance in the bogs could have won an Oscar.'

But this praise for his dramatic skills only seems to annoy Padre Pio. Instead, he throws down the duffel bag, takes out the gun and points it straight into my chest.

'See this, see this McManus! This is called the Silver Lady. It has a very proud history, this weapon has. THIS is what got us out of trouble because it made them two Orange bastards piss themselves with fear. THIS is also going to get us our freedom, McManus. As Trout so often says, "Words divide, actions unite!" THIS is why those two gave us respect.'

'Holy fuck, put that away, will ya?' I beg him. It seems to work, as his anger subsides and his glare disappears, and he slips the gun back into the bag.

Instead of pushing on towards home ground, however, he insists that we sit on and finish our burgers. He spears the pineapple on top of his meat and holds it up, waving it towards my face. 'I'd love ta put these on the tits of some bird and them bite them off, Ruin. Would you do that?'

'Nah, I'd rather put the pineapple around the shaft of my dick and get her to nibble it all the way through to the end.'

'Did you do that with yer woman?'

'What woman?'

I can see he senses my panic and says, 'Don't worry, McManus, relax yer kacks. I don't mean with my ma. I mean did you do that with that arty bird you were banging up in the Holy Lands last summer when you disappeared from us all for a while?'

The mere mention of his ma has me shuddering, so I try to joke it off. 'Nah, she was allergic to exotic fruit.'

He flicks the pineapple off the plastic fork and it lands exactly where he intended it to: right onto my army trousers. A circular stain appears on the left knee. Before I get the urge to fire back my pineapple slice onto his army coat, we hear the yell of '*Tele* ... *Tele* ... *Tele* ... Ulster, Ulster, last edition, Ulsterrr.'

'Ireland's Saturday night,' yelps PP. 'There will be pictures from the cup final.'

We burst out laughing again when we see the spasmodic paper seller clip-clopping along at an angle over Donegall Square East, one lame arm turned in on itself like a crab's limb, the other holding on to a large grey bag stuffed with the cup final edition of the sports paper. PP beckons him over. The giant man-child has ginger banjo-string hair stretched across a bald pate, and the tip of his fattened tongue is wedged between his lower lip and gums. PP shows no mercy and puts on his finest retard voice.

'Yo mate, any chance of an "Ulster" there to see if I made the front page?' PP says, with his own tongue hanging half out of his mouth.

He hands over ten pence to the paper seller, sits back down and flicks through the pages of the cup final coverage. Every photograph, including the front-page celebrations of our players at the Kop end, the goal-mouth action, Tony Bell's match-winning strike and the snapshots of the Red Army in the terraces behind the nets, are studied meticulously. Padre Pio descends into a rage; there are no pictures of him.

I try to calm him down. 'PP, there's the *Sunday News* tomorrow. They'll have better coverage of all the aggro.'

'Well, you can fuckin' buy it and bring it round to our house,' he says sullenly. He throws the remains of his Hawaiian into the pages, smearing the faces of the Cliftonville team, who are proudly holding the cup aloft, and then dumps it all into a nearby rubbish bin.

'Right, let's head back home and bring this thing in. There's important work ta be done,' PP grunts, making off towards May Street. He clocks an Ulsterbus stuffed with glum-looking Portadown supporters to whom he jiggles off a few wank-hand signals before scooting down Alfred Street and into the edge of the safe zone. All the way along Hamilton Street, across Cromac Square and into the 'other side' of the district he is singing a familiar pop tune out loud, 'Come on Silver Lady take my word, I won't run out on you again believe me. I've seen the light.'

Eventually, outside our old primary school, as I am about to head towards my house, Padre Pio blocks my path and puts his bony hand on my chest.

'Whoa there, chum. We're not finished yet.'

'Finished what, PP? I told my da I'd come home as soon as I could. I've gotta check if that cousin of mine made it back safely from the flats.'

'Don't worry about that English cunt, McManus! Or should I say that "Judas cunt". Isn't that what you called him once for riding that bird you used to be mad about?'

I want to scream at him that he probably never 'rode' her, but what would be the point. Instead I plead, 'Look, it's not him that I'm worried about. My da will just give me hassle if he isn't back in tonight. He'll start thinking his beloved nephew has been picked up by the Shankill Butchers and will end up with his throat cut up an alleyway. If he is killed, I'll never hear the end of it.'

'Sure that would be a good result for you. Anyway, listen to me, McManus. I told Trout you were coming along on this operation, and that's exactly what you're going ta do, right?'

'Thought you said you don't take orders from Trout.'

He is shaking his head again in fake sorrow while he fumbles around his pockets. I'm suddenly expecting a blade to be produced.

'Ya still don't get it yet, McManus?'

'Get what, PP?'

'All this! The wee trip to the flats; facin' up to them Orangemen in Lord Hamill's; movin' the Silver Lady from Divis down ta here. Don't ya get it?'

'Get what?'

'It's all about being game, McManus. You've ta prove ta me and also ta Trout that you're game. That's what Trout wants ta know. I told him you'd bolt from me, but in the end ya didn't bottle it. Trout wanted ta know if you were a fence sitter just like yer da.'

'So did I pass then?'

Padre Pio is staring down at his diminutive DM boots, his eyes fixated on something that is not quite there. His face is getting redder as heat rises up to his ears. With nostrils flaring, he croaks,

'Not yet, McManus. There's one more thing ta be done and you have ta play your part.'

Reluctantly, I follow him up to an alleyway at the back of two rows of terraced houses. We come to a back door on which someone has spray-painted 'Splinters – UTE'. Padre Pio clambers on top of a bin close to a wooden door and then hoists himself onto the wall before disappearing into a yard below. A couple of seconds later, he yanks open the door and beckons me inside with a jerk of his head. We hunker down as we pass by a kitchen window. The light on and there is the sound of running water hitting something metallic.

Looking up, I see a grey-haired woman in a pink housecoat filling a kettle. Her wrinkled hands are shaking slightly as she holds it under the tap. Then she takes it to the stove behind her. PP takes two black balaclavas out of the duffel bag and tosses one to me.

'Put that on now!' he growls, before rolling his own over his shaven head.

When I shake my head in protest, Padre Pio gets up close and whispers, 'You don't want to let any traitors see your face.'

I am about to retreat and escape out the wooden door, but it's already too late. He has pulled open the door to the kitchen and is already yelling, 'This is a takeover for an operation. Do as you are told and you won't get hurt.'

The first thing I do when I follow him through the door is to turn off the gas ring on the cooker. A TV is blaring in the next room. Crystal Gayle is singing 'Don't It Make My Brown Eyes Blue' on the *Val Doonican Show*. The elderly woman facing the television set seems paralysed; she is neither shaking nor trembling, demonstrating no kind of visible fear. She's ancient, in her late-sixties, with dyed blonde hair that looks like whipped ice-cream, and she's actually staring at me as if to ignore him. She seems more shocked to see me entering her living room than him pointing the Silver Lady at her. How can she be so indifferent to the presence of a gunman before her? It's as if she has been expecting him but not me. To avoid her stare, I look at the oak sideboard behind her. Two vases of dying flowers are on either side of a glass rectangle on a plinth; my second embossed Padre Pio of the day. Just in front of the holy man's image is an open packet of Embassy Regal with eight cigarettes left in the box and an empty ashtray, a present from Rome.

Just after PP opens his mouth and fakes a nasally accent, I see the photograph and I realise who she is. I am filled with fear, utter dread and disgust.

'This is the Ulster Volunteer Force. We need your house for an hour before our target passes by. If you do exactly what we say, you will not be harmed,' Padre Pio says, before nodding towards a table and chair by the door.

'Bring that chair over here, Geordie,' he commands, and I carry the chair to the centre of the room.

'Right, madam. Sit down and keep quiet in front of the TV. Val Doonican will be on soon, singing in his rocking chair.'

With one hand still holding the pistol, he takes out a pair of woman's tights from the duffel bag. He ties her wrists tightly to the armrests and then reaches over beside the Padre Pio plinth to reef out a few handkerchiefs from a box of Kleenex. He surveys his captive and puts the barrel of the Silver Lady to her lips. Now, she finally starts to shake violently as he forces open her mouth and shoves a bundle of hankies into it as a gag.

Placing the gun between the holy man's plinth and her cigarettes, PP pulls out one more thing from the duffel bag – a video cassette. He slots it into the video player. I am frozen as I watch him work the controls. I note that beside the machine there are a number of other cassettes. Thin white labels with handwritten black capital letters identify them as, 'Holy Communion', 'Pilgrimage to Rome 1976' and 'The Song Of Bernadette'.

Val Doonican suddenly turns to snow, 'Paddy McGinty's Goat' dissolves into a hiss and then the screen finally goes black.

Suddenly, King Dong appears, ramming his member into the petite blonde from behind. The sight of the black porn actor at his work produces the first twist of resistance from PP's prisoner. She swivels this way and that to avoid seeing what has been put on in front of her. PP gets up from the floor, stands behind the elderly woman and whips off his balaclava. As she tries to shut her eyes to King Dong and his groaning blonde, PP is softly whispering to her, no longer with the accent of a UVF intruder but with his very own.

'This is what they did ta me. This is what the "good holy men" did ta me. This is what your friends, who you sent me down to, did ta me. Think about that! Better still, take a good long look. Fuckin' look at it!' His whispers have turned to screams. He picks up the pistol from the sideboard and puts it to her left temple.

I remain rigid.

'If you don't open your eyes and look at it, I am going ta pull this trigger,' PP snarls.

All I can do is stare at the balls of handkerchiefs peeking out of the cuffs of her pink housecoat. She must have stuffed them up there throughout the day. I can only look at them as he is forcing her to open her eyes. Her tears fall onto her grandson's hands. As I glance back to the kitchen and the open door, Padre Pio senses my thoughts.

'And don't you think of movin' anywhere, chum. You stay exactly where you are.'

In this transfixed state, I've no doubt he would shoot me down like a dog straight away if I move another muscle, just like he would pull the trigger and splatter his grandmother's brains all over her pink housecoat without compunction. Her eyes are now as wide open as the blonde's, who is reaching climax, and King Dong's arse cheeks contract again and again as he thrusts deeper and deeper towards the explosive end.

'When you go to bed tonight and say your prayers to him over there, think of me bent over a chair like that. Think of what your dear friends down in the monastery were doin' ta kids like me. The ones you sent me away to so that they could make me good. Think of the wee ones the main brother told you he'd already straightened out in the end. Well, he straightened them out alright. He stretched a few of us out too, just like King Dong over there is doing. Only we were just kids, straightened out over Brother Ignatius's bed. Yeah, your good friend Brother Ticklebum. But he did more than tickle us down there, didn't he? It's about time you were told all about him.'

He unties her wrists and she spits out the hankies. She is croaking and gasping for breath but dares not get up from the chair, even when Padre Pio bends down again to turn off the video player.

So this was his plan. I was meant to see all of this. I am his chosen witness and his accomplice. I am trapped in the amber of his anger and his agony. I am finally made to 'understand' why. I want to run, but, after all this, I can't be certain that he wouldn't put a bullet into my back. I am welded to the spot. I scan the living room to avoid his gaze, and hers. The television is back on and there is a party political broadcast by the British Labour Party. I decide to think about the general election. It is not long now to see if Trout's prophecy will come true. Maggie Thatcher the Milk Snatcher is odds on to be the next Prime Minister. My father calls them 'the party of the rich for the rich by the rich' and predicts a new assault on the working class. I want to go home. My father warns of an imminent crisis of late capitalism. Unlike Trout though, he is not so confident that the workers will revolt. I want to go home. I long to be with my father right now, sitting in front of our TV and debating this with him. Instead, Padre Pio steps directly in front of me. I can't see the TV, only his mouth, which is breaking into a seditious smirk.

'Would you take that fuckin' balaclava off, Ruin. It only makes ya look even more ridiculous,' PP says.

'Shut up, man,' I hiss at him, shocked that he has uttered my nickname.

'No bother, Robert McManus. She's not goin' ta say anything, is she? And who to? The cops? The mother of an on-the-run they've been hunting for years? You think they'd care about her? Besides, she knows what she has done. She knows it's all her fault,' he roars.

'PP ... please,' I implore.

'She's not game enough ta squeal or even tell my ma because if she did, it would all come about how her friends down in the monastery were "sorting me out" in that special school for bad boys. Isn't that right, Rita?' he says to her.

I want to interject but am lost for words, dumbstruck, because it suddenly dawns on me that this has, in some shape or form, happened before. There was no shock in her face over him wailing on about Brother Ticklebum or the rest of the monks. Now, she's just sitting there, immobile, untethered but frozen, staring at the TV, watching *The Rockford Files* begin. Isn't she going to clutch her chest? Isn't she going to collapse or keel over right there in front of us? No she isn't. She isn't, because this has happened before. It's fucking happened before, and he's not finished yet.

'Hope ya enjoyed King Dong's dick, Rita. I bet ya did! I bet deep down your oul fanny was throbbing. I think I saw your nips poppin' out when he whipped out his monster cock out of that babe's hole. Well, at least she was gettin' paid for takin' a hammerin' up the shite pipe. We weren't paid for anything. We just had ta take it or else the brothers' canes would come out and then we'd really suffer. Yeah, that's one to think about: the cane. Maybe the next video will be a nice kinky caning. Would ya like that, ye oul cow? Would ya like ta see what the swish of a cane does to some tight young arse cheeks?'

I want to bawl over to her that I am so sorry, that I want no part of this and I had no idea what her maniac of a grandson was planning for tonight by locking me inside this nightmare. All I can do, however, is plead with him to let me go home.

'I gotta go, PP. Dad will be worried,' I say.

'Aye, you go back to your perfect family, Ruin. Go on. Go back to your da or visit your oul ma's grave. Or go see if your dear cousin who skanked your bird is back from his lick-out session in Paki's flat. I'm just goin' ta sit here on the sofa and watch *The Rockford Files* and drink a few cans with Rita; the ones she gets in for us every Saturday night. You just bettle off out of here and leave us alone but say fuck all to nobody. This is our wee secret, isn't it Rita? Just like the good Brother Ignatius and his lads kept their secrets.'

I glance back and see Padre Pio on the sofa, one arm wrapped around his grandmother's quaking shoulders and the other on the trigger of the Silver Lady, which he is aiming directly at me. He winks and makes that 'sna-ha' sniggering sound, and I realise it's not so much that he is done with his grandmother, but, rather, he is done with me.

23

'A NEW CAREER IN A NEW TOWN'

August 1978

Sabine had asked my dad for a 'Purple Nasty' when he was getting the first round in the Blackthorne Inn. She was in the mood for celebration after posting off her portfolio to St Martin's College in London. The night after she had arrived at my door with *Low* as a peace offering, Sabine had walked all the way up to the Knock dual carriageway with her camera and tripod, until she found her spot on the footbridge not far from Rosetta Road. Waiting until it was almost dark, she had taken dozens of long-exposure, light-trail photographs of the traffic building up on either side of the road. Then she went back to Jerusalem Street and sat up for the rest of the night printing the whirred, molten images to add to her application. 'Circulation', she told me in the pub, had been an inspiration for her and she was grateful for my input.

I watched as she walked back from the ladies. She looked invincible, so sure of herself. She was so confident that her portfolio would give her a racing chance of getting a place in the prestigious art school across the water. It was beautiful, particularly the side-profile portraits of her father and 'circulation': the streaks of red, white, green and amber coursing along the city thoroughfare, the colours slicing through the darkness. It seemed like the most important thing in the world to her that Saturday afternoon when she joined my father and his comrades for their weekly get-together where they could moan and groan about how the workers of the Western world were constantly letting them down. She was humming when she sat back down beside me.

'What's that you're humming?' I asked, straining to hear the melody.

She smiled. 'Track 7,' she replied.

'"A New Career in a New Town",' I said, barely audibly. I felt disconcerted, uncomfortable and powerless to prevent what I knew deep down was eventually going to happen.

My father returned from the bar with a Skol tray weighed down with two pints of Guinness for himself and Marty Johnstone, pints of cider for Rex Mundi and myself, and a beetroot-coloured concoction which Sabine convinced us all that she only drank on special occasions.

'Robbie tells me you've something to cheer about,' my dad said jovially as he handed out the drinks.

'Not yet, Mr McManus. I'll have to go over for an interview if they summon me,' Sabine replied, after leaving a line of lipstick on the rim of her glass following a sip of her purple poison.

'It's Peter, never mind the mister. Call me Peter, or else comrade will do. So, how did you two meet?'

'Ah, it's a long story, Da. Boring too,' I said quickly.

Immediately, my father could sense my panic. All those nights when I said I was in Padre Pio's house but was sneaking into The Harp or The Pound in all my underage glory was about to be revealed.

Evidently, however, there were no flies on my father. 'Listen, Robbie, I don't give a shite where you went this summer. In fact, I'm glad you've been spending more time with this lady and less time in that other fellah's company. The less you see of him the better.'

'What other fellah? Have I something to worry about here? A rival?' Sabine jibed.

'Just the bogey man I warned you about. The one I avoided a few days ago when you were down,' I said.

'He is serious bad news, that boy,' Marty Johnstone interrupted, as keen as always to run down PP. Johnty tapped his left temple and added, 'Not the full shilling if ya ask me. Small wonder when ya think about it. His own da was a bit of a looper too.'

I was desperate to change the subject and divert attention away from the lineage and the insanity of Padre Pio McCann.

'Rex here says he's off back ta England on Monday,' I said.

This news seemed to change the atmosphere at the table or at least deflate the elation Sabine was showing over her portfolio. My dear cousin's imminent departure appeared to darken her mood.

'Are you really heading back so soon, Aidan? The summer isn't even over yet.'

'Yeah, I might as well. I've got this chance to do roadie for a band from Horsham that I know. They're gigging all over the south coast. They might even be playing up in London. They've been offered to back up Chelsea at a gig up in Hackney. I might as well take the chance to make some cash. It'll pay for my ticket to Germany.'

Sabine took a couple of gulps from her purple drink and smiled back at him. 'Give Robert the dates of the London gigs, as I might be over there at the time for my interview. Ring him up or, better still, ring me.' She took out a diary from the inside of her biker jacket, tore off a blank page and scribbled her home number down. It was only then that I realised that she had never given her telephone number to me.

'Sure I could even come with you,' I butted in.

Neither Rex Mundi nor Sabine even acknowledged this suggestion, and I wondered if I had uttered it out loud.

Tom, the bar owner, turned on the television for first race of the afternoon. We sat in a silence for a while as Johnty and my da went next door to the bookies for bets, leaving us alone with only Peter O'Sullevan's galloping commentary for company.

'Did you know that John Cooper Clarke models his poetry performances on Peter O'Sullevan's delivery? He said it was the voice of his childhood, his teenage years, that his oul boy had the racing on all day,' I said, to elevate the mood. Again I was ignored.

'So when will you be back over here again, Aidan?' Sabine asked.

'Oh fuck knows. My brother Mick is trying to get me a job in West Berlin working on a building site. I might go over there, even though Uncle Peter here might not approve.'

'Might not approve of what?' my dad said, returning to the table to crush the first beaten docket of the day into an empty ashtray.

'Our Mick reckons he can get me a job with some Irish subbies he knows on the building sites of West Berlin, but you might not like that with you being a communist and all that, Uncle.'

'You can go where you like, Aidan. It's none of my business. Just don't let them tell ya it's an island of freedom when you get there,' my dad retorted.

'Just like I won't let the Beasty Easties tell me that I'm entering the workers' paradise when I cross over at Checkpoint Charlie,' Rex Mundi quickly bit back.

The pace of his reply seemed to impress Sabine. 'Oh, touché, Aidan!' she said, before turning around to my dad. 'You're not seriously a communist, are you Mr McManus?'

'It's Peter, and, yes love, I certainly am. So is Marty here and some of the other comrades in the bar today. So was your boyfriend too, for a while, before he discovered all that posy anarchy, chaos and destruction malarkey. When he grows up he might become a good Marxist again. He could have a great future in the party.'

Sabine leaned across the table, sipping away at her Purple Nasty. 'So what do you believe in then, Aidan? What makes you want to storm the barricades?'

Rex Mundi shrugged his shoulders and took off his biker jacket to reveal a T-shirt with two cowboys with their flies undone and their cocks rubbing together. He started to piece together a joint.

I don't know what annoyed my dad more: the sight of his nephew rolling out the Rizla papers and softening up a lump of Leb Gold with a lighter, or the homoerotic image on his T-shirt.

'Would you mind covering yourself up when you're in this bar, Aidan, or else Tom will have a fit and make us all leave.'

'Yes, Aidan, show a bit of respect for others,' Johnty said, backing his comrade up as always.

Rex Mundi looked across at them and snorted, 'Haven't you two heard of the Tom Robinson Band? "Glad To Be Gay"? He's a communist.'

'And you're not gay, Aidan McManus. You're just wearing that thing because you think it will freak people out. And you can stop doing what you are doing with them drugs right now. Drugs are for mugs,' my dad said.

'Really, for such a bunch of so-called progressives you two are just a couple of uptight conservatives. All you communists want to do is tell people what to do,' my cousin responded.

'When you are in my company, under my supervision, you do not take drugs, and you do not go about deliberately insulting people with things like that bloody T-shirt.'

Sabine came to Rex Mundi's rescue, which surprised me given the obvious affection she had shown for my father. 'What's wrong with the image of two men who are into each other? It's all fine and dandy if the newspapers print pictures of girls with their tits out, but how come men with their knobs out on somebody's T-shirt is offensive?'

My dad appeared stung by her intervention. 'Look, I've nothing against the gays. Burgess was gay and he was a hero in my book for helping the Soviet cause. That eejit over there is not gay. He just likes freaking people out. And by the way, love, I would never buy one of them type of newspapers.'

Rex Mundi stood up, threw his biker jacket over his shoulder and shoved the Rizla and dope into his pocket. 'This is boring. I didn't come here for a lecture. I'm going up to watch the stripper in The Harp. Anybody coming with me?' he said, only looking at Sabine.

Her answer left me feeling temporarily relieved. 'See you in the bar later. Page 3 birds and strippers aren't my thing. We're gonna stay here for a while and talk to Peter about slaughterhouses.'

After Rex Mundi went out the door sullenly, Marty Johnstone was still shaking his head. 'That boy is totally out of control. Does your brother know that, Pete?'

'Comrade, he's not a bad lad really. I don't think he ever got over what happened to him and the family back in 1971 when they were saved by two gunmen we used to know.'

'No! You saved them! If it wasn't for you, Pete, they could have been burnt to death in their beds,' Johnty said.

Dad looked embarrassed when he realised Sabine was staring in wonder at him. He turned to explain to her. 'It's a long story, a golden oldie. We need to get away from all that kind of stuff now.'

'What kind of stuff?' Sabine asked.

'All that stuff about hero worshipping gunmen. There's too much of that about these days. Real change won't come from the barrel of a gun, at least not here,' Dad said.

'Did you used to believe in the use of arms?' Sabine continued to press him.

'Well yes, but only for a short time. I wised up pretty quickly that guns weren't the answer. I only wish the rest of the daft lads would do the same. Maybe one day they will.'

'Fat chance of that, Da,' I interrupted. 'They won't listen to the likes of you anymore. Just like I don't think our Aidan listens to you either.'

My father steered the conversation away from armed struggle to ask what Sabine wanted from him.

'Well, Robert tells me you work in a meat plant. Is there any chance I could go in there with you? To photograph what goes on inside? I think the images would make for some amazing paintings!'

'I very much doubt that management would want anyone seeing what really goes on inside there, love.'

'But Peter ... OK, you could get a camera inside. I could give you a Polaroid to take a few sneaky snaps. That's all I'd need to get going.'

Sabine did have this knack for getting men to do things for her, and I could visibly see my dad's resistance crumbling.

'Oh, I don't know. I might get sacked if they found out.'

'Peter, it would only take about five minutes. Maybe on a quiet shift or something? I'm just looking to get some ideas from inside there. Please!' Sabine pleaded.

'Go on, Da. Take a few snaps for her and I'll be in her good books forever,' I added.

He turned to look at his oldest comrade for some guidance. 'What you do think, Marty? Should I risk a well-paid and unionised job for this gorgeous young woman sitting in front of me here?'

'When ya put it like that, comrade, I don't think you've any choice,' Johnty replied, and at that Sabine hugged him first and then my father.

After a second round of drinks, this time paid for by Johnty, Sabine set about planning the entire operation. She instructed my father on how to use the camera and the various ways it could be concealed in his overalls, as well as the different angles she wanted him to shoot the assembly line from. My dad became so immersed in her strategy that he used a couple of empty betting dockets to draw out rough sketches of the slaughterhouse's interior, paying particular attention to the area where the animals were stunned before being butchered. I felt for the first time in years that my father was once again enjoying some female attention, and looking back now, I wonder if he too was not a little smitten by Sabine himself.

She sat back in the chair with a triumphant expression on her face, smiling as my father sketched out a rudimentary map of his workplace. She was in complete control and I admitted to myself that she certainly could make men do her bidding if she tried. Observing her poring over Dad's mini-blueprints of the plant, I felt a strange mixture of both pride and fear about her. I knew I would never be able to 'own' her fully, even if I wanted to. I would only be able to follow in her wake.

When the sketching was completed and the order of battle was drawn up, Sabine and I left the two comrades, who were already doing their world-tour analysis of Anglo-American imperialism and the new Cold War. Outside the Blackthorne, Sabine said she was going up to Boots to buy some more Polaroid film while I opted for the subway to see if any of the punk crowd I hung around with were about. After she left, I descended into the underground passageway running underneath the road towards the Albert Clock, but the only character down below was a spotty paranoid kid from Carrickfergus in a torn-up biker and a Sid Vicious T-shirt. He was blowing into a glue bag and threatening to 'knock my fucking head in' if I came any closer. Paddy Rae's pub, up above, would be packed with Saturday afternoon racing punters who objected to the presence of punks, so I was left with only one alternative: The Harp, with Rex Mundi and the stripper. As I backed away from the glue-sniffer and headed towards the other entrance upwards to High Street, I spotted some newly scrawled graffiti written in thick black marker with the all-too-familiar abundance of exclamation marks: 'M60's kill Prods!!! FTQ!!! Padre Pio!!!!'

24

'THE SPEED OF LIFE' II

August 1978

Gyrating to 'Young Americans', with only the stars and stripes covering her tits and gash, the black stripper in the cowboy hat appeared to have a hard-on. It was only when she approached a table of old codgers and put her hands down her star-spangled panties that I realised it was a banana. She pointed the yellow fruit at the oul boys, who were all decked out for the day in standard issue OAP creams and browns. They were clapping in-between generous sups of Guinness Red Heart. The stripper started to shoot them with her bendy yellow 'gun', and one coffin dodger after another faked a bullet and collapsed into his chair. Then she moved to the other side of the bar, stripped the skin off the banana and asked a middle-aged man in a dogtooth jacket, with greasy banjo strings combed over his bald head, if he would like to eat it. When the excited punter leaned towards her boobs and gobbled up the banana, I knew I'd seen his face before.

I had been fixated on Black Bessie's show while Rex Mundi feigned misery and rolled yet another joint. As she peeled off her starry knickers and threw them into the half-empty hall, I spotted the banana-muncher heading back to the bar. I elbowed my cousin to follow me.

'Here lad, come to the bar with me. This is goin' ta be a real laugh,' I sniggered.

'Go up yerself. I'm fucked.'

'How many bastard and well spliffs have you had since you got in here?'

'Three, possibly four. I can't remember.'

'You're hardly goin' ta make it through the night with any of those punkettes you pulled last time, are ya?'

'Balls to that. I can get some speed later to waken me up. Fancy some?'

'No, just cider for now. Come up and see this. It's going to be a geg,' I implored.

Reluctantly, Rex Mundi slid out of his plastic chair and followed me to the bar. Our luck was in: an older woman was pulling pints rather than Tommy Nasty, who would have instantly refused to serve us given the state my cousin was in. I leaned on the table and watched the man in the dogtooth jacket order half a pint of Bass and a Castella cigar. His voice confirmed my suspicions.

'Mr Feeney? Mr Jude Feeney?'

The man turned around, visibly panicked at the sound of his name being called out.

'Robbie McManus, sir. Senior 3A. Geography a few years ago. C-block wasn't it?'

My old teacher pretended not to recognise me at first. 'Who are you again? I don't quite recall anyone of that name,' Feeney pleaded.

'Ach sir, you must remember me. You once had me up in front of the class. You pointed to the exercise yard of the Crumlin Road Gaol and told the rest of the class it was my most likely destination once I'd be kicked out of the college.'

Rex Mundi interjected, having come to a bit thanks to his first gulp of cider. 'You weren't far wrong there, Mr Feeney. The way we're going we'll all end up in the Crum, just like my brother Mick did.'

Feeney lifted up his half pint and tried to take a swig, but I wasn't letting go. This unexpected Saturday torture session was tremendous fun.

'You had our class in stitches the way you mapped out my future. We always said you were good craic. Honestly, sir, we really did.'

'Well, it doesn't really matter what I think, boys. I mean this is a show for adults. Are you still at the college, er … McManus? Yes, it is McManus, isn't it?'

'Oh aye sir, just like yerself. I didn't opt for Geog in the A levels though. Sorry about that, Mr Feeney.'

'Well, I really must go, lads, and pick up a few things in the town for dinner tonight,' Feeney said, hurriedly knocking back the rest of his Bass. 'Look McManus, does your mother know that you go to places like this?'

'My mother's dead, sir,' I said, unable to resist keeping up his torment.

'Well, look, I'm very sorry, truly sorry to hear that, McManus. But what about your father? Surely he wouldn't approve either.'

'He's a communist, sir. His mind is on other things.'

Black Bessie appeared at the bar and ordered a soda water and lime for herself. She came over to Feeney and elbowed him gently in the side.

'Hello there, stranger. I haven't seen you in here for a while,' she said in a thick Birmingham accent.

Feeney's voice was quivering as he twisted his wedding ring round and round. 'Well, you see, I came in here to check out this punker scene. You read all about it in the papers and most of it is inaccurate. They're really a good bunch of eggs these punks, when you get to know them. I just didn't realise that there was also this exotic dancing thingy here in the bar.'

He then slammed the glass down and popped the cling-filmed cigar into his breast pocket.

As Feeney got up to leave, the stripper pulled out another banana from her handbag and tossed it in his direction. 'Here ya go, mister. Happy munching.'

Once we recovered from being bent over laughing, Rex Mundi offered to buy Black Bessie a drink.

'No thanks, children. I'm no longer working, at least not until later,' she said.

'Can we come along?' Rex Mundi asked in a childish voice.

'I really don't think a couple of hundred horny squaddies would welcome your sort on to their army base, lover. Even with that south-coast accent of yours.'

'No harm in asking,' I added, before she disappeared into the staff room to change.

'I never thought I would ever say this, cousin, but I actually can't wait to go back to school. The sight of Feeney doing hall duty or supervising a free period in the library will make it so worthwhile.'

'Wish we could have filmed it, mate. Now, I'm going out to get some speed.'

Rex Mundi went in search of the Hells Angels who normally drank up in the Club Bar and doled out acid tabs and lines of amphetamines. I went back to the Blackthorne to tap my da for a few quid, and to tell him about my old geography teacher, of course.

'For Christ's sake, Robert. You should have left the poor man alone with his pint and not embarrassed him like that,' was the predictable reaction of my father. Feeney belonged to the teachers' union and therefore deserved some sort of solidarity, apparently.

There was now a ragged pile of betting coupons beside him. They all had sketches of areas in the slaughterhouse from different angles that Dad had been working on for Sabine.

'You've been busy, Da. Are they all for her?' I asked.

'Sabine can look over them tomorrow when she comes down to our house,' Dad said. 'Do you think we should get something special for the Sunday dinner in case she stays?'

When I failed to answer, he just went on with his plans. 'Here look, go and get a nice pork fillet for the Sunday lunch.'

It was then that I spotted an advantage. 'What's it worth if I go?'

'You can take a tenner out of the change, son,' he said, as Marty Johnstone shook his head again and tapped his temple to indicate he thought Dad was mad.

By the time I got to the Fountain, I had made up my mind what I was going to do with the tenner that I had just swindled out of my father. I would add it to the money I managed to get off him the night before when he was wasted, and I would go down to Caroline Music and buy Sabine something for her upcoming birthday. She had mentioned the release of the debut single from Siouxsie and the Banshees – 'Hong Kong Garden' – so that would be a good start. She was always raving about their stint on the John Peel Sessions last February. But first, I needed to buy the cheapest pork fillet I could find.

I started to slowly slalom through the hordes of spides and their birds, all in town to menace everybody else's Saturday. Then, from across the street, I saw them. They were sitting together in the window seat of the Lite Bite restaurant. I stepped back into the entrance of the Masonic Hall to conceal myself and watched them. He was feeding her skinny chips, one after another. She was laughing and giggling at his show-off antics.

I was frozen by the Masons' door, my face burning, my brain swirling and my ears aching from the blood beating like a boiler about to blow inside my temples. The pain in my head was compounded by the hellfire-and-damnation preacher wearing thick cola-bottle glasses and a sandwich board over his body. Harsh black letters informed everyone that 'The Wages of Sin is Death', and he kept howling through a loudspeaker, 'Yer all gonna die! Yer all gonna die!' which raised cheers of derision from some of the younger poseur punks dotted around the Fountain.

I dared to look across the street again and saw them getting closer over the table, playing rock-scissors-paper until my cousin snatched Sabine's wrist, held it tight and then, with no resistance from her, stroked her palm with his forefinger. At first I thought about storming in there, but I didn't want to make a dick of myself in public. I would lose the advantage if I barged right in there, so I decided to bide my time. I would let the hare sit, as my da always advised whenever I came home from primary school with a bloody nose, swearing vengeance on the bullies; at least, that was until Padre Pio started to blade them up the arse with a protractor.

'Oh, I'll get the two of them. I'll get the two of them shitheads in the long grass,' I murmured to myself, biting my lower lip till it nearly bled, before heading off to Littlewoods.

Once I picked up the cheapest, mankiest-looking pork fillet from the butchers, I went straight into the off-licence and bought myself a bottle of Strongbow. I took the alternative route back to the Blackthorne, through two entries and eventually crossing at High Street, still cursing and swearing at them in my head. I dropped off the fillet with Dad, who was too engrossed in an argument with a college student about the Vietnamese boat people to notice the cider. My father had no time for 'those that left', even while their boats were sinking in the South China Sea. Nor did we in the Red Army, for that matter. On hearing down at Mourneview Park that Glenavon Football Club welcomed some Vietnamese boat people who had settled in exile in Craigavon, the Cliftonville support started chanting, 'We're gonna sink yer boats. We're gonna sink, we're gonna sink, yer boats.' I tipped a nod to Johnty, who was hanging on dad's every word, and made straight for the Baby Subway, vowing that this time no wannabee Sid Vicious glue-sniffing wee ballbag would scare me away from my subterranean haven.

Fortunately, Tip and Tap had arrived off the Portadown train and had already scared off the Evostik-sniffer out of our subway.

'Ya luck like yiv seen a ghost, boy, and I don't just say that cos yer hair is stickin' up,' Tap said, offering me a swig from his QC bottle.

'Boys a dear, yer a shittier shade of pale, Ruin,' Tip added. 'What happened? Did ya get run by a gang a Belfast spides?'

I declined the QC and cracked opened the cider, which I drank almost a third of in one greedy gulp.

'No, I just saw Judas!'

'Did he kiss ya on the cheek, boy?' Tip asked.

'Nah, he'll probably be kissing someone else's cheek now. Or somewhere even worse.'

The two culchie punks then cried out in unison, 'Wimmin trouble, wimmin trouble.'

It was far too humiliating to relay the details of what I had just seen through the Lite Bite window and what it all confirmed in my head. Instead I just stood with my two friends from Portadown, knocking back our bottles of QC and Bow, bitching about the plastic Saturday punks with their expensive *NME*-ordered bondage trousers, biker jackets and fart-flaps, as well as the piss-poor quality of Harp in The Harp. We debated whether New Wave was just providing an excuse for any oul *Top of the Pops* groups to spike up their hair, wear plastic sunglasses, sneer into camera close-ups and try to appear edgy for the kids watching at home.

Later inside The Harp, I passed the evening beside her once more, listening to a band from Bangor railing against the bombs and the bullets and the men-with-woolly-faces. Tip and Tap pogoed themselves into a sweaty steaming stupor on the dance floor while Rex Mundi sat beside us, deftly rolling joints without even looking down at his work, as if he was carefully constructing a crude but lethal explosive device. During the band break, the DJ played 'The Speed of Life', having clocked Sabine in our company. Yet she was too stoned or drunk or both to get up and shimmer and quake as usual.

Rex Mundi had clearly failed to score any speed from the Hells Angels, if he had ever bothered his arse searching for them at all when he was with her. As the opening tune of *Low* faded and was consumed by the start of the reggae set, the punks were 'allowed' once more onto the floor to dance to a different kind of music. I saw Tommy Nasty coming towards our table, no doubt intending to eject both Sabine and Rex Mundi from the bar. I stood up, blocked his path and held up my hand.

'I'll take her home from here, mate. I'll bring her out now.'

'And what about cunty beside her?' Tommy Nasty asked, headbutting the air towards my semi-comatose cousin.

'Ya can do what ya want with him. I'm not his keeper,' I replied.

An older bouncer on the door, one of those squashed-nose ex-boxers that Belfast produces legions of, kindly used the payphone to ring us a taxi for the Holy Lands. I managed to drag a doubled-over Sabine outside and see her decorate part of Hill Street with puke. I was secretly delighted that her guts and her head were hurting her.

'Take me home, my love. Take me to bed. I'm so sorry about this, so sorry.' Sabine winced as her voice cracked and her throat burned.

25

'WHAT IN THE WORLD'

August 1978

I had left Sabine snoring upstairs and spent the night and early morning hours wrapped up in a sleeping bag and unable to sleep downstairs on the couch. I had stayed up like a sentinel on night shift, waiting for a knock on the door or the sound of him trying to fiddle the key into the lock, as I imagined she had given him one. I had sat curled up in ambush mode, ready to pounce if he made it into the house, and then we would have it out once for all, all three of us. But there was no sign of him, and, before she rolled out of bed and into her first bout of boking up in the toilet bowl, I slipped *Low* back on downstairs to muffle out the sounds of me scanning through her artwork and personal papers for any signs of treason.

Eventually, I came across a diary with a home-made cover composed of Bowie on the front of *Heroes*, which she had pristinely cut out from the pages of a music magazine. I flicked through the pages for July and August for any evidence of two-timing, but there was only banality. The entry dated 26 July read: 'Dad and I at lunch down in Strangford with an old army buddy of his. At Mum's favourite spot. Fab!' In the front of the diary were all her vital details, including home address over in the east, telephone numbers of her house there and here in Jerusalem Street and that her blood group was O/A.

There was a longer entry for the next day, prefaced with a little symbol Sabine had sketched in red ink of a clenched fist inside a circle with an upturned cross stretching out from its edge. I had expected to read more about her thoughts on her father but she had surrounded her reflections with red-inked speech marks because she had something more important to record.

'You don't own me! No one owns me! You won't slap a label on my back. No one will hang a placard around my neck. You won't know where I am really from. No padlock and chain dangling down, no dog collar clamped around my throat. I want to be from nowhere that is pure, cleansed or filled in only by either Orange or Green. You will not find me in any fixed co-ordinates. I come only from the shimmering, blurred hinterland. All you can say is that I am She.'

I closed the diary and put it back where it belonged. I realised then and there that two-timing was the last thing that would threaten my fantasies of a future with my Sabine. Some of her artwork included an album of black-and-white photographs of punks in various settings around Belfast, as well as several of her father; all of the latter were side profiles. One showed him in driving gloves and sporting sideburns while holding up a revolver. The length of the gun barrel was almost the same as his Roman nose, and the collar of his brown suede jacket was pulled up to his ears as he stood by a TR7. Sabine must have had *The Professionals* in mind when she composed the picture, so that her father looked armed and mean up against his sports car. I peeled off the protective film around it and popped it into my pocket. I had no idea why I had taken it.

I had just managed to return her personal things to their places when Sabine finally made an appearance. She looked thinner, paler and more delicate than ever. I greeted her with the track about 'a little girl with grey eyes' even though hers were red-rimmed, blood-shot and shiny emerald green.

'Ya look liked death warmed up,' I said.

'You really are the silver-tongued charmer, Robert. Any chance of making me a cup of tea there?' she said, caressing both her temples. 'Did you sleep down here last night?'

'Aye, you were very restless in bed and I thought you'd need the full space. I came down here and quickly conked out.'

She surveyed the living room and the kitchen a couple of times and then added, 'So where did Aidan sleep? The spare room?'

'What am I, his social worker? He wasn't here last night. I'm sorry, but he didn't come home,' I hissed at her.

Appearing not to have picked up on my sarcasm, Sabine continued, 'So where did he go then? Hope he was OK and safe wherever he ended up.'

'Maybe I should have put a tracking device on him. I haven't a clue where he ended up and, to be honest, I really don't care where he is now.'

It was the disappointed, disapproving look on her face more than her words that set me off. 'But Robert, you know what he's like when he starts and if he was wearing that silly T-shirt someone might have taken offence and attacked him. We should have been more careful about him.'

'You seem far more concerned about him than me these days.' I said as loudly and wounded as I could.

'What's that supposed to mean?'

I lost it. I couldn't help letting it out. 'Don't play dumb, Sabine. You were holdin' hands and gigglin' like a schoolgirl with him in the Lite Bite yesterday, so maybe I shouldn't be so surprised about your deep concern for him.'

I didn't realise that by the end I was roaring like a lunatic at her. 'That's right, isn't it? You were holdin' hands and strokin' his cheek the way you do to me. Wasn't that a pretty picture yesterday down by the Fountain? My girlfriend having a romantic wee date with my cousin.'

She may have appeared shaken at first, but when Sabine eventually recovered, she hit back so hard it left me stunned.

'You are a possessive baby.' She hammered out each of those words slowly as if she was trying to talk to a class of retards.

'As Joan Jett says – you don't own me! Nobody does! I never said we couldn't hang out with other people. I never agreed to being your possession, Robert. And I certainly don't like the idea of you or anybody else spying on me … ever! And I don't own you either, Robert. I don't tell you who not to talk to you or where to go or not go. Isn't that what this thing is all about? Or are you so-called punk boys just like the spides deep down, the way you wanna control your women? I thought we were supposed to be different from them.'

'You're one two-faced bitch, Sabine. You really are. Telling me how much you think Boy Bondage has a chip on his shoulder and is such a poser, and, oh aye, that he hates you so much, but then there you are, hand in hand like a couple of geeks from *Love Story*. You're a fuckin' hypocrite. He's my fuckin' cousin!'

'You don't own me!' Sabine snapped back, and, at that, I lashed out with the back of my hand and caught her on the left cheek with a stinging slap. She retaliated instantly with her right winkle-picker connecting to my bollocks. The seething agony felt like my ball bag had been pierced. When I recovered, ever so slightly, and the pain abated to a dull ache that throbbed across my groin, I looked up to see again that bloodless tight-lipped expression of defiance on her face.

'Get out of my house. Get the fuck out of my house now, Robert, and don't come back,' she said, emphasising the words 'my house' for added, hurtful affect.

The continual pain in my balls forced me to do a Charlie Chaplin walk through the Holy Lands, along Botanic Avenue and down the Dublin Road. The streets were empty, and the detritus from Saturday night was still blowing around. The only sign of some human life came from the schismatic, dissonant sound of various church bells ringing out across all of South Belfast. To my shame, a small part of me really hoped that her fears for my cousin's safety were real, and that he would be found eventually up some entry somewhere, battered and sliced and diced up for slobbering to the wrong sort the night before. Because she never denied anything I had said about him, because she had managed to turn an insult to me into an affront to her. Whatever had happened to him would be her responsibility now; it would be her fault for getting so drunk that she had abandoned him back in the bar, all curled up and comatose at home while he staggered drunkenly outside to his doom.

My dejection was compounded on returning home and seeing him safely and smugly laid back across our sofa in the parlour. His face was covered by the sports pages of *The Observer*, and there was a pint of water and a packet of Anadin on the coffee table beside him.

'You comfortable enough there?' I asked him as I interrupted his Sunday recovery snooze behind the newspaper.

Without moving an inch, he replied, 'I see Spurs are really signing Ardiles and Villa from Argentina. Two World Cup winners in the Tottenham team, eh! Fucking hell, the Yids are going to be even more unbearable than usual this year. In a way, I'm almost glad we didn't get promoted this season. At least we won't have ta listen to them bragging on about their men from the Argentine.'

Ignoring him, I went into the kitchen where Dad was preparing Sunday lunch. He was listening to the wireless: news reports about the ongoing struggle of the MPLA in Angola and the story of how the heroic people of Vietnam were now fiercely resisting the chauvinist Chinese invaders along with their mass-murdering Maoist allies in Cambodia.

'Where on earth is Sabine?' he asked, while poking a sharp serrated knife through the pork fillet.

I was shocked by Dad's question. I lied to him, just in case my cousin overheard us. 'She's not coming. Not feeling too good after all those Purple Nasty drinks you bought her yesterday.'

My dad looked puzzled and said, 'Well that's odd because she just phoned there a few minutes ago and said she was on her way.

She said her dad was driving her down. When I heard you come in I thought the two of you had been dropped off.'

I wanted to tell my father that there was no way I would ever be allowed into her daddy's TR7, but then I was gripped by a fear that Sabine was coming to our door to inform him that I was now a woman-beater.

I went upstairs and flung myself on the bed. Johnny Rotten was sneering above me. I sneered back at him. I couldn't relax. I fished out the photo of her dad that I had nabbed earlier and threw it into a drawer. Then I left my room and went into the spare, which Rex Mundi commandeered a few weeks earlier when he had turned up unannounced at our door. I spotted one of his T-shirts draped over the bottom of his unmade made and grabbed it. After spraying my torso with Brut deodorant, I slipped on the Troops-Out T-shirt with its helmet and visored North Britain bashing blood-splattered Ireland next door. Then I waited for the doorbell to ring.

After less than fifteen minutes, the rattle of her knuckles on the glass of our internal hall door heralded her arrival and I rushed down to greet her. Sabine had a small cotton bag with her, which resembled the ones retired footballers used to fish out balls from, standing alongside overweight chumps in FA blazers in the annual live TV draw for the third round of the cup.

'Is that another peace offering?' I said, pointing to the bag, but this time she didn't reply. She kept staring down at the oversize T-shirt, the one she knew fine well belonged to Rex Mundi.

'No, this is for your father. It contains the Polaroid and some film,' she said with cold firmness.

'Here, Dad,' I cried out behind me. 'Sabine is here with her camera. Looks like she's got her way once more!'

'Oh stop showing off, Robert,' was all she could say.

'I'm not. Just go inside and talk to him in his kitchen. That's his domain. He's gettin' lunch ready for all of us, including your lover boy dossing down in the parlour there. Wanna call him and see if he's OK too?'

Sabine brushed past me and politely tapped the kitchen door, which was already open.

Rather than listening to her slaughterhouse instructions for my father, I made my way outside to where the TR7 engine was still purring. Her father was wearing driving gloves and was nervously tapping the steering wheel while listening to Jimmy Savile on Radio 1. I stood facing him with both of my hands behind my head, affecting the pose of a man who has been P-checked and spreadeagled up against the wall by an army foot patrol. The message from my T-shirt was unmistakable for him as it billowed off my body in the wind.

'Alright there, boss?' I shouted towards the driver's seat.

Despite his confident, playboy bearing, there was a visible nervous tic throbbing near one of his sideburns, and sweat was developing on his forehead. He stared furtively into the rear mirror in case anyone was approaching from behind.

'I'm fine, old chum. You wouldn't kindly tell that daughter of mine that we have to go or we'll be late for our lunch,' he said, without tearing his gaze away from the windscreen.

'Oh, so you're not stoppin' ta eat here then. And my dad has made a big lunch for all of us.'

'I'm afraid not, old son, earlier plans and all that,' Sabine's father said before pressing down the klaxon and sounding two impatient beeps of the horn.

I turned around and saw Sabine in the hall hugging my dad and then smiling up at my lanky bare-chested cousin standing at the door of the parlour.

When she came outside, Sabine patted me on the head, indicating that she wanted me to drop my under-arrest pose. When I refused to budge she said, 'I know what you're doing, Robert. I really wish you were more like your father and grew up a bit. Anything that went on between you and me has nothing to do with my father.'

'Did you tell my dad or even your own what happened earlier this morning?'

She whispered back, 'You mean up at Jerusalem Street? No, don't worry, your covert wife-beating remains a secret, Mr Ruin.'

Her voice had softened for a few seconds before it hardened once more. 'Just stop showing off by thinking you can freak my dad out with a T-shirt that doesn't even belong to you. I know you're not like that. You aren't one of them.'

'Who do you mean by THEM?' I challenged her.

'Them – the terrorists and their supporters, Robert. You're not part of all that. And you never will be.'

'Who says I'm not. How do you know who or what I belong to?'

'Because they are not you, Robert, that's why. Deep down you know that as much as I do. You hate them as much as I do.'

I finally took my hands away from the back of my head and pointed down to the T-shirt hanging off me. 'You know nothin' about me, Sabine, or what I truly believe in.'

The car horn sounded again and I saw Sabine's dad throw his head back and his eyes roll up to heaven.

'I really have to go, Robert.' she said.

'Is this it then, Sabine?'

'No, no, it isn't. I'll call you, Robert. I do care about you very much but let's meet in town soon, even this coming week. Bring your dad's pictures when he gets a chance to take them. And then we really need to talk.'

'Talk about what?' I asked, but by then she was already inside the passenger seat of the revved-up motor. Her father released the handbrake and the TR7 edged to the corner with Stewart Street. He took a left and sped off, far far away, into the safety of the east.

26

THE DOGS IN THE STREET

29 April 1979

My father makes it through each night thanks to the crackling static and hiss of his short-wave radio. Alone in the darkness, he visits the capitals of the socialist countries by tuning into their airwaves. This faithful bedside companion is the only thing that has been keeping him company up there for years now, at least ever since mum cut herself adrift from him, long before she got sick. Sometimes his little black portable portal to that 'other world' is still on when the first shafts of light break through his Venetian blinds, and he wakes up to the pling-plong chimes of the East German national anthem on Radio Berlin International or the cool jazz big-band balalaika bars of interval music on Radio Moscow just before the English-language news from the USSR. He will revisit in his mind once more all those places that he toured around, marvelled at and paid homage to, and then further into the morning he will eventually call out to me.

This morning, however, when I go up to his bedroom, his bed is empty and unmade, and I hear the radio downstairs. He is up and out earlier than usual for a Sunday. This is normally the time where, from his pillow, after I give him *The Observer*, we engage in our only serious man-to-man talk of the week. This is when he quizzes me about my A levels or my choices for universities on the UCCA application form or what I should be studying at college or why it's vitally important that I cut all my ties with the one he labels 'Hitler Youth'. He never asks about my feelings about mum and I am eternally grateful for that. If he mentions her at all, it's normally about one of her old boyfriends who has swaggered past him on the street but can't look him in the eye. He will expand on his Saturday afternoon theoretical discussions with Marty Johnstone, all conducted in-between horse races and Peter O'Sullevan's break-neck, breathless, flawless commentary. He often pleads for me to have interest in his interests, including that of the party, which, truth be told, I couldn't care less about. Then when finally he accepts that I have no interest, his final thing is to urge me to escape this town, to get as far away as possible from the madness, to 'get the fuck out and don't come back', and even to forget him and leave everything behind me. There was to be no such conversation this Sunday, however, so I return to my own bedroom.

I pull back my curtains, scan the backyard and notice that the back door is lying open. Dad and Rex Mundi are standing together watching some commotion in the alleyway. There is more static rippling across the air, not from Dad's short-wave radio but from the pack on the back of a Brit soldier who is crouched down beside a lidless, iron bin. The soldier is at the end of a foot patrol blurting out messages in the NATO alphabet, and our entry is filling up with cops, including one in a white boiler suit who is carrying a camera and moving towards the end of the back of our house. White tape is being strung across the entry.

I am still half-dead with lack of sleep. After what I had seen last night, I feared that I would slide into the suffocating sponginess of darkness and night terrors. I stayed awake, terrified of my childhood nightmare when out of the crevices and cracks of a giant sponge would come wagging tongues, all of them fattened and distorted, purple and black, toxic and menacing. Only this time, when my head finally hit the pillow, I imagined there would be a pair of eyes visible amidst this mocking gallery of ululating tongues – those of Padre Pio. Maybe I would also hear the 'sna-ha' sniggering – the sound he made when I turned my back from him inside his grandmother's house a few hours earlier. Whatever happened out there in the alleyway, I'm amazed I slept through it.

When I go out into the yard and ask my father what happened, he replies, 'Were you too drunk to hear anything then?'

'Or maybe too stoned, Uncle,' Rex Mundi adds treasonously. 'Or maybe both!'

'Oh aye. You're my perfect cousin, aren't ya? Did you enjoying lickin' out that pregnant bird last night?'

Rex Mundi turns to face me and then backs away shaking his head in mock disappointment.

'Will you two idiots knock it off? I'm sick of it,' my dad pleads, while keeping his gaze fixed on the cops who have sectioned off the top of the entry with white tape. The peeler in the boiler suit starts taking photographs of one of the puddles that is now a mixture of red seeping into black. At its edge, a skimpy mongrel dog is lapping up the polluted water and blood.

'Would one of you take that fucking mangy mutt out of here?' one of the cops bellows towards the army patrol. A soldier in a black beret, his SLR rifle pointed down at the ground, steps over the white tape, goes to the puddle and boots the dog up the arse, making the animal yelp in pain before it tears off past us.

'Bloody Brits, eh! Even our dogs are unfree!' I say, but my father just glares at me and then goes back to staring at the streaks and splatters of blood around the pool of water and the walls surrounding it.

'And you didn't hear a thing last night?' he asks me.

'Here what, Da? You sound like one of them peelers.'

'The shooting. The shooting! Some poor bastard got shot up there last night.'

'Dead? Did he get nutted?'

'No, fortunately not, but they nearly killed him. He was in some pain and was yellin' about it only supposed to be a wee flesh wound or something. It looked like they'd taken off half of his leg in the blast. They must have fired into him at very very close range.'

'You went to him?'

'Of I course I went to him, after the goons that shot him had scarpered. I rang the ambulance for him, the poor bastard, whoever he was.'

Suddenly, the sight of the mangy dog lapping up the victim's blood replays in my mind and I am on the verge of retching as I sense the presence of Rex Mundi over me.

'Never interrupt men at work, dear cousin,' he says. 'And for your information she was quite sweet. Well, her bits down below certainly were. Now I fancy getting out today, maybe go into town.'

'And do what exactly?' I say. 'Even the kids can't play in the playgrounds on Sunday because the bible thumpers on the council lock up the gates for their Lord. There's nowhere ta get a drink unless you're goin' to the Provie or Sticky clubs, or if ya really wanna try your luck, the loyalist dens. Anyway, I'm staying here ta watch the match again.'

'What for? We know the score!' Rex Mundi sneers.

'What! You don't wanna see yourself being chased around the pitch again by the peelers and the stewards?'

My father scowls at Rex Mundi and me. 'What the hell was going on there yesterday at Windsor? If your father found out you were getting involved in trouble ...'

'Relax, Uncle P. I'm still here, aren't I? I'm not in Her Majesty's custody. Besides, yesterday was nothing compared to the rucks I've seen at the Goldstone Ground between us and the Palace. You oughta get over there soon, cousin. Hook up with me and some of the Brighton firm when the Eagles have landed.'

'He'll do no such thing, Aidan. He is getting his head down and studying to finish his A levels, and that will be him off for good,' my dad says.

Ignoring what my father has just said, Rex Mundi walks barefoot into the alley wearing his Troops-Out T-shirt and starts talking to the Brit radio operator by the bin. 'Where you from, mate?' he asks the soldier.

'Southend! Why, what's it to you? You're obviously not from around here either then?'

'Nah mate, seriously, born and bred in Belfast,' Rex Mundi answers.

'Well how come you've got that south-coast accent then?'

'I've been living in Brighton since 1971. I'm an adopted Seagull, chum. Here, what do you think of my T-shirt?'

'I don't think it's very hospitable, is it now?' the soldier says.

The cop who had ordered that the dog get a boot up the hoop moves in-between the Brit and Rex Mundi. 'Do not let that clown here rile you, soldier. He's just trying to stir shit. You get back inside your house, sonny,' he says, chewing gum.

The peeler is enormous. His two hands are shoved into his flak jacket. He eyeballs Rex and spits out his gum at his bare feet. My father senses an arrest so moves towards the cop and holds up his hands.

'I'm sorry, officer. He's been away too long. He doesn't really understand what's going on in this town anymore.'

'Why should I go back in cos he says so?' Rex Mundi protests. 'This is our yard and our alleyway. We're not doing anything wrong standing here.'

The entire patrol now stands up from their crouching positions while the cop moves directly over to Rex Mundi.

'If you don't get back into that house I am going to have you arrested while making sure that piece of shite you're wearing is ripped off yer back,' he barks into his face.

But my cousin stands defiant. 'And I'd like ta rip off that piece of shit on top of that Harp on your hat, officer.'

My father shoves Rex Mundi aside and pleads with the peeler, 'Officer please, as I said before he's been away far too long. I'll make sure we all go inside – now!' He turns to us and yells, 'You two dicks go inside. This is my house and these are still my rules.'

Surprisingly, Rex Mundi just shrugs his shoulders, about-turns and saunters back in through the kitchen door while I follow. I don't close the door. Instead, I stand inside and listen to my father and the cop chatting.

'So once more, sir. Did you know the victim?'

'No, never seen him before in my life, officer. Can barely remember even what he looked like. It was still dark when I heard the shots and then him screaming outside.'

'So you have absolutely no idea who he is?'

'None. He certainly wasn't from this district. I'd have recognised him if he was local. All I can remember was that he had a moustache and this strange blue dot in the middle of his forehead. And oh aye, he kept yelling about Judas bastards and that it was only supposed to be a wee flesh wound.'

'Ah, fuck!' I say under my breath. 'A fucking dot. Jesus!'

'Thank you, Mr ...?'

'It's McManus. I'm surprised you don't already know that.'

'Not really, sir. It's actually good to meet people who you don't know anything about. You're the ones that I don't have to worry about.'

When Dad eventually comes in to start lunch, Rex Mundi is fishing out two cans of Harp from the bottom of the fridge.

'You want one too, Uncle Pete?' he asks.

'I just want you, Aidan, and your cousin here, to stop being cheeky sods around the Brits and cops. The last thing I want is for them breaking down our door in the middle of the night.'

'Sweet. Will promise to be a good boy,' my cousin says.

We head to the sofa to wait for the Irish Cup Final highlights on BBC1. I can feel him sizing me up, waiting for the right moment to talk to me again. My stomach is in knots and I feel lightheaded.

'So then, after the game. Fancy getting out of here for a few hours and going for a drink?'

'Which venue do you suggest? The subways? I'm all out of Evostik and Timebond glue,' I tell him.

'We could grab a couple of cans and sit in the City Hall Gardens. Watch out for some babes going by.'

'What for? Are you joking? I'd rather sit here and get quietly merry watching the game again. Maybe I'll even get to see the goals properly this time around.'

'As the Pistols would say, NO FUN. You are seriously no fun anymore, Robbie Ruin. In fact, you are as dull and grey as your pallid face today.'

I know he's right because I could feel it, even though I had avoided my reflection in the mirror since I got up. I felt all the blood in me draining down into my feet. My skin felt waxy and wafer thin. My hands seemed shrivelled like an OAP's, and my eyeballs covered in a skein of spittle-lick liquid. When the TV flickers into life, I can barely make out the opening sequences. I no longer want to be beside my cousin or my father. I don't want to listen to Rex Mundi's inane commentary. I want to wipe out all the memories of what I had said and done yesterday afternoon and evening because it was all leading to one single horror show whirling in my head. There is only one way to press the stop button and rewind the nightmare: I have to go to him now and confront the bastard. I have to tell him that I want out of his insane orbit forever. I must break off into anonymous void. I want to hear no more of his excuses or protests. I will refuse to understand him.

When I get up, just as John Bennet in the studio hands over to the match commentator and the whistle blows, Rex Mundi tries to pull me back onto the sofa.

'Get off me. I have to go out,' I say, barely able to look at my cousin.

'But the game's starting. Where are you going exactly? As you said yourself, the pubs are shut and there is fuck all else to do.'

'You can horse every one of those cans into ya. I have to go and see somebody,' I say.

Rex Mundi winks at me slyly, cocking his head slightly to the side in a movement that suggests sudden knowledge and awareness. 'I know what the score is here,' he says. 'You gotta see that cock-head and interrogate him about what happened to a certain person in that alleyway out there.'

'You're startin' ta sound like one of them cops out there.'

'It's true, isn't it? You're off to see that retard and get the low-down on what happened out there. Because he knows, he knows for sure.'

'Would you ever fuck back off home to England!'

'Oh, that's nice,' he says. Then he shouts to my dad, who is preparing lunch in the kitchen while humming along to an orchestral piece on Radio Moscow.

'Here, Uncle Pete! Robbie has just said "Brits Out" to me. He thinks I'm an occupying force in this house.'

My dad refuses to respond and whacks up the volume to drown out both us and the match commentary.

'No seriously, Rex. Would you ever fuck back off to England? Do it for me as a big favour.'

He stands up to face me. There is a look of genuine hurt on his face. 'You seriously haven't got over her, have you, cousin?'

'Her?'

'Yeah, her ... Sabine.'

'What has any of this got to do with her? Why bring her up?'

'You still think in your mad jealousy that I fucked her, don't you?'

When I move for the door, he yanks my arm and pulls me back into the centre of the room. He stares directly at me and smiles the smile of someone who has to let go of something, the smile of release.

'I've been a cunt to you, Robbie. I know that. I kept you hangin' in the air over her. I left you wonderin' if I really did her. Well, I never did. Yeah, we kissed and flirted a couple of times last summer, but that was that. I'd no interest in her really. I faked it, even though I really think that she was up for it. But as I told you the first time I met her, she was not going to hang on for you or anyone else who crossed her path. You were just her summer pastime.'

I push his hand off my shoulder and turn away. 'Go up to your other uncle's after the match and don't come back. I'm sick of the sight of you,' I yell, loud enough for my dad to hear too.

'You're just sick of hearing the truth about her,' Rex Mundi yells back with equal force. 'You don't wanna believe that you weren't so special to her. God help you – you poor, sad, lovesick bastard. You fucking child!'

I race to my bedroom and lock the door. I go to my LPs stacked up against the wall and flick through them until I find *Low*. I sit on my bed, whip out the vinyl and smash it on the wall. It breaks into two distinct pieces. I take the cover and rip Bowie's face in two. The man who fell to earth falls onto the floor, and I leave him there. I open my dresser drawer and fumble about until I find what I am looking for. It is the picture of her father in *The Professionals* pose that I had taken from her apartment in Jerusalem Street last summer. Thoughts of treason and revenge are ricocheting in my brain, pinging from one plot to another, from her to PP, from his grandmother tethered to a chair, to his mother on the sofa in their front parlour. I put the photo on my bed.

Downstairs, I hear a roar from the crowd on the TV as the first goal is scored. Dad is clattering around in the kitchen. I stare at the album, her peace offering, now two sharp jagged-edged pieces, each one a perfect missile to hurl at the enemy, whoever that may be.

I pick up one of the jagged black curves and place it in the inside pocket of my army jacket that is hanging up behind the bedroom door. It is the coat I will wear to go round to his house and finally confront him about all of this. My dad hates this coat because it is the same as those worn by all the OCs and operators who were once the objects of my mother's affections; the men who still can't look him in the eye as they swagger past like they're on permanent parade duty. I put on the black zip-bondage trousers, slip on a Destroy T-shirt and lace up my DM boots. I pick up the photo from the bed and slide it into my back pocket. With my army jacket under my arm, I unlock the bedroom door and tiptoe downstairs and out of the house without my dad or my cousin noticing.

Outside, the dogs on the street are barking now as I turn the corner and walk past the front of Inglis's bakery with its great steel gates shut tight today. The dogs on the street are heading east. They are moving in packs towards the old bus station. They are yelping and howling and puncturing the Sunday dreams, the hangovers, the post-Mass siestas and the solid stodgy lunches being served all over the district. The dogs on the street are being led towards some unknown quarry by the grey and black skimpy mongrel who had lapped up fetid water mixed with the blood that seeped from the legs of Padre Pio's cousin.

27

COMMS 7

1987

The gentleman who is responsible for me being in this place is reported to be having second thoughts. At his own request, the so-called supergrass has been moved off the wing mainly reserved for the bull-roots and so-called ordinary decent criminals. He has been shipped out to an army base, where he continues to enjoy the fruits of his treachery: a video-recorder in his cell, an endless supply of blue movies, Johnny Walker whisky, cigars, dope, wank mags and the same grub served up to the Brits in their mess halls. Yet we hear he has lost a lot of weight while in military custody. He fears the food and has become paranoid he will be poisoned. No doubt he has heard the rumours about the Prods putting a toxin inside the porridge destined for one of their own supergrasses. The screw delivering it to the loyalist tout's cell noticed that the porridge had turned a strange green colour and handed it over to the cops for examination. This incident seems to have spooked our traitor. His lawyer has let it be known now that the hooding thieving bastard who was never officially in the movement has cold feet about going into the witness box. So, we live in the hope that this particular State-paid perjurer might have lost the bottle to point the finger at us in court. However, he does know a lot – thanks to the conversations in his flat over the years, which I now assume must have been bugged.

Normally those guilty of treason deserve one thing and one thing only – but if he did do a U-turn, I would make an exception in this case, and that is my recommendation to the leadership on the outside. We have already transmitted this message through a family channel you are aware of and stated that if he is prepared to withdraw his testimony, turn up at a press conference with the local and international media in front of him and denounce the whole rotten show-trial system that ensnared him, we would then allow him to take the boat and not come back. Naturally, we could hunt the fucker down sometime later in the future. After all, we have long memories and infinite patience.

But ask yourself who is ultimately responsible for this traitor? I think you know the answer to that one already! It all flows back to one day eight years ago, when a certain person got a wee bit over-zealous with the Silver Lady he was given and exceeded his orders. The target was only meant to get a wee flesh wound but instead ended up almost bleeding to death thanks to our former comrade.

The original sin was handing Skyscraper the Silver Lady in the first place, and that he be allowed to carry out the operation personally. Granted, he did a better job with it when he wasted that off-duty Brit soldier - a prime hit for the organisation. He was always trying to prove he was game - and we took advantage of the zealous wee shite. Who then can blame our traitor for seeking revenge? The funny thing though is that in all the depositions relating to his statements to Special Branch, the informer never mentions Skyscraper once. It's me he obsesses about. He hates me for giving the order but says nothing against the one who pulled the trigger. Family loyalty, eh!

Yours in incredulity ... Comrade T.

28

'WARSZAWA'

August 1978

I retreated once more into the treacly black bleakness of the waste ground adjacent to the Blackstaff river, separating the street where I was born and the Belfast Gasworks. I often took refuge there on the roof of the abandoned mini-station beside the rusting redundant rail tracks, where coal buckets were once transported along the sidings to feed the giant tanks providing gas for the entire city. In summer, when the 'Blackie' was dried up from the heat, the gamer boys of the district would hop across the flat mounds of drained mud and effluent to get into the complex, which was guarded by British soldiers and was used, way back in the early days, by armed loyalists as firing points to rain bullets into our area. From there too, the older, bolder boys would launch a battery of stones, bottles, bricks and anything else they could use as missiles, not only against the Brits in their base but also up and over across the Ormeau Road and into the Donegall Pass. Once, they even bombarded the roof of the Ram's Head pub, hoping their payloads would land on the heads of patrons frequenting the bar.

It was also where three Provo bombers died after their suspect device prematurely exploded, blowing them and one of the gas tanks up, and sending a giant 50-foot flame into the Belfast night sky. I was about to sit down at home to watch West Brom hammer Manchester United 4-0 on *Match of the Day* when it started raining fire and black tar. The heat from the vertical firewall melted the tarred roofs of the houses in those streets closest to the gasworks' walls, creating hot black rain. Pious, elderly women ran from their houses in a panic to douse the district with holy water, praying for protection from what must have felt like the end of the world. Those more mobile than them fled westwards towards the city centre, onwards to families and friends who lived as far up the Falls and Grosvenor Road as possible, in case another, more lethal, horizontal blast would set off the other gas tanks.

It was the same place where Padre Pio chose to 'swear in' the younger volunteers to his own personal youth movement, ordering them to lift anything they could find on the slimy, tar-slicked ground below to launch over at the 'other side' across the Ormeau. It was his very own secret HQ, his 'testing centre' for those game enough to join him.

And it was here I went walking around in numbed circles after her final words to me. It was where I imagined I could always be somewhere or somebody else; marooned on some strange, decaying dystopian zone of solitude. Meanwhile, Bowie's 'Warszawa' kept playing and replaying in my head.

I longed for the childish, sci-fi games my cousins and I had played here before all this desolation. On this blasted, sulphur-reeking, snorting, hissing, machine-throbbing landscape, we pretended we were astronaut-soldiers exploring a hostile planet with our home-made wooden ray guns. I always insisted that they referred to me as a cosmonaut, which pleased my father greatly.

On that last day of summer, 1978, I walked around until the soles of my feet throbbed. I stumbled over the sharp, jagged bricks and stones studding the carbon-scarred earth. I picked up a half-brick, which wasn't as slimy or blackened as the thousands of others, dropped the 'halfer' into the pocket of my army jacket and then clambered up onto the wall, eventually reaching the roof. I was already supposed to be back in school for the first day of Upper Sixth. I was supposed to be lining up for new books and stationery or listening to a rousing pre-A levels speech by our Director of Studies about all the challenges ahead. Yet, here I was with 'Warszawa' droning in my head, drowning out the imperatives of my father, his consistent advice to 'get out, get the fuck out'. Instead of dropping up to school, I had slipped quietly out of the house around 7 a.m. that morning, long before dad woke up after his night shift in the slaughterhouse. I had hours to kill before my scheduled meeting with Sabine.

She had arranged to see me at lunchtime in Lord Hamill's burger bar for what she had said on the phone would be an important wee chat. She had asked me to bring along the Polaroid pictures my father had managed to secretly snap inside the meat plant earlier in the week, as well as the camera Sabine had given him for the undercover shoot. I must have shown these weird Polaroid pics to, and had the camera examined by, every civilian searcher at every entrance to the ring-of-steel security barrier that was erected to slow down the rate of Provo firebombing in the commercial heart of Belfast. A Brit soldier at the fortified entrance leading into Victoria Square even made light-hearted banter with me, asking if 'there were any naughty ones in that collection, son?' I had lain out the laminated, slightly blurred images of animals being strung up on hooks, of the stunned and sliced beasts, for a female searcher to check. After she had scanned them, the Brit snatched the camera off me and pretended to photograph the lady searcher who swayed and jived about in the early morning sunshine with her hands on her hips as if she was posing on a catwalk. She sniggered back knowingly at the English soldier when he told her to put her finger in her mouth, and I instantly pictured him riding her from behind in the back of an army jeep. When she handed the pictures and the camera back eventually I hit a major reddner when I realised she was staring down at the visible steamer swelling in my black nylon school trousers.

Once inside the closed security zone, I ambled past the Cornmarket Fountain where I had hung about on alternating

Saturdays with other punks from across the city and beyond. Then I returned to The Harp on Hill Street with its concrete-filled beer barrels and security mesh-wire fencing, constructed to ward off car bombers and gunmen. Tommy Nasty was helping the delivery men offload beer kegs, which they dropped onto a filthy grey pillow to cushion their impact as they were rolled off the back of the lorry and into the pub. I nearly retraced the whole of the route I took every morning on my way to school – north through the art college gardens in the shadow of St Anne's Cathedral, across York Street and into Donegall Street, but instead of continuing north towards Carlisle Circus and the Antrim Road, I took a left down Union Street and the back of the *Belfast Telegraph*, where the early editions were being dispatched into red vans waiting to deliver stories of assassinations, kidnapping, torture, bodies found up entries, fireballs tearing through ballrooms, roasting the revellers inside, and riots erupting in towns and cities across the north.

I killed a few hours in the Central Library, flicking through the news magazines – *The Economist*, *Newsweek*, *Time*, *New Statesman* – reading about rumours of slave camps in Cambodia, the birth of the test-tube baby, the dithering of Jim Callaghan, who was delaying a general election, and the murder campaign of a maniac who was butchering women in Yorkshire. I was deeply grateful and relieved for this long parade of horror, terror and technological miracle splashed all over the pages, as it took my mind off what was coming – what I knew deep down would happen and yet still kidded myself would not come to pass once she looked at me and had a change of heart. Later, among the publications, time started to really crawl as if to mock me. I fantasised about jacking in school, borrowing dosh, selling off everything that I owned so I could follow her to London. When she heard my plans she would definitely change her mind. I tried to convince myself of all this as the sound of 'Warszawa' faded and was replaced by the muffled announcements and the flickering signs for Carlisle,

Lancaster, Stafford, no change at Crewe, Rugby, Watford, Euston. I imagined the line of stations that I had been pulled along with my dad on our first visit to Aidan and my uncle in Brighton the summer before when the Sex Pistols were screaming 'God Save The Queen' to rain on Her Majesty's Silver Jubilee parade. I saw myself following those same signs to be near her, towards a life far away from where I knew Padre Pio was leading me, to do finally what dad had always advised: 'Get out, get the fuck out.'

These words always came in his darkest moments. They were an admission of defeat and impotence against forces that he and his comrades could never tame. Of all people it was Padre Pio who made me understand why my father had fallen out with the people. In our early days in the Red Army, I once asked PP what drove him to do those mad game things, and his reply was just one word: 'Hatred!'

Carlisle, Lancaster, Stafford, no change at Crewe, Rugby, Watford, Euston.

I remembered the blurred faces of late-night commuters on these platforms, as our mile-a-minute British Rail special hurtled past them. There were the incomprehensible squiggles of graffiti on the pillars, the entrances to tunnels and the sides of bridges as we went by. Then came the sensation-assaulting adverts as we slowed on our approach into Euston. When the train pulled in to a shuddering halt, I heard the dissonant din on the platform as the indifferent black mass of travellers thickened on the concourse and moved towards the exits to the streets and the underground stations. Soon, all of this disorder would swallow Sabine up, and, one day, I must follow her into the morass.

'Warszawa' returned when I left the library and made my way round to Queen Street, pausing at the window of The Model Shop. This was where I had bought my first ever Airfix box of soldiers. They were Russians of course, and later I used the mantelpiece in our parlour to re-enact Stalingrad. I took ashes and dying embers from the grate to affect the destruction wrought by the great heroic battle. I strategically placed the Soviet soldiers at the side of clocks and ornaments, including snipers who hid behind Lenin's shiny baldy dome, and even a plastic statue of St Martin de Porres was deployed to provide the heroic defenders of the city with some cover from German fire. A few weeks later, after saving up my pocket money, I went back to The Model Shop and provided further cover for my little grey troops with glued and clipped-together models of MIG fighters and YAK bombers, all of which naturally made my father very proud of his son.

Now, I carried a present from my father to her: the wedge of Polaroid photographs of stunned beasts, strung up along lines of metal piping, gliding towards their deaths; of buckets full of bleeding black-and-brown offal and wooden block tables on which white-coated men were slashing and slicing their way through skin, flesh and bone. All of them bloody offerings to my love from my dad.

Sabine was sipping a thick vanilla milkshake in a seat near the toilets. The strip lighting flickered to the sound of 'Dancing In The City' on the radio. Her half-eaten Hawaiian burger left grease stains on the stars-and-stripes wrapping. When she rolled her mouth around to free the straw from her lips, I noticed she left a deep purple line of lipstick on its edge.

'Robert, please sit down,' she said in a tone as grave as a doctor about to announce a terminal diagnosis.

When I said nothing she nodded over to the counter. 'What would you like, Robert?'

'Nathin'. I'm not hungry,' I replied sulkily.

'Why so surly, Robert?'

I ignored her question, took out the Polaroid snaps and lay them out in a fan shape on the table.

Her green eyes darted back and forward in fascination at the instantly captured images of the doomed cattle. 'Wow, this is great stuff; great material to work with,' she said excitedly. Her breasts raised slightly in her low-cut T-shirt underneath her biker jacket.

'It's as well you're not a vegetarian, Sabine,' I said to interrupt her fixation.

'You tell your father that he has a great eye for the camera. They are all perfectly composed,' she said, not taking her eyes off the images.

'Will do. He'll probably put that down to all the snaps he's taken through the years with his East German camera. Any excuse to praise the optical genius of Carl Zeiss Jena and the technical brilliance of the GDR.'

'He can't in this case. He only took Polaroids,' she reminded me with casual brutality.

She lifted the burger up and took a small delicate bite. Juice from the pineapple ring crushed between the meat and the bun trickled down one side of her mouth and onto her chin. I had to stop myself from reaching over and gently wiping the clear liquid away from her pale, freckled skin. Instead, I handed her one of the napkins from her tray.

'Thank you.'

'No worries, love.'

Sabine seemed to recoil over my reply. 'Robert, please, you need to stop saying that!'

I pretended not to know what she was on about. 'Saying what, Sabine?'

'That word.'

'What word?'

'You know what word.'

I noticed that she had stretched out her hands on her side of the table. The tips of her fingers touched and strained at the edges, creating too much distance for me to reach across and stroke them. When I tried instead to stare into her eyes, those green irises flickered but avoided mine while she shifted uneasily in her plastic seat.

'Robert, I —'

'You what? Go on say it, Sabine. Say it!' I was ashamed to hear the sound of my own voice croaking.

'Robert ... I'm going in a few weeks. I doubt I will ever be back. You have to stay here and finish your A levels and then you'll be free to get out too, to go wherever you want, to do amazing things with your life. It's just that we can't keep this up anymore,' Sabine said while leaning slightly forward, her guard only temporarily dropping.

It was then that I finally burst. 'You used me! You used me this summer! You used me to get those pictures from the abattoir. You used me to get close to my darling cousin. You used me that night in The Pound because no one else was talkin' to ya because they all think you're a fuckin' stuck-up weirdo. You used me because ya didn't want ta be on your own up in yer house in the Holy Lands, while all your fancy art college friends were away on their holidays or back with their families in England. See, that's all you are – a fuckin' user.'

By the time I had finished she was shaking and teary eyed. The two flicked ticks of eye liner were smudged and dribbling black streaks towards her cheekbones. Other diners were staring at us.

'Robert, please, that is not true. That is just not true. Don't make this any harder for me. Don't say horrible things like that. I truly care about you. Please don't be so hard.'

'Hard! Hard? You are the hard cold bitch. You're the one dumpin' me here in front of a lunchtime audience,' I snapped back. 'You're the fuckin' user! You don't care about me. I was just there for you ta pass the time before you moved to London.'

Then she did exactly what I had wanted her to do: she collapsed into a roaring sob, her head down on the table, her entire frame now juddering. In that moment, I kept telling myself that this was an act, one of her art-house spectacles she often talked about, just a performance, merely a show. Then one of the staff, a rake-thin girl with spots, stopped wiping down a nearby table and went over to Sabine, resting one hand delicately on her left shoulder.

'Are you alright there, love? Is he bothering you? Do you want me to ask him to leave?' the waitress said softly while glaring over at me.

I took no notice of the threat and hissed into Sabine's face. 'I'll tell you one thing about my Judas cousin. He told me this would happen. He told me he'd clocked you from the start and that you were a user. He wasn't far wrong now, was he?'

Sabine suddenly resurrected from the table and shot me a withering look. 'You're lying. You're such a liar. Aidan would never say that about me!'

The mere mention of his real name forced me out of my seat and towards her, but instead of striking her in the face I karate-chopped the slaughterhouse pictures on the table. When the Polaroids went flying onto the floor, the waitress pointed her finger in my direction and said, 'Right, that's it. If you don't leave now, I'm callin' the manager and then he will call the police.'

'You can call the peelers, the Brits or the UDA for all I care,' I replied. 'I'm outta here. And fuck you, Sabine. Fuck you ... you Orange bitch!'

As I got up I was shocked to see that Sabine's face had changed from being teary eyed and reddened to that same familiar cold stare she defiantly adopted when provoked or slighted. It was the last sight of her I would ever have.

Outside in the lunchtime sun, a big burly motorbike cop was leaning into the driver's window of a TR7 sports car whose engine snorted impatiently while its exhaust spat out black smoke. The man behind the wheel wore driving gloves. He fished out something from the inside pocket of his navy blue blazer and flashed it at the peeler, who then saluted before moving back towards his bike. Before I made an about-turn, manic, I caught the driver's eye. He was smiling – not at me, but about me. Instantly, I felt she had brought him along just in case, and he was enjoying himself. Bastard! I was livid.

Along Wellington Place, heading for home, the wailing and weeping of 'Warszawa' returned. As I walked through town, I imagined that everyone around me had witnessed my disgrace inside the burger bar. Every laugh and snigger I heard became an insult. Even the Brits and the civilian searchers sharing a joke at the cage into Royal Avenue was about me. I needed to be far away from them all. I wanted desolation. I yearned for the waste ground – to be back among the coal-streaked stones, the tarred debris and the smell of sulphur mixed with the stench of bilious green water – to where no one else would dream of going, on this, the last day of summer.

Hours later, when I stood back up on the roof of the abandoned mini-station, I gazed out behind the bridge over Cromac Street where a number 38 double-decker bus was stuck in traffic. It must have been after half past three, as I spotted a row of amber and black school uniforms in the upper deck. In that instant, I plucked the 'halfer' brick out of my pocket, swivelled my body like a discus thrower and hurled it with force straight into the second-last upstairs window of the bus. When I heard the sound of glass shattering and the squeals of a child, I dropped off the station wall and tore across the glass, brick and stone-studded ground. Seeking sanctuary, I arrived eventually at the house of my one-time tormentor but now best friend and comrade.

29

HOLY LANDS

29 April 1979

No more excuses. No more understanding. No more bye balls. No more sympathy. No more root-of-it-all reasoning. No more sad backstory. All I want to do is take this jagged crescent of shiny vinyl and slash it across his throat and cut out any more explanations.

I walk up the street by the engineering factory towards the house where he first showed us the video of *The Exorcist*, where, after the film was over, he took a crucifix down from the mantlepiece and pretended to be Regan's demon wanking herself while all the time urging Jesus to come and fuck her. Scared shitless as we were about to leave, we promised each other to all walk home together. Then he went into the hallway, opened up the fuse box and trip-switched the electricity, leaving us in complete darkness. He left us for a couple of minutes while we fumbled around his parlour, trembling, shaking and cursing as he informed us in a croaky, demonic voice that all our mothers sucked cocks in hell. Eventually, he threw back the switch, blinding everyone with a sudden explosion of light, and then came that familiar eruption of his 'sna-ha, sna-ha' cackling at the sight of his friends wrapped around each other in terror.

And now, after this real-life horror show last night, he will still want me to believe in him; that it is not his fault, his sin; that, like Regan, he is infected with a demon far beyond his control. He will try to convince me that none of this is actually his fault. He will try because there is no one else prepared to listen to him; there is no one else who will pay him any attention, and he knows it. But there are no more excuses, understanding, sympathy or reasoning here. There's just this shit that rains down in buckets until I am up to my neck in it. Aptly, I sidestep a steaming pyramid of horse dung on the street. The chimes of the ice-cream van echo in the air, reminding us all about the dour oppressiveness of Belfast Sundays.

I stand in his hallway waiting on him to answer the door, but his mum appears instead, dressed in a blue polka-dot dress and dolled up to the nines in her make-up for Sunday Mass. Her arms are exposed, and I notice a scalding scar visible on her right one. The skin tissue is still red and mottled from an incident that obviously only happened a short time ago.

She puts her hand on her hip and shakes her head. 'If you're lookin' for him you're out of luck, Robert. He's gone back up to Divis Flats this morning to see his cousin Paki. And if you're lookin' for me, I'm sorry but I'm a bit tied up with Mummy in there, as she's feelin' a bit poorly today.'

'No, no, it's alright. I'll get to him later,' I croak, while looking down at her feet. She swivels a blue stiletto heel and I instantly feel a steamer coming on.

She bends over and I can detect that compound of vodka and Regal off her breath. She has started early today.

'Don't be a stranger, Robert love. Just not today. I've my hands full with Mummy. Maybe later in the week?'

'I'm sorry to hear about Rita.' My voice cracks. 'Tell her ... tell her I hope she feels better soon.'

'You're very good, Robert. The sooner she can go back to her own place the better for both of us.' Then she winks at me and adds, 'Unless you wanna go around to her place in an hour or two and I'll meet ya there. I can leave the key under the bin at the front of the house. I'll be upstairs waitin' for ya.'

'I'd love to but my dad is cookin' Sunday lunch.'

I nod towards the still-glowing, rectangular scar on her arm. 'What happened to you?'

Her face turns the same colour as the seared tissue. 'Just a wee accident this morning pouring the spuds into the colander. It's nothin' ta worry about, Robert. Pity about later. We had a free house at my ma's. Maybe this week some time, love?'

'Aye, maybe later this week. I'll call when he's not in.'

'You do that Robert, and I'll tell him that you called,' she replies, before retreating back into the hall, prompted by the whimpering cries of her mother from the living room.

I stand frozen at their doorway for a few seconds, realising that he didn't stop all night – from the granny to his ma and finally Paki, lying on the ground near a pool of fetid water up our entry. He's still probably buzzing even now on his way back to the flats, ready to report on the completed operation. I can picture him delivering the bad news to Colleen and Stephen in their flat as he smirks and secretly sniggers over what he did to Paki. I put my hand inside my jacket and rub my forefinger along the jagged edge of the broken vinyl. I think about the crimson scarred tissue on his mother's arm, and I now know that my moment has passed. The paralytic fear has returned once more.

At the wooden gate leading to the keg room of Mooney's Bar in Eliza Street, a couple of young teenagers are re-enacting yesterday's cup final. They have used chalk to mark out a goal area on the gate. One boy even wears a yellow Arsenal away top and has written the letters CFC with thick black marker over the blue logo of the Gunners' cannon. He lives next door to the pub and, like me, has been spiking up his hair all through the season. He wears the same type of DIY uniform of the poorer punk kids who can't afford to buy bondage trousers or biker jackets via the pages of the *NME*. I spotted him among the crowd at Windsor Park yesterday.

He and his friends scarper after an orange-and-black Striker ball as it trickles across the road to the stables where the trotting horses are looked after. The ball rolls to my feet and instantly I lash at it and cry out, 'Tony Bell bags the winner.' Unfortunately, the ball connects with the boy in the yellow shirt instead of Mooney's gate, and he buckles over with the impact on his groin. Before I get the chance to run to his aid, his mates surround him and tell me to fuck away off. His mother emerges from his house to see what has happened to her son. She is the woman who makes the communion and wedding dresses but recently turned her hand to stitching up red-and-white fabric for Cliftonville flags. Her scowl is directed towards me even though I try to explain that it was an accident.

'Did you do that deliberately? I saw you from the window. You hit that ball straight at my son. You're as bad as that maniac that lives up the street there. Is that who you learned it from? To hurt a child like that.'

The kid with the sickening pain in his cock and bollocks begs his mother to shut up, reminding her that not only is he no longer a child but that I am nothing like Padre Pio. But his mother is like me, not in the mood for any excuses, even while I try to help the kid get to his feet again.

'You tell that maniac to leave all these boys alone. Do you hear me?'

I shake my head in feigned bewilderment. 'Missus, whatever he has done to them has nothing to do with me.'

'It's not what he's done to them that worries me. It's what he's tryin' to lure them into. He's the Pied Piper tryin' ta lead them into the sewer. Comin' round here, kickin' ball with them when everybody knows he has no interest in football. All the time askin' them to come ta wee meetings with him. Well I don't want my son involved ... ever!'

Ah, PP's waste ground youth movement. 'I'm not involved in anything either, missus,' I protest. And I'm not lying. For all his supposed fence-sitting, my da has eyes everywhere, and he threatened dire consequences if he heard I was anywhere near what he termed PP's Hitler Youth. I also suspect he had a word about it with Padre Pio because my invites to the waste ground ended a long time ago.

Her son nods in agreement. 'Ruin, there, is not involved cos his da is a commie, Ma.'

This doesn't deter his mother, who keeps up her rant. 'Involved or not involved, you just tell that maniac to leave my son and his friends alone. They're not joining anything while I'm around. Leave them alone. Do you understand?'

Silently, I nod my head in agreement. If Padre Pio is still recruiting, I know fine rightly that nothing will stop him from luring them in if given the order to do so.

I pass by the pub and onto Cromac Street, heading southward in the country direction. I'm driven on by a new force that pushes me away from the gravitational pull of Padre Pio up towards the place where she used to be, to where I had never been happier. As I march on to the university area, pealing bells are piercing the sonorous silence of Sunday in the Holy Lands. Their tinkling chimes are so unlike the solitary dull dong of the bell from the Catholic church where I was baptised, confessed my sins in a box that we called 'The Tardis', swallowed 'God-the-biscuit' on Holy Communion day and had oil rubbed on my head by an elderly man with reptilian skin and an enormous Liberace ring. All these rituals followed many home battles, as my mother insisted I was to be brought up in her faith: a belief system she still clung to right to the bitter end when she only had a mini-statue of St Martin de Porres for company in her death room. Dad, of course, always surrendered in the end to her demands. I was thankful for that because I didn't want to be left out, to be the only weirdo in class who never got Communion or Confirmation.

Entering Jerusalem Street, I pass by the VW Beetles and the Citroen 2 CVs belonging to the academics and the teachers who have colonised this uniquely mixed corner of the south of the city. The stickers on their car windows let everyone know exactly which European city they visited on their last summer holiday, while others proclaimed, 'Nuclear Power No Thanks' and 'What Price Peace?'

Last summer! I know only too well what really propelled me back up into the street again. Her father might be coming to collect the rent. He has to call around some time to number 66. So I cross the street but hesitate before banging on the brown door. Through a grimy window I can see the television is on, but instead of the cup final highlights, those inside are watching a black-and-white film with Bing Crosby dressed as a priest. Two people are sitting in the lotus position on the sofa where we used to crash, kiss, cuddle and fumble. One girl has a green Mohican, and the other has pink crimped hair. On the table, I spot two tall cylinders of hairspray, a bottle of Woodpecker cider and a fat unlit spliff sitting in an ashtray. They must be friends of hers surely. They might be fellow students from art college or just old mates from The Pound and The Harp. They are bound to have kept in touch with her. They are certain to know where exactly she is now. But I stop myself from pressing the bell or lifting the knocker. I see an image of him forming in my mind, him in his *Professionals* macho-pose with that smug smile. And I think back to that day last summer, to the last time we met, when she ate a burger and broke my heart in front of a lunchtime audience while her father waited outside in that fucking car, smirking. I take the jagged vinyl out of my pocket, and I slide *Low* gently through the letterbox. I turn away and head back towards the Lagan. He'll be home again by now. I am going back to Padre Pio with some vital information.

30

COMMS 8

1987

A final word this time on personnel selection, comrade. Thinking about our reluctant supergrass got me wondering about who might want to volunteer and join this mission. The answer was obvious – the informer's offspring.

If you are looking for someone with a motive, who is also an expert driver, then here is the perfect person bearing a personal grudge. When they tell me that nothing is personal in this struggle, in this war, I have to laugh sometimes. As a man with a history degree, you know better than most that soldiers are always more willing to kill and be killed if there's some personal connection to the war. Think of all those Soviet soldiers that murdered, raped and robbed all the way from Stalingrad to Berlin. How many of them had personal stories to tell about their own families, their own loved ones in the former occupied lands, who were shot, burnt, hung, tortured, butchered or enslaved by the Germans!

There is plenty of the personal invested in our very own self-cleansing operation. The image of Duffy, all alone, tortured and slaughtered then dumped like a dog, should inspire all those involved in our movement, in our game. This is exactly why I believe this young volunteer might be the ideal candidate for the job. Not only due to his obvious hatred of Skyscraper but also the need to erase the shame caused by his father. He has something to prove against his da's treachery. After all, the kid refused all requests from the traitor for jail visits. When this tout first opened up to the cops, the family came under savage pressure in the flats. They had their door daubed with graffiti and later shit, and the boy was threatened. All of this of course turned out to be entirely counter-productive to our cause and only strengthened the quisling's resolve to turn us all over. So, do make the approach. I hear the kid is a whizz behind the steering wheel, having been a wee joyriding hood for a couple of years ... like father, like son! If I was in this boy's shoes I'd be horny for this job. He will surely enlist!

Yours ... Comrade T.

31

PICTURE AND POSTCARD

29 April 1979

I appear at Padre Pio's door with purpose. He looks older and harder, more pensive and withdrawn than I've ever seen him before. We are in his front parlour with the blinds pulled down. One candle is burning on the table by the window as if the house is holding a wake. He is stretched across the floral sofa where his mother cajoles me to kiss, finger and lick; where she whispers in my ear, 'Don't worry about it, Robert love. It's just a bit a sex.' He is studying the picture that I have handed over to him at long last, and, as he holds it up to the candlelight, a smile breaks over his face.

'Trout is going be very pleased with us,' he says. His head is reclined on a pillow and he's speaking up towards the ceiling rather than directly at me. 'Are you absolutely certain that he is a Brit?' he continues.

I plant my feet onto the table and barely grunt out, 'Aye, sure of it.'

He continues to stare in fascination at the photograph as the faint strains of *Songs of Praise* are audible from next door where his mother and grandmother are sitting.

'And the address? You sure about that too?' he asks.

'I'm hardly goin' to forget it now, am I?'

'Aye, right enough, Ruin. You spent quite enough time up there last summer.'

He clears his throat and then hackles into a hanky he is holding in one of his bony hands before leaning back again. His glare is still fixed above, on the fake crystal chandelier hanging from the ceiling.

'I'll take this up to Trout myself and he'll pass it on. I'll mention you in dispatches, when it gets there.'

'What about Paki?' I say without thinking.

On the mention of that name he shoots up like a vampire rising from his coffin and trains his stare on me. 'What about HIM? He was given fair warning. Anyway, what's he to you?'

'I just wonder why he got done in our entry of all places?'

'Oh, I wouldn't know anything about that.' He smirks and adds, 'I'm saying nothin' and signing nothin'. And that's the way you need to think too, McManus.'

He is back with McManus! He switches once more from nickname to surname just to let me know the score.

'Think how, PP?'

'If you ever get lifted and the peelers are bangin' the cell table or threatenin' ta throw you out of one of their jeeps in the middle of Sandy Row or the Shankill, shouting, "Here lads, there's a Fenian!" Your one thought is sign nothin' and say nothin'. The bastards can hold ya for up ta seven days in Castlereagh interrogation centre. Would you be game enough ta tell them to fuck away off, to make it all picture and no sound until yer solicitor walks through the door?' Padre Pio says.

'I'm game,' I protest, genuinely stung by his accusation of no balls, no guts and no spine.

Padre Pio hoists his legs into the air and starts doing bicycle kicks. 'Sure you are. You proved that yesterday, Ruin. And now, with this new information, well, I know you're game and so will Trout.'

'Did ya watch the cup final highlights?'

'Aye, I saw the match up in the flats with Trout and Paki's boy. Trout was minding him while the rest of the family were up in the hospital visitin' Paki. It was a really good game, wasn't it, mate?'

Trout minding him! The man who gave the order for his father to be shot was looking after the son, sitting in the flat watching Cliftonville win the Irish Cup, probably promising the young lad he'd take him up to Solitude next season.

'I can't wait for Seaview and the County Antrim Shield final, Ruin. There's goin' ta be more aggro down there on the Shore Road. Here, the *Sunday News* is predictin' the UDA might attack us. There's going ta be more than just a riot, and if we're there, then too fuckin' right there will,' he boasts.

'I'll be there too, mate,' I add, and then we both break into a verse of 'Oh when the Reds went up and won the Irish Cup we were there ... we were there.'

A rap on the door disturbs our chant and in comes his mother with a silver tray of square-cut sandwiches, thick steaming hot cuts of re-heated Sunday roast wedged between white pan bread, the melting butter oozing from them onto the tray in yellow streams that trickle towards two mugs of scalding tea.

Padre Pio shoots upright and reaches over for his mug, the one with green-and-white hooped Celtic colours and the club's shamrock crest. His mother hands the plain white mug to me while leaning over just far enough to expose the black lacy bra she is wearing under her blue polka-dot dress.

She winks at me when she says, 'Now eat up, Robert. You're a growing boy.'

I smile back at her and notice that Padre Pio is staring at the two of us, but strangely, without a trace of menace or disgust. Instead he is shaking his head slightly and almost smiling at us. He takes a gulp of tea and belches as loudly as he can, and his mother beats a retreat out of the parlour leaving us to the roast meat sandwiches. Suddenly, all I can think about are those Polaroid pictures of the strung up and slaughtered beasts that my father had smuggled out of the abattoir for Sabine last summer.

'Fuck sake, eat something, Ruin. You're witherin' away here. You'll need ta build yerself up for Seaview and oh aye ... also the struggle,' he says in a mocking way.

'The struggle?' I'm forever and will always be perplexed by the absurdity of that word.

'Are you simple or a mong or what? The struggle! You're in, Ruin. Trout wants ta bring ya into the group, and that's before this photograph. He'll be well chuffed with that. You've proved that yer game to him and now he wants ta swear you in personally. Not just for being game but also for keepin' yer mouth shut. Ya proved that too last night over everything and that's good too in our eyes.'

I look over to the photograph that I have handed to Padre Pio and realise that there is no turning back for me now. I'm 'game' and I'm 'in'. My mouth goes dry. I get up from the chair and tell him that I have to go, muttering about that mongoloid cousin being on the missing list. As I move towards the door, he is still staring at the face of the man that Sabine had captured on film. He doesn't even say goodbye.

When I finally return home, there is no sign of Rex Mundi anywhere inside. The spare room is bare, the hangers inside the open wardrobe empty, his holdall gone, the few books he had brought over with him from Brighton – *The War of the Flea* and the works of Richard Allen: *Punk Skinhead* and *Suedehead* – all taken away. Only a few discarded Rizla skins and curly flecks of tobacco on the bedside table are evidence of his one-time presence. The bed, of course, is unmade, but when I shake up the blankets and pull back the pillows to straighten them up, I spot a postcard lying underneath one of them. It is rectangular, much larger than the usual ones. It is a montage of different images from day and night. I pick it up and read the words in-between the four square pictures of different cityscapes: 'Berlin. Hauptstadt Der DDR.' Then I flick the card around and recognise that familiar pristinely compressed handwriting in sky-blue, fountain-pen ink, and my heart sinks.

'Crossed over Checkpoint Charlie today to send this to you from the east. Thought you'd appreciate that! Will bring back memories for you. I gave up course in London and settled in West Berlin where I'm working in a photographic studio close to the Wall. They gave me exhibition space for pictures and paintings based on your slaughterhouse snaps. Thinking of you all back at home. Hope Robert is OK. My address is on a little sticker at the back of the envelope. The East German post office made me use the envelope to send this postcard. Love Sabine xxxx'.

She had also attached a tiny heart sticker beneath her signature, alongside a drawing, which had escaped the East Berlin postal censors. It was a mini-sketch in red ink of a clenched fist inside a circle with an upturned cross stretching out from its edge.

Downstairs, there is the hiss of water and the clatter of crockery as Dad tidies away the Sunday dinner plates. I hear the jabbering bursts of foreign words from the radio tuned to somewhere across the Iron Curtain. I go down and join him in the kitchen.

'Where is Aidan?' I ask.

'After the match, he took your advice and decided to go up and stay in his other uncle's house up in the Malone. I think your constant reminding that his uncle's drinks cabinet had more to offer him than a few cans from our fridge did the trick. So he's gone and I don't think he's coming back.'

'Good riddance to him. When did this arrive?' I hold up the postcard with the four images of East Germany's capital on the front of it. 'Was this sent to him? Did she have the cheek to send it to him here in this house?'

His answer sends a shockwave through me. 'It wasn't posted to him, son. It was a postcard for me.'

I wondered where he had put the envelope with her address on a sticker on the back of it, but I wouldn't ask him that.

'For you! Why would she send it to you?'

My father sticks to his kitchen chores, either unaware or else indifferent to the heat and anger rising throughout my body.

'Maybe because she was grateful for me helping her with them pictures from the meat plant. I thought it was nice of her.'

'So why did I find it in his room then? Were you both keeping this from me?'

Dad carefully puts down the tea towel and looks at me. 'It only arrived this Friday and you two had other things on your mind like a certain football match at Windsor Park.'

'Oh, so when were you going ta tell me that she'd been in touch after all this time?'

'I'm not sure, son. I was going to tell you this morning but that incident in our alley threw me a bit, and I forgot.'

'Why did that dick see the postcard first?'

My father steps a bit closer to me and for the first time since we dumped soil together onto my mother's coffin, he puts his hands on my shoulders.

'It was already opened when I realised who it was from. Aidan must have got up early and saw the envelope and the address on the back. He stopped me in the hall on Friday as I was going out to work and handed it over to me. I put it in the drawer beside the telephone for later. OK, I didn't know what do with it. I was worried. I was worried for you. Worried about what you might do, son.'

'What was I going to do exactly, Da?'

'I dunno, son. Maybe go out to West Berlin after her. You threatened to do it when she was in London. You are less than a month away from your A levels. The last thing I want is for you to start begging, stealing and borrowing to go over there just as your exams are starting. I was just trying to help.'

I push both his hands off my shoulders and get up in his face, teeth clenched. 'By hiding this from me? Is that your idea of help? So where is it? Where is the envelope with her address on it?

Where is it now because I wanna write back to that bitch. Has he taken it up with him to Malone?'

'No son, he doesn't have it. Don't blame him. I burnt the envelope. I threw it in the fire. And I didn't take a note of where she's living either.'

He is trying to sound confessional but I am in no mood to absolve him. 'How dare you interfere between me and her! Isn't it a pity you weren't more interfering when it came to my ma and all the things she used to get up to supposedly behind your back!'

At this I am expecting a dig into the bake, instead he just shakes his head, that martyred look returning to his ridiculous face.

'Do not bring your mother into this, Robert. If she was alive even she would agree with me here. This is about you having no distractions for your A levels; for you to get out, to get the fuck out of this place for good. It's not about acting the hard man, which you are not, whether it's over at Windsor or down at Seaview. Even your mother in her worst state would have told you that.'

'Fuck the A levels. Fuck university, and don't think of coming down to Seaview so you and your comrade can keep an eye on me. If you do, I'll raise hell. And oh aye, I'm going down there for the Shield final and we're going to wreck the fuckin' place!'

All he can do to retaliate is grab the tea towel, throw it into my face and walk away in disgust while muttering, 'You're a moron if you do, Robert. You're a moron if you keep following the Hitler Youth around. You are a real moron if you waste this chance to escape.'

'The lads are so right about you,' I call out as he turns his back on me. When he ignores that, I press on harder. 'They say that you're such a fuckin' fence sitter that you've splinters permanently up yer arse!'

Without bothering to turn round to face me, he points out towards the yard from the kitchen window. 'It's better to be sitting on a fence than lying up an entry like that poor bastard in the early hours of this morning. And that's where you're going to end up too one day, if you're not careful,' my father shouts back.

I retreat up to my room and bolt the door behind me.

32

COMMS 9

1987

It was a clever move by you to relay the offer of talks through that third party across the Irish Sea. Our go-between, as you so rightly point out, still has romantic notions about a great reunion, about the burial of bygones in the cause of the greater struggle. It shows how far removed your cousin is from the facts on the ground here. He actually believes his own rhetoric and, in doing so, has delivered us this planned meeting with Skyscraper and his chums.

It reminds me of that summer a year after the hunger strike when he brought over a 'fraternal delegation' of supporters, principally from northern English polytechnics, who had come to rally behind our banner rather than the rosary-bead rattlers, who had suddenly also turned red! Skyscraper took charge of their accommodation for their fact-finding mission to Belfast, and we had to dip into the war chest to pay for the B & Bs in the university area. On their first night, Skyscraper organised a party for them at a house in the Holy Lands. It belonged to a wealthy lawyer who still represents several of us locked inside here and who, due to his leftist student past, still harboured sympathies for the movement. There were about six of them, four of them were women and all were keen to 'fight racism, fight imperialism!' They were eager to meet our 'soldiers' at the sharp end. We only found out about a planned encounter with Skyscraper's personal team much later, when a stewards' inquiry was held into the incident. Anyway, this clique arrived late up at the barrister's house, having just robbed an off-licence on the Ormeau Road. They bounded into the lawyer's home armed with stolen bottles of Smirnoff and Paddy Whiskey. Instead of regaling our English comrades (some of whom must surely have been MI5 plants) with tales of the armed struggle, Skyscraper let his boys off the leash. At least two of his praetorian guard almost raped a girl in an upstairs bathroom while the Skyscraper himself went around goosing the other women. One of their boyfriends objected to his behaviour and inevitably ended up receiving a head butt and a drop kick to the balls.

I never thought your cousin was as naive or as gormless as the students he brought over in 1982 to meet the movement. But as you say, he hasn't suspected a thing since you made contact and relayed our request. And to think that not a million years ago, in our presence, he used to harp on about how much he despised Skyscraper. It's funny how things go!

Comrade T.

PS: Fingers and toes are crossed inside here for your important task ahead. Naturally, none of us are praying for you. We would never go that far!

33

COMMUNIQUE – REVOLUTIONARY COMMAND COUNCIL

16 MARCH 1987

'At approximately 12.45 today, our armed activists carried out an operation to bring to an end the attacks and threats on our movement in recent weeks and months.

'Our cadres ambushed a car in which a gang of renegades were driving north of Dublin Airport. They proceeded to execute the trio of traitors: Padre Pio McCann, Paul 'Yeti' Larkin and Roy 'Pig Face' Green.

'The Revolutionary Command Council claims responsibility for their execution at this time.

'This course of action was not taken lightly, as the vista of Irishmen killing Irishmen is an appalling one. The core of our struggle should always and will always remain focused on our main enemy: the Crown Forces and their local collaborators. However, the leadership of the Revolutionary Command Council had no choice in taking this decisive internal initiative. Our intelligence department had solid and irrefutable information that Padre Pio McCann and his small band of followers were planning a major murderous assault on our members as part of his egotistical bid to seize control of our organisation. This treacherous plot was about to be put into place by McCann and his cohorts either this weekend or the week ahead. Fortunately, for the cause of authentic revolutionary socialist republicanism, we found this out just in time.

'In addition, the leadership of the Revolutionary Command Council point to the abduction and disappearance of Alex Duffy in Amsterdam over a year ago. Comrade Duffy was a dedicated volunteer who worked across Europe to provide logistical support to our armed struggle back at home. Duffy's refusal to hand over war materiel to McCann and his flunkeys in Amsterdam cost him his life. Despite hours of torture and degrading and inhumane treatment, Comrade Duffy demonstrated the same kind of courage our revolutionary forefathers, like James Connolly, showed as they faced the British firing squads in 1916. Comrade Duffy would not disclose the whereabouts of weapons and other resources that were secreted across the continent. He knew, as we now know, that such an arsenal in the hands of the likes of Padre Pio McCann and his cohorts would be used to sully our struggle.

'In life, actions always have consequences, and the reactionary, evil actions of McCann and his men in Amsterdam had consequences for them.

'Finally, to those who might have any semblance of loyalty to the McCann gang, we say a number of things. Firstly, anyone with information as to the exact whereabouts of Alex Duffy's body can pass it on without any fear of retribution. You can use your parish priest, your solicitor, or contact *The Irish News* to furnish them with any details that can lead to the recovery of his remains. We implore you to think humanely and imagine the agony of the Duffy family who have no body to bury, no grave where they can go to grieve.

'As for those who are contemplating striking back at our movement after this operation, we say – desist! All those associates of Padre Pio McCann must also contact a parish priest, solicitor or indeed the media, and make it crystal clear that they wish to disassociate from his gang. We call on that band of renegades to immediately disband forthwith or face their own consequences. Any attempt to kill or maim our members and their families will be met with a ferocity never imagined.

'There will be no more communications for the foreseeable future until this internal business is completed. The leadership of the Revolutionary Command Council will then issue a manifesto for the future, based on the principles of establishing a broad, popular front that will unite all the forces fighting British Imperialism in Ireland. Saturday 16 March 1987 will then be seen in the history of our struggle as the turning point in our war to free our country. Long live the Revolutionary Command Council. Long live 16 March!'

NOTE TO EDITORS: The code word your newsrooms received by telephone ahead of this statement will remain the same one for all future communiques from the Revolutionary Command Council.

ENDS

34

COMMS 10

17 March 1987

A horse box! A horse box! My kingdom for a horse box!

That was a masterstroke. Luring them into thinking both sides would meet up inside Dublin Airport, where it would be safe due to the security there for all concerned, and then staging that ambush on the road near Slane was truly inspired. I hear our young, vengeful volunteer who did the driving would give Senna a run for his money. Those reports of him steering the jeep with the horse box in tow to overtake Skyscraper and his chums in their Ford Fiesta were magic. He has certainly proven he is well and truly game. The details are also chilling, especially when the horse box was crashed from the back into them and the boys then dropped the door down to come out from inside and let fly with their AK-47s. Ask yourself this: who in their right minds among them is going to stand up for the remnants of Skyscraper's gang now, after reading all of that?

The cheering on our end of the landing inside hasn't stopped since the news broke on the radio on Saturday evening. There was more whopping and hollering for joy than when the Celtic score came in half an hour later. The prisoners are saying it is small wonder your nickname is 'The Professor'! Having a degree in history is one thing – but making history is quite another.

Yet we cannot be complacent even while we offer the remainder of them on the outside a way out of all this. The priests and the boys of the old brigade who mediate on these matters have been contacted. The party line is that if any of Skyscraper's remaining goons want to stay on this earth a while longer, they should contact their local parish priest, a solicitor, one of the old IRA men or even *The Irish News* to make it clear they are taking early voluntary retirement. A comm. has come in from the exterior to confirm that this offer has now been transmitted. We shall see if they have any capacity to fight back now that our old friend and his two praetorian guards have been iced.

Speaking personally, none of this gives me any satisfaction, even knowing what they did to Duffy. But then I sit here in this cell and wonder what Duffy's family must be thinking, knowing full well that their son and brother's chief tormentor has been put in his box permanently. Hopefully his family won't come off with any of that father-forgive-them-for-they-know-not-what-they-do guff. That's all we would need at this crucial stage of the game. They above all others are now entitled to gloat.

Meanwhile, watch your back, keep the head down and stay put wherever you are holed up. They will try to kick out, no doubt, so remain on standby just in case.

Once again, massive congratulations on a superb operation.

Yours fraternally ... Comrade T.

35

SEWER RATS

19 March 1987

Graveside oration by Aidan McManus, Chairperson of Brighton & Hove Against Imperialism and South-Coast Co-Ordinator Republican Socialist Solidarity Group.

'It was into a life of repression, occupation, state terror and fear that Padre Pio McCann came into this world. Even by the time of his First Holy Communion, Padre Pio had personally suffered at the hands of British Imperialism. His father was the first in the family to take up the armed struggle against the occupiers and in 1970, following a gun battle in Belfast's Lower Falls, his dad was forced to flee the occupied jurisdiction for the Free State. So, from a very early age, Padre Pio McCann's life was already being shaped and his revolutionary consciousness was developing. He had lost a father thanks to the battle that was, in reality, only beginning.

'The Padre Pio McCann we came to know was a freedom fighter – not a terrorist, as the media likes to say. The Padre Pio McCann we knew was an energetic vibrant personality who loved life. He was devoted to his mother, who had lost her husband to exile, and to his grandmother, who loved him dearly. Wherever he went alongside his comrades he always found the time to seek out the nearest telephone to call and make sure his mum and granny were safe back at home. A loving son, a caring grandson – the truth is a far cry from the capitalist press's stereotyping of him as a blood thirsty, callous, cruel, apolitical gunman.

'Here are some facts for those in the media gathered here around his graveside today in Milltown Cemetery – facts that we are proud to put on the record for them. It is a fact that Padre Pio was a militant activist in the Revolutionary Brigade. It is a fact that he engaged in armed actions against British Crown forces as his father had done before him in the earlier phase of the struggle. It is a fact that among those operations was the assassination of a locally recruited British Army captain in 1982. It is a fact that Padre Pio McCann came under fire from this undercover British officer in the Holy Lands district of South Belfast, but, fearless in the face of bullets whizzing over his head, our late comrade removed this veteran military intelligence operative from the earth outside the door of a house in, of all places, Jerusalem Street. The location of that successful operation should remind us all that Padre Pio McCann was never parochial in his mindset when it came to armed struggle. An instinctive socialist, he often quoted how the Palestinians fought against all the odds to keep their dream of a homeland alive and how the peasants of Cuba and later Nicaragua managed to overthrow their masters by the sheer determination to be free.

'Comrades and friends, we would have expected to be here mourning Padre Pio McCann after he fell at the hands of the British Army, the RUC or their loyalist proxies. He was, after all, in the British state's eyes, a 'marked man', especially after he had dispatched one of their officers back in 1982. However, it pains me to remind you all that Padre Pio McCann died not at the hands of our historic, traditional enemies but rather by sewer rats masquerading as Irish revolutionaries!

'It is even more painful for me personally to tell you that amongst those who conspired to murder Padre Pio McCann and his two comrades in the notorious ambush last weekend was someone once very close to him and related by blood to me. We all know to whom I am referring: the king rat of the sewer rats behind this murderous treachery last Saturday. So, on behalf of Brighton and Hove Against Imperialism and indeed all the solidarity groups in Britain aligned to the Revolutionary Brigade, I have a message for him and his cohorts: You may kill the revolutionary but never the revolution! Your treason will be paid for in blood. Your demands that the Revolutionary Brigade disband in ignominy are laughable. Your allegations about Padre Pio McCann are fictions aimed at confusing the Irish working class and obscuring the truth about who the real revolutionaries are.

'Even in death, Padre Pio McCann is inseparable from the rest of us. In life he was unforgettable. I will always remember cup final day in 1979, when we were callow, young football supporters marching defiantly towards Windsor Park. Even back then I was amazed by his energy and his courage as well as his organisational skills, particularly the way he helped organise a mass impromptu protest against the playing of the British national anthem before the cup final. I can still hear him yelling at all those around him on the Kop as 'God Save the Queen' struck up: 'Sit down the lot of ye. Sit fucking down.' And of course they did! He was also by nature what they call in Belfast 'a raker' and enjoyed a joke at others' expense, most usually his own comrades.

'Finally, let me turn to this line of gentlemen in their helmets, shields, suits of armour and batons surrounding us today as we pay tribute to one of our fallen. Let me make it clear to them that once the Revolutionary Brigade have dealt with the renegades that took the life of Padre Pio McCann and his comrades, we will return to what we do best – resisting you with all our might! Be under no illusions, boys, that you are our prime enemy and that we will kill you! You might be enjoying the sight of us laying one of our own to rest today, as I can see so many of you with smiles on your faces. Yet your very own gravediggers are all around you here in this cemetery. They are the revolutionary youth who are inspired by the example of Padre Pio McCann and his life of resistance. They will join with all the other gravediggers of capitalism from the docks of Liverpool to the pit villages of South Yorkshire, from the slums of Glasgow's East End to the tower blocks of Dublin's Ballymun and the streets of Ballymurphy. They will be the vanguard of a new anti-imperialist broad front across these islands, working on a minimum programme that is forged in the interests of the working class. Such a broad front will bring about victory and with it the only true fitting tribute to Padre Pio McCann. So onwards to that victory and to the memory of Comrade PP! *Venceremos! No Pasarán!*'

36

'SUBTERRANEANS'

1 September 1994

I imagine my father's deteriorating brain transmitting fainter and fainter neurons across the cortex at thirty frames a second. I picture images flashing backwards beneath his skull, rewinding from the colour of the 1990s into the sepia tones of the 1960s. I imagine time shuttling into reverse in my own mind, as his shrunken body heaves and groans under wires and an oxygen mask. Only the bleeps and beeps of the life-support system interrupt my reverie, my imagined visualisation of Dad's final interior moments. Today will also be the first day of their ceasefire: their war will end with his death.

I hear the lift ping and the doors slide open. The familiar soft tread of shoe leather announces the arrival of my father's greatest friend: Marty Johnstone has come to say goodbye. I lightly touch my dad's forehead and feel repulsed as one of my fingertips pops a bead of sweat close to his left temple. It is the nearest I want to come to any physical farewell. When I retreat to the window, I stare outside towards the mountains beyond. Johnty starts to weep quietly behind me with the muffled semi-repressed cries of a man who knows he is now completely alone.

I turn around to Johnty. I want to say something comforting to him, but I'm not sure I can even manage anything coherent. Something catches my eye amid all the Get Well Soon cards on top of my father's bedside locker. I lift it up. It is a business card with a picture on the front of it of a red-brick building that I have known since my primary-school days. Above, printed in machine block font, is the name – 'Sabine'.

Holding it closer to the light from the window, I flip the card over to see four square images on the back: the Mir space station; the blurred frame of animal carcasses hanging up on meat hooks; a masked man handling a Luger pistol which obscures his mouth and, in the final mini-quadrant, the face of another man that I can never forget. Above the four frames, the headline reads: 'Marooned: An Exhibition by Sabine Schneider.' Beneath all the images at the bottom of the card are the dates: 31 August–6 September 1994.

I turn to Marty Johnstone, but my question is really aimed at the man whose last minutes of consciousness are ebbing away, hurtling backwards into oblivion at thirty frames a second.

'Did you know about this?' I ask, pointing the card at Johnty.

Johnty suddenly pulls himself together and serves me a stunned glare. 'Is there something wrong with you?'

'Oh there's nothin' wrong with me, Marty. Just tell me if you knew about this?'

'I don't even know what "this" is, Robert, and I really don't care what "this" is either. I didn't even notice it. Haven't you more to be thinking about?' he says, his voice cracking as he gestures towards my father.

I don't respond and he nods back towards the exit. 'Anyway, shouldn't you be out there with yer mates celebrating whatever it is they think they've achieved?'

'What's to celebrate?' I say glumly.

'Oh aye, I forgot. You're one of those who are still standing by the Republic!' he says, before placing a hand tenderly on his best friend's shoulder. Gently patting my father, Johnty keeps his eyes focused on him while speaking to me. 'I'm sorry. It's just when I see that crowd out there partying as if Celtic had won the

European Cup again and then seeing this man lying here in this state ... well, it's just too—'

He pauses and looks over his shoulder to me. 'He must have brought that card in with him when he first took bad, before he went into the coma. So, what is it then?'

'It's nothing, Marty. Just a message from an old friend of the family. At least it's not a Mass card.'

This appears to make Johnty smile. 'No, never a Mass card. That man there wouldn't have approved of somebody sending him that kind of thing. Not his scene. What did he call them, Robert? Witch doctors! He would say, "Marty, whatever you do, keep me away from them witch doctors." You make sure you do that too, Robert.'

'No sweat, Johnty. When the time comes, I will do as he bids. There will be no witch doctors. No masses. No nuns. No priests. No rosary beads. I wish his last day would have been May 1.'

'"Long live May 1" – he always said that on May Day,' my dad's best friend says in a near whisper.

I pop Sabine's card into my breast pocket and move to the door. 'I'll be back up later for another visit,' I lie to him, while delivering a gentle supportive slap to Johnty's back. I know this is going to be the last time I ever see my father alive. Instead, I leave him with his loyal friend to deal with the final moments.

Inside the lift, I take out the card once more and wonder if my dad had left it there deliberately for my benefit before his condition worsened, before the second stroke took him over into death's antechamber. How did it come into his possession? Had he met her? I'd never be able to ask him. My mind swirled as I exited the hospital.

Outside, the crowds on the Falls Road are far thinner than yesterday, but the odd black taxi still whooshes by with a tricolour flapping triumphantly out of its back window. There are a few onlookers bent over the school barriers outside St Dominic's, politely applauding a solitary flute band as it files slowly down the road to the beat of a single snare drum. It is all berets, white shirts, skimpy black ties and shiny brogues tramping on the tarmac. On the hospital side, at the band's right flank, is a small boy barely into his teens with his drumsticks wedged underneath his left armpit. He looks like a mini sergeant major with his regimental baton. The band, who are playing in memory of some martyrs or others, comes to a complete halt, and, after a minute or two, when a tubby man batters the big bass drum, the flute players strike up a tune and the side drummers rattle in unison.

My mind hurtles backwards at thirty frames a second to twenty-five years ago. I see another boy, his head shaved in a short back and sides, wearing a summer T-shirt and shorts. He's hammering on a red tin drum with toy soldiers with painted bearskin helmets. There are two older boys who are blindfolded with rolled up tea-towels wrapped tightly and tied across their eyes. The pair are being led to a garden wall. Their executioners are on either side, armed with plastic Winchesters, pop guns and even a toy SLR, the latest treat from Woolworths. The 'prisoners' are put up against the ivy-flecked brickwork and their 'guards' form a firing squad in front of them. The little drummer boy sidles up to the firing party and starts to beat at a more frenetic tempo. When he stops, the drummer boy shouts, 'Fire!' and the 'prisoners' finally cry out, 'God Save Ireland'. Aidan and I had won the right to be martyred that day. We had desperately wanted to be placed in the firing line rather than the firing squad, so that we could die for the cause that summer just as the real business was about to kick off all around us. We had yearned to be gunned down inside his family's back garden that August while his older brother, Mick, played 'The Foggy Dew' on his tin whistle while hanging out of his bedroom window, providing us with the soundtrack of our mock execution.

The roar of buses and the whine of a filterless motorbike drown out the faint strains of that very same lament for the rebels of 1916 as the flute band now parades past St Paul's chapel and onto the junction of the Grosvenor and Springfield Roads. As I follow them south, back towards the city centre, along the same route we followed on our way back from Windsor Park fifteen years before, I sense that someone is approaching from behind. For an instant that shiver of fear ripples down from my neck to the base of my spine. When you have stalked so many targets of your own, you will surely scent the day when you become the quarry. Before I get one behind the ear, I start to slalom slowly around women pushing prams and groups of teenagers. Just when I think that I've zigzagged sufficiently to dodge a bullet in the back or head, I hear my stalker cry out, 'Robbie Macara, Robbie Ruin!'

My stalker still has that hollow tone in his voice, similar to that day in April 1979 when I first met him, drawing jets of blood spurting from his father's legs. I turn around. The boy has caught up with his dad, looking similarly withered, drawn and haunted. Paki's son stretches out a hand. His smile reveals jagged discoloured teeth and he sports a beard that has been trimmed neatly to offset the trauma of premature balding. For a young man still only in his early twenties, his face reveals that he has seen and done far too much already.

'Well how's our Formula 1 star?' I ask as he grips my hand a little too tightly when we shake. This is a dodgy encounter – dangerous even. Considering his direct involvement in the hit, he is probably as much a target as I am for those who might still seek revenge over Padre Pio.

The mood of Stephen, son of Paki and nephew of Trout, instantly darkens. 'For fuck's sake, Robbie, don't even think that, let alone say it out loud, will ya! There are still a few of their relatives knockin' about this road. One of them started on me the other week in the supermarket when she clocked me in the aisles. "Look me in the eye. Just look at me, ya bastard. Ya don't have the balls ta face me, do ya? You traitor. Judas. Murderer. Renegade." And yada, yada, yada ... I got the whole heap. Do these people ever move on?'

I say nothing but just elbow him in the ribs and nod towards Dunville Park. After we cross over Grosvenor Road, I choose the exact bench where Padre Pio and I knocked back our carry-out on the way to Paki's flat after the cup final. When we sit down, Stephen takes out a tin from his black bomber jacket. It was the very same one, with Cuchulain engraved on it, that his father rolled up from in Divis Flats that Saturday evening when we first met. Stephen takes out the papers, deftly glues them together with the help of his saliva, rolls out shag tobacco and then sprinkles it with grains of Fools Gold-flecked Lebanese dope.

'Dear Uncle Trout used to tell me we were funding the armed struggle in Lebanon and Palestine by smoking this stuff,' he says, taking his first long draw from the joint before passing it over to me.

I decline the offer and stare over towards the hospital where I wonder if my father has died yet. 'The Ruts had a song on their first album, the LP before Malcolm Owen killed himself. It was called 'Dope For Guns'. I think it was about Lebanon,' I say.

'Who the fuck were The Ruts? And who the fuck was Malcolm Owen?'

'Ach, just a band that I liked when you were a kid, when I first met you in the flats on the day of the cup final. Do you remember what you were doing on the floor that evening?'

He turns to me with a bewildered expression. 'Jesus Robbie, I can barely remember what I did last week. These days most things are a big blur thanks to this great shit. Do you wanna blast?'

'No thanks. I used to smoke joints with your uncle Trout and a certain other person, but if truth be told I never really liked the stuff.'

'You were just a social toker then?'

'Aye, something like that. Tell me this, Stephen – you were drawing pictures of your dad being shot and then later other ones of the Reds lifting the cup. Did your da ever bring you to a game like he promised?'

'When I reached fourteen, I used to go up to Solitude on my own, just like you used to do with that certain other person. I would beetle across Millfield and dodge the Orangemen coming down from the Shankill Road. But only on my own, never with Paki. He was always up to some dodgy moves on Saturdays. One of the best days for business, he used to say. Working moves for Paki always came first before me or my mum.'

He stops to take the longest of drags before billowing out a bulging membrane of acrid blow up into the air. 'Truth be told, he really was a fuckin' waster. It was only when I joined the struggle that I realised that. He was a hoodin' bastard who was only in it for himself. No wonder he turned tout. No wonder the movement stopped protectin' him from the bigger tigers.'

'You mean the movement that stood by and let the 'RA shoot your father dead,' I remind him a little too coldly.

He takes another blast of the joint and says slowly, 'I didn't see you tryin' ta stop them.'

If that had been Padre Pio, his retort would have been loaded with threat, but my companion today says it without a scowl or a stare, without a muscle or nerve flickering on his face, without any menacing gear change in his voice.

When I stare straight at him, he smiles back reassuringly. 'Don't worry about it. We're comrades. I'm sorry. You weren't in a leadership position back then when they finally clipped poor oul Paki.'

I put my hand up to interrupt his apology as two members of the martyrs' band go by. With their performance now finished, their shiny black flutes are tucked under their arms. When they swagger onto the Grosvenor, making for the Springfield Road, Stephen nods towards them.

'They hadn't a fuckin' clue who we were, Robbie. It's as if we don't count anymore,' he says.

I shrug my shoulders. 'WE WERE! That's about right. You've hit the nail on the head there, Stephen. Personally, I couldn't care if they don't know us and even less that we don't count anymore. Don't you just want to be left alone? Didn't you say that yourself, in a way, when you told me about that fishwife balling you out in the supermarket? What's the matter with lying low?'

'I suppose you're right, Robbie. At least I wasn't with my other half when that woman started on me about her dead husband.'

'Your wife?'

'Nah, never had a wife, just a wee bird I knocked up the spout ... twice. What about you, Robbie? Did you ever get hitched?'

'No way, Stephen. I never bought into that racket and that means no kids either. Well yes, plenty of one night stands, but I'm just too toxic for any woman who happens to find out what I'm really like.'

Stephen laughs, imagining I am making a joke, and says, 'The local female masses just don't appreciate what we did for them back in the struggle.'

'Too right, Stephen. Not that we ever asked them for permission to do whatever it was we did for them in the first place,' I say, as I notice that his joint is burning down and he has already laid out the papers for a second one.

'They were charging 1969 prices in their social clubs yesterday to celebrate the ceasefire. That's the only reason I went out yesterday along with the masses. It was for a cheap afternoon on the gargle,' Stephen says, still fixated on his next creation. 'But that's about all it was, Robbie. All of them flags, them balloons, them good-luck banners, even the teddy bears. None of it was about victory, it was simply relief. Hardly a glorious way to end the revolution, was it?'

When I don't reply, he starts on in that same drone tone as his uncle Trout, who is like a brother to him and is still currently incarcerated up in the Maze, wondering, hoping, if yesterday's cessation-of-violence announcement might be the key to unlock his cell door too.

'Ask yourself this, Robbie. Did we engage the British armed forces and did we take on the renegades within our own ranks just to end up with balloons and teddy bears?'

I interrupt what I fear is going to be an oration stretching all the way back to Wolfe Tone, 1798 and the long, long litany of betrayals and sell-outs through history. 'If yer da was such a waster, Stephen, then why did you volunteer to drive the boys on that job? Why did you come forward to us to take part in that operation to fill in Padre Pio and his gang?'

There is a long pause until Stephen eventually responds. I'm shocked to see he is shaking and on the verge of tears.

'It had fuck all to do with my dad,' he says. 'On the odd occasion when Paki took my ma out for an evening, he'd drop me down your way to be minded, rather than leave me in the flats with my grandad, because he was always pissed as a newt. Most of my sleepovers were in Padre Pio's house.'

I freeze, fearing what's coming next.

'We'd go into his front parlour after tea and play a wee game. He said it was called 'punishment beating'. Sometimes he'd let me wear the balaclava and I'd do the beating. But most times it was me bent over his sofa. You know? The one with the floral patterns. My bags and trunks would be pulled down and it was usually a wire hairbrush belonging to his ma that would be his weapon of choice. That same hairbrush he'd make me use on him now and again. Not very often mind ya, compared to the times he had to "sort me out". That's what he said he was doing, ya know – sortin' me out.'

I lie to him and tell him I am shocked to hear someone so close to family, someone so young himself, could do such a thing. I tell him that I don't blame him for volunteering for the operation.

'And no, Robert. He didn't slip me one inside. Not with me anyway. I don't know about the others.'

The others? I say nothing. I don't know what to say.

'Skyscraper the raper, eh! I don't think that dumb fuck even realised why he got that nickname. With me though, all he did was deliver a severe whackin' to the arse. Oh aye, that and him furiously wankin' himself with his own bags down around his legs. Over and over, he'd tell me I was just another wee hoodin' bastard that needed sortin' out, just like my thievin', toutin' da. He didn't slip me one but he was still a skyscraper! That's what Uncle Trout always called him, so Uncle Trout must have heard something – about the others at least! He never knew about me.'

Oh Jesus fuck! That parlour! Where I used to lie down with his ma after she had one too many Smirnoffs; where I handed over the photograph to him that Sunday after the cup final. That picture! The image that became my entry visa into the movement. In that very same parlour, a couple of years after I had handed him that photo, Padre Pio gripped my arm and said, 'We did it, comrade. All thanks to you. We fuckin' did it and it was all your intelligence, Ruin. The movement hit the jackpot.'

I have to get out of this park! I can still hear Padre Pio whispering into my ear on this exact same bench and in that fucking parlour. I think about his sign-nothing-say-nothing lecture. When I hear 'say nothing' now, I don't think of PP. I think of his mother. I can still see her, with that withering Medusa look, as she stood in front of me with her arms folded on the day they were getting ready to plant her son up at Milltown Cemetery. Yet she never uttered a word of hatred towards me in public or even confronted me for an explanation. A certain person, after all, had sent her an anonymous letter asking her if she knew what her son had got up to with her own mother, his granny.

'Robbie, how does it feel to be a sewer rat?'

I get up from the bench. 'Oh, I'm the king of the sewer rats! Haven't you heard? What does it matter what they say any more about us?'

'Or us about them?' Stephen adds acidly.

'I need to go, Stephen,' I say.

37

MAROONED

1 September 1994

When I inquire how much the entrance fee is to 'Marooned', the girl at the desk with pink hair and nose piercing says the exhibition is free and directs me to 'The Installation Room'.

Before entering, I close my eyes for a few seconds. It is the smell I notice first: the scent of space – wafts of hot metal and welding fumes being pumped through the air vents. Then the music assaults me, unsteadies me – the soundtrack from 'our summer' in 1978. I feel the jagged edges of *Low* on my fingertips. I step into my trench. Constantly changing pictures are dissolving onto the walls of 'Marooned'. Lights are flashing, faces are flickering and snatches of a very familiar voice break up the mournful, groaning, synthesised lament of Bowie's 'Subterraneans'.

Astronauts have reported a reek of sulphur or a faint acrid aroma lingering on their suits after returning from a spacewalk. Cosmonauts must have noticed it too whenever they were back safely through the airlocks of Mir, which is now spinning slowly on the art gallery's brick walls. The image of Mir dissolves into the moving image of a man in a sky-blue tracksuit who is floating inside the oxygenated gravity-free confines of the space station; a man who will eventually fall towards a very different earth. Beneath his right shoulder, sewn on to the arm, is the only flag that my father would ever stand to salute: the emblem of the Bolshevik Revolution, the red banner of the CCCP, whose scarlet colours are about to fade out of power down on the earth below, leaving Sergei Krikalev marooned amid the stars as the last Soviet citizen left in the universe.

When Krikalev was finally lifted out of his space capsule, he had orbited the earth 5,000 times and spent 803 days in space. He had returned to a world where even his home city had been renamed St Petersburg; his entire country, as he had known it, had ceased to exist. As I watch the image of the pale, emaciated, bewildered-looking cosmonaut being hoisted out of his Soyuz module, I remember my father suddenly switching off the *News At Ten* report in disgust over that historic touchdown in the now independent Kazakhstan. 'They'll be pulling down Lenin's statues and putting up ones of the fucking Ayatollah Khomeini there next,' my dad shouted at the blank television screen.

The scraps and scratches of human voices of 'Marooned' mingle with the bleeps and beeps of earth-to-orbit communiques. It sounds like those noises emitting from the machine that had been keeping my father barely alive on this planet. The confident, wonder-struck words of Yuri Gagarin, who is marvelling at being the first man to travel through space, are interspersed with those of Krikalev talking to ground control at Baikonur cosmodrome three decades later. Then there are other fragments of conversation, different ones, recorded off a telephone call between two women, one of whom I once imagined had loved me that summer.

'Aunty Iris, tell me what Daddy was like when he was a wee boy?'

'He was always playing with soldiers, you know. Ever since I can remember, he was taking them out of their boxes and placing them all over the front parlour.'

'So he always wanted to be a soldier?'

'Oh, you should have seen his collection of toy soldiers. Every Christmas it was always something to do with toy soldiers or an Airfix model.'

'An Airfix model?'

'He got his first Airfix Spitfire in 1953, I think. The first of many. He was still collecting toy soldiers when he married your mum.'

Airfix models! I think back to Trout's weird military crib in honour of those in the H-Block on that cup final morning as Sabine's voice repeats her aunt's words, 'Toy soldiers when he got married to mum ... Toy soldiers when he got married to mum.'

The picture rippling over the Victorian brickwork changes from Krikalev to a shockingly familiar one of a man in his pristine prime, with sideburns, a fawn polo neck and a tweed jacket. She must have developed it from the negatives in Jerusalem Street. Like a secret agent in *The Professionals*, he was holding up a revolver; the same gun he had fired in vain to ward off his executioner twelve years ago this summer.

Sabine's voice returns once more – this time a solitary whisper over her father's frozen profile. Her words are not about him or his memory, rather a message freighted with meaning for another to hear and remember.

'You were not one of them ...You were not one of them ... You were never one of them ... Which was worse ... Which was worse.'

Then her father's image disappears and the installation is plunged into complete darkness. The odour of space is still wafting through the pipes and Bowie's 'Subterraneans' rises to a higher volume. The last track of *Low* re-emerges out of the babble of voices from space and from earth at three minutes, eleven seconds – just at the point where the saxophone sways onto the track. She once whispered breathlessly, during an intimate moment in bed, that the mournful jazz sax echoes were meant to evoke the sense of loss and entrapment among those left behind on the eastern side of the Berlin Wall.

As I stand here while Bowie's sorrowful vocals fade into the sax-climax, amid the blackness and the faint reek of space in the air, I know I will never see or hear from her again. This is her final message, her last transmission to me. I also know that while Krikalev is no longer a cosmic castaway and the East Berliners, whom Bowie gently wept for on *Low*, are finally free, I am marooned.

One last image appears on both sides of the room, surrounding me. It is an enlarged Polaroid snap of carcasses on meat hooks, hanging above the carving tables in the slaughterhouse. At the edge of the picture, the blades of the butchers' knives can be seen approaching. Despite the horror depicted, it is beautifully composed. Suddenly, imploring squeals of livestock envelope the room. It is the relentless sound of futility, and, from deep within, I hear my da begging me, imploring me to, 'Get out. Get out. Get the fuck out of here.' Then all the images of 'Marooned' flash by on the wall in one rapid final sequence, accompanied by all the sounds entangled together. Darkness and silence returns – a cold, still, eternal void that is the end of the future.